# MY SOUL TO KEEP

# KRIS NORRIS

# OTHER BOOKS BY KRIS NORRIS

## SINGLES

CENTERFOLD

KEEPING FAITH

IRON WILL

MY SOUL TO KEEP

RICOCHET

ROPE'S END

## SERIES

### 'TIL DEATH

1 - DEADLY VISION

2 - DEADLY OBSESSION

3 - DEADLY DECEPTION

### BROTHERHOOD PROTECTORS ~ Elle James

1 - MIDNIGHT RANGER

2 – CARVED IN ICE

3 - GOING IN BLIND

### COLLATERAL DAMAGE

1 - FORCE OF NATURE

### DARK PROPHECY

1 - Sacred Talisman

2 - Twice Bitten

3 - Blood of the Wolf

ENCHANTED LOVERS

1 - Healing Hands

FROM GRACE

1 - Gabriel

2 – Michael

THRESHOLD

1 - Grave Measures

WAYWARD SOULS

1-Delta Force: Cannon

COLLECTIONS

Blue Collar Collection

Into the Spirit, Boxed Set

COMING SOON

Delta Force: Colt

Delta Force: Six

# MY SOUL TO KEEP

KRIS NORRIS

My Soul to Keep

Copyright © 2016, Kris Norris

Edited by Chris Allen-Riley and Jessica Bimberg

Cover Art by Kris Norris

Published by Kris Norris

Released in print ~ June, 2017

*To Siobhan. For all the little things you do that make the world shine that much brighter. Thank you for being the kind of friend we all aspire to be and for never losing your faith.*

# CHAPTER ONE

"Bloody hell."

Detective Caitlyn Decker shook her head before pressing her fingers against the bridge of her nose, closing her eyes as pain throbbed through her temples, not that it'd do much good. The headache had already taken root, somehow pulsing with every beat of her heart. Nothing but time or drugs would touch it now. And, somehow, downing half a bottle of Motrin while working a murder scene didn't seem like a viable solution. She glanced at the paper again, rereading the words scribbled across the crisp white sheet.

*Some choices are easy, some aren't. Can you guess which one this was?*

Christ, she'd officially seen it all.

A male snort drew her attention, and she shifted her focus as Detective David Truman knelt beside the body, giving it the once-over. He gazed up at her, exhaling loudly as he gained his feet. He stuffed his hands in his pockets, nodding at one of the CSI technicians as they snapped some photographs.

He turned to face her. "Not exactly the kind of case you want to grab at the end of a shift, huh?"

She shrugged. "Thinking there isn't a right time for a case like this, period. We both know that note means trouble."

Truman glanced at the paper, nodding. "Just another Wednesday as far as I'm concerned."

She frowned at his hollow tone, spinning slightly toward him. "You sound more cynical than usual. Everything okay?"

"Peachy. You?"

She shook her head. "Fine. Keep secrets." She toed the pavement. "So, you aren't on shift for another two hours. Why the early start?"

"I needed to get out of the house, and I heard the call come through over the radio. Thought I'd check it out... see if you wanted me to take it for you."

"And let you have all the fun? That's crazy talk." She nudged his elbow. "You and Clare okay? We can go grab coffee after if you'd like."

"God, who are you, Dr. Phil? I'm fine." He glanced over her shoulder, cursing. "Looks like the feds just pulled up. You sure you don't want me to take this? Their presence here probably means a joint endeavor, and seeing as you got stuck with the last one..."

Caitlyn did her best to calm the sudden pounding of her heart. The last thing she needed was to sound breathless. And all because of who *might* have just arrived. "I'm good. But I can count on your help if I need it, right?"

"It'll cost you."

"It always does."

Truman gave her a mock salute before trudging off toward his car. She heard him murmur a token hello to the fed he'd mentioned, the gravelly reply beading her skin with a sudden rash of goosebumps. She took a few soothing breaths, only to jump when a rumble of thunder sounded off to the east, the promise of rain heavy in the early morning air. A nearby streetlight buzzed as it flickered, casting odd shadows against the brick building before settling, again. She turned up her collar against a blast of cold, damp air, tucking her hands in her pockets. After a few weeks of summer-like weather, the sudden shift into more typical spring temperatures felt even colder than usual. Or maybe it was just her. A reminder of how little else she had in her life to make the endless string of homicides bearable. To chase away the incessant chill that seemed to have settled bone-deep inside her.

Footsteps scuffed the pavement behind her as the fed moved into her peripheral view. She didn't turn to greet the man. Couldn't. Not when her face felt more than flushed. Special Agent Deacon McGraw—or Deke as he usually went by—headed the violent crimes unit for the Seattle branch of the Federal Bureau of Investigation, and he seemed to be the bureau's prime choice in interagency ventures. Not that she had a clue why he was here. As far as she was concerned, this was just a routine killing in an alley of one of the poorer districts the city had to offer. Nothing to suggest it fell under federal jurisdiction. Her gaze strayed to the paper lying beside the victim's bloody body, the words glaring at her. Perhaps routine wasn't quite the correct term.

Deke cleared his throat as he crouched beside the corpse, using a pen to twist the paper slightly. He cocked his head to the side, glancing at her as he stood. "Just what this city needs, a killer with a twisted sense of humor."

Caitlyn crossed her arms over her chest. "I'll admit. I found the note...odd."

He chuckled. "Odd? It's creepy as hell, though I think we both know the answer to his question. The way the throat's been sliced damn near through to the vic's spinal column, the arcs of blood against the wall, not to mention the fact the guy's been virtually gutted... thinking it wasn't a hard choice for the bastard that did this."

"I don't know...all that defensive bruising along his arms, the marks on his head. The guy fought hard. Could suggest reluctance on the part of our perp."

"Or the killer's not as strong as he thought he was."

Caitlyn snorted, waving at the guy spread out across the black asphalt. "The victim's easily two-twenty and those muscles aren't fake. The guy obviously put in some heavy hours at the gym. And that faded tattoo on his wrist means he was part of the Fifth Street gang at some point. That kind of street tough doesn't ever really go away. Thinking there aren't many people who'd even consider taking him on. Lord knows, I wouldn't want to have met him in a dark alley."

"At least, not to fight."

"Seriously, Deacon? He's not even cold, yet."

"But he was pretty. Thinking guys like him would want that noticed, even under these circumstances." He winked at her. "Especially by a sexier-than-hell cop."

"That's detective to you, G-man. Besides he's not my type."

"That so? What is your type, *Detective?*"

"Still breathing would be a good start."

Deke grinned, the simple gesture making her heart race. Damn, but the man was handsome. Shaggy brown hair, the perfect amount of scruff, and those eyes—so fucking blue it made her stomach flip-flop. She'd had an *unfortunate* crush on the guy since they'd worked an assignment together six months ago, and bumping into him every few weeks on any potential crossover cases only made the fire in the pit of her gut burn hotter.

She drew in a much-needed breath, turning to fully face him. "So, there something about this case I'm unaware of? A reason I'm going to have to play nice with the bureau?"

Deacon placed his hand over his heart, the wind tousling his hair around his face. "And here I thought you liked playing nice with me. That hurts, Caitlyn."

She did her best to ignore the way his words curled over her flesh, making her skin prickle as if he'd actually touched her. Damn, she shouldn't react to him like this.

She glanced at the body again. "Is this where you tell me there's a slew of other bodies just like this one scattered across the country? All with cryptic messages that make your skin crawl? Which makes this whole damn mess some jurisdictional bullshit? Because honestly, if that note is any indication of what direction this case is going to take, I might be inclined to just hand it over to you. No fighting. No whining to my superiors."

His expression sobered, the lines of his face becoming slightly harsher. He scanned the alleyway, motioning her to join him in a relatively unoccupied area off to their left. Caitlyn followed him, unsure whether it was curiosity or the inklings of fear making her stomach tighten. Or maybe it was just him. He stopped when he reached a dumpster, looking up and down the narrow road again before focusing on her. Those crystal blue eyes of his made her breath hitch, the intensity of his expression bordering on lethal.

She reached up, palming his shoulder, wondering why he suddenly seemed so serious. As if the previous banter had just been for show. "Hey, you okay?"

"I was better before I got here."

She pulled her hand back, tucking it in her pocket. "Thanks, Deke. Way to boost my fragile ego."

He chuckled, leaning in dangerously close. His breath feathered over her cheek, rustling the wisps of hair that had pulled free from her ponytail. "Sweetheart, you're the only silver lining in this whole mess."

Her face heated again as his jaw brushed hers when he eased back, palming the brick behind her head. The position virtually trapped her between him and the building, his chest grazing hers as she inhaled deeply. Her pulse kicked up as her breasts rubbed across his pecs, the slight friction making her nipples peak against her shirt. Thank God she had on far too many layers for him to notice. She cursed inwardly. Now wasn't the time or the place to consider anything other than the task at hand. But damn...every new case, every lost soul just seemed to be a hollow echo of her life. Claimed a bit more of the part of her she'd tried to lock away— keep safe. And she knew that, sooner or later, there'd be nothing left of *her*. Nothing left for her to give to anyone other than an empty shell of the person she'd once been.

She scanned the area, expecting someone to start yelling suggestive comments, but no one seemed to notice them. Or maybe everyone was simply too focused on the dead body splattered across the pavement to spare them a passing glance.

Caitlyn schooled her features. "Obviously, there's something much deeper going on here than one creepy note and a dead body. So spill."

Deacon tilted his head slightly, a hushed sigh sounding between them. "It's...complicated."

"Everything with you is...complicated."

He arched a brow. "I could say the same thing about you, but..." He raked his free hand through his hair. "For the record, this isn't the first body. Or the first note. There's just one catch."

"There always is." She moistened her lips, quirking her mouth into a hint of a smile. "And..."

"The truth is, this is the thirteenth victim in a string of killings, all of which have the same MO and the same type of cryptic note."

"Thirteenth? Strange how I haven't heard anything about it. Not so much as a bulletin over the wire. There a reason for that?"

"The murders began about sixty years ago. The killer seems to target fit, young males in their prime. There were six deaths, then nothing for about forty years. Then suddenly, there were six more. An agent tied the two cases together, despite the first file being buried beneath a bunch of high security red tape, but he was killed during the investigation. The bureau pretty much back-burnered the whole thing when the killings stopped as mysteriously as they'd begun. In fact, there hasn't been another case... until now."

"And you know all this how? Please don't tell me you actually spend your days off scouring through unsolved files, especially ones that have been collecting dust for twenty years because that...that's even more pathetic than my life."

Deke straightened, giving her some much-needed space as he glanced at the body over his shoulder before staring down at her. "The agent that unearthed it all, who died twenty years ago, was my father...and I still have all his notes."

"Shit." She offered him an apologetic smile. "I'm sorry about your dad. That's a hell of a legacy to leave."

"I can't tell you how many times I've looked through his findings. I just never really thought..." He motioned to the remains. "I'll be honest. I'm not sure if I'm relieved to discover he wasn't batshit crazy like they'd claimed or scared shitless that it's started, again."

"A healthy dose of both would be wise." She blew out an exasperated breath, nodding at him. "You know this little confession explains a lot about you, right?"

"You're, of course, referring to my dedication to the job."

"I was going to say stubborn obsession, but..." Caitlyn pursed her lips, releasing a weary breath. "Sixty years? You realize that would make the killer at least eighty years old. No way someone that age killed this guy, who could probably take on three attackers at once." She arched a brow. "You thinking it's some kind of pact? Continued by family members or friends or something?"

"From the notes my father has, he deduced it was the same killer both times."

"I don't know. If the victims all resembled this guy in physique...I'm not sure that's possible."

"Yeah, puzzling as hell. But, there's the body. And there's the note. I find it hard to believe it's merely a coincidence."

"So you *are* taking over the investigation."

Deacon sighed, closing his eyes for a moment before meeting her gaze. "Unfortunately, the bureau isn't quite ready to pull out all the stops. Seems they've done the math and come to the same conclusion—"

"That the cases can't be connected do to the length of time. The age of the perpetrator."

He nodded. "They *did* give the go ahead to join the investigation if the detective in charge welcomed my help. Strictly as a consultant, if you'd like."

"You? Just consulting? That's not the Deke I've come to know."

"Whatever it takes to get me on the team."

Caitlyn shook her head. "Something tells me I'm going to regret being on call tonight." She offered him her hand. "Guess this makes us partners."

"Partners? You sure?"

"Keeping you stuck on the sidelines as a consultant... huge waste in resources. Besides, I have the feeling I'll need all the help I can get on this one."

"Partners it is, then." He smiled, his roguish facade firmly back in place. "For the record, I like the sound of that."

"Yeah, well don't get all warm and fuzzy just yet. I

have a feeling neither of us is going to like where this leads."

"My dad died trying to find justice. I'll take this wherever it goes."

"We can start with coffee, and you're buying. And I want to see those notes. If you're right, this is just the first in a series of six killings. It'd be wise to try and get ahead of the killer, if we can." She pushed past him, heading for her car.

"Caitlyn!"

She looked at him over her shoulder.

He gave her a genuine smile. "Thanks."

"For what?"

"For having enough faith in me to give me a chance."

"Faith is easy. Results? Much harder."

She turned away again, cursing the butterfly feeling in her stomach. He was right about one thing. She was more than willing to take this wherever it was headed. She just hoped it didn't end like his father's case had.

# CHAPTER TWO

Deacon McGraw scrubbed a hand down his face, sliding into the driver's seat. He didn't miss the way his hands shook slightly when he shoved the key in the ignition, listening to the hum of the engine as it sparked to life. Music echoed through the cabin, the telltale twang of his favorite country station soothing the raw feeling still gnawing at his gut. After convincing himself it'd all been a screwed up figment of his father's imagination, to actually see physical proof...

Deke raked a hand through his hair. A dead body. That's what he'd been staring at. It wasn't proof of his father's sanity, and it sure as hell wasn't something Deke should be happy about. In fact, now that the initial shock had worn off, he couldn't deny the restless feeling in his stomach. The clammy press of his palms against the leather steering wheel.

He glanced in his rearview, watching Caitlyn pause at her vehicle, talking to one of the CSI guys before reefing open the door and sliding in. Her long hair fluttered across her face, the deep auburn color contrasting perfectly against her pale skin before she brushed the strands out of the way, revealing soft features and striking green eyes. Christ, he'd never seen eyes that vibrant, that beautiful before. And he loved that she always held his gaze, studying him as if he were a complicated puzzle she needed to figure out.

He groaned, wondering if the sensation in his gut was from the case or just her, cursing when it flip-flopped as she looked up, nodding at him in the mirror. Fuck...this wasn't the time to delve into *that* line of thinking. Sure, she was smart, sexy and had the kind of beauty that made everything around her seem almost two-dimensional. But he needed to focus. On the case. On the damn murders. Do everything he could to prevent another five bodies from ending up like the one in the alley—like the twelve before them that flashed relentlessly inside his head whenever he tried to have a normal life.

He sighed. Nothing about this case was normal, and he'd just signed Caitlyn up to be part of his insanity. He only hoped once he told her his suspicions, she didn't call his superiors and have him carted off to the local psychiatric ward. God knows, he wouldn't blame her. Hell, he'd probably go willingly.

His phone chimed, the accompanying vibration jerking him out of his thoughts. He pulled it out of his pocket, smiling at Caitlyn's text.

*You just going to sit there, checking your makeup, or are you going to buy me some coffee?*

He glanced in the rearview again, smiling when she held up her wrist and tapped it. Damn, she turned his insides to mush. His brain, too. He touched the screen, sending the message without even thinking.

*Don't hate me because your shade of lipstick goes better with my eyes, sweetheart. Now buckle up and follow me.*

He looked in the mirror, watching her response— grinning when she laughed, her gaze lifting to his. She nodded, starting her car then waiting for him to lead the way.

He tucked away his phone, slowly pulling into traffic. He maneuvered through the throng of techs and other police still milling about before angling onto the street. He didn't really concentrate on where he was headed, his mind still lost in thought. Only it wasn't just the case that held his attention. He couldn't resist glancing at the mirror, catching glimpses of Cait as she followed him, varying emotions playing across her face. He damn near ran a red light when she started nodding her head, obviously singing along with whatever music she was listening to. The woman was stunning.

Fuck. He was good and rightly fucked.

The rising sun glinted off the windshield as Deke continued eastward, finally pulling into a small side alley, then an adjoining lot. He shoved his Wrangler into first, killing the engine as he reached into the back pocket of the passenger seat. When he'd heard the call come in over the radio, he'd shoved the old files into the seat rest with little more than a glimmer of hope he might actually get to use them. He really hadn't counted on this being anything more than another dead end. A routine killing. God, how long had he kept that folder in the drawer at his desk?

He pushed away the thought, holding the folder tight

as he stepped out, waiting until Cait had parked beside him, her head still bobbing to the beat of the music. She seemed indifferent to the fact he was watching as she belted out a few more phrases before hitting some imaginary drum and finally turning off the car. An easy smile graced her lips when she turned toward him, those green eyes sparkling in the early morning sunlight. Strands of hair framed her face, the shorter pieces bouncing as she grabbed her purse off the passenger seat then opened her door.

The wind lifted her ponytail off her shoulders, carrying a sweet, floral scent over to him. It reminded him of summer and heat, and he wondered why he hadn't noticed it at the crime scene. Hell, he'd been a lot closer to her. Unless... Shit. His damn dick stiffened against his zipper. Just the possibility that she'd put it on for their "coffee date" made his pulse echo inside his head. The girl was trouble with a capital T tattooed across her forehead.

She motioned to the folder. "Are those the notes you mentioned?"

"More than you'll probably want to go through. You can have a look once we're inside."

She stared at the building, scrunching her nose as she adjusted her purse. "Are you sure this is the place?"

He smiled, wondering if she realized the picture she presented. Adorable lines creasing the bridge of her nose as she stared at him as if he'd lost his mind. Which, arguably, was fair in light of what they were going to discuss, but...

"Pretty damn sure." He cocked an eyebrow. "Don't you trust me?"

Her own brow arched in response. "Wow. First you ask to join my investigation, and now you're asking for my trust. Is nothing sacred to you?"

Deke moved over beside her, crowding her against her car door. He didn't miss the way her breath hitched or how she snagged her bottom lip as her head tilted back, her gaze rising to meet his. The green seemed darker, more like jade now.

He leaned in, stopping an inch away. "So is that a no?"

Her fingers landed on his chest, the tiny pads pressing against his shirt as the sides of his jacket hung open. "Let's see how coffee goes, then maybe I'll give you an answer."

He chuckled, stepping back, but not before he caught a hint of regret flash in her eyes. He motioned to the back door. "Shall we?"

She frowned again, heading for the restaurant. Another confused look crossed her features as she stopped just shy of the door. "Call me crazy, but the place isn't even open yet."

"I know." He held up a key, unlocking the door before opening it for her. "After you."

She glanced inside, tentatively crossing the threshold before turning. "Do you own this place?"

"Not quite."

"But you have a key…"

"Just get inside. Trust me."

"There's that phrase again."

She shook her head, making her way down the hall and into the main area. Dishes clattered off to her right before a woman stepped out from the kitchen.

The girl stopped, staring at Cait as her mouth hinged open. "I'm sorry, but we're closed—"

"Hey, Stacy."

Her gaze swung to him, relief gentling her expression. "Damn it, Deacon. You scared me half to death." She darted over, giving him a hug and a quick kiss before swatting him with a towel. "I never should have given you a key."

"Now, Stace, that would hurt if I didn't know you loved me."

"You use that excuse far too often for your own good. One day, I'm just going to kick your sorry ass out of here." The woman gave him a shove, eyeing Caitlyn before sighing. "You going on shift or coming off?"

"Off, I hope." He grinned when she motioned to Caitlyn, eyes widening slightly. "Where are my manners? Stacy, this is Caitlyn. Cait. Stacy."

Caitlyn shook the woman's hand, eyeing him suspiciously. He held back the chuckle bubbling in his chest. He knew he hadn't provided near enough information regarding who the other woman was, but he couldn't help it. He wanted to judge Caitlyn's reaction. See if there was any hint that she might see him as more than a fellow officer she bumped into every few weeks. A flash of annoyance colored her eyes before she schooled her features.

He nudged Stacy. "I was hoping you'd make some of your famous coffee for us while we go over some files." He gave her his best puppy eyes, grunting when she punched him in the shoulder.

Stacy glanced at Caitlyn. "Oh, so you two work together?"

Caitlyn looked at him, her lips quirking. "That remains to be seen."

He smiled, ushering her over to a table. He eased out a chair, holding it for her while she slipped into it then pushed it forward.

She snorted, placing her hands on the table. "And I thought chivalry was dead. Who holds a chair out for anyone, anymore?"

"Not everything from a simpler time is necessarily obsolete. Besides, you can hold mine out for me, next time."

"Jackass."

"That's partner jackass. Though, from the sounds of it, you're already having second thoughts."

Caitlyn sighed, thanking Stacy when she ventured back to the table, setting down a couple of mugs, some milk and sugar, and a pot.

She dropped another kiss on his cheek, tossing a "stay safe" over her shoulder as she walked away.

Cait watched the other woman leave, a hint of irritation creasing her brow as she sighed and added some milk and sugar before taking a cautious sip. Her eyes bulged wide, a throaty moan sounding between them. "Dear God. This is the best cup of coffee I've ever had." She took another sip, another luscious rumble breaking free. "Seriously. Christ, it might be better than sex."

He coughed as his coffee caught while swallowing, the gravelly noise she made spiking his arousal, again. "If that's true, you need to find a better bed partner."

"That would imply I currently had a bed partner, which I don't." She inhaled as the words left her mouth, looking as if she'd realized she'd revealed too much. She placed the mug down. "So, this is obviously more than just a place you frequent." She glanced at where Stacy had disappeared behind a set of swinging doors. "She seems nice. And she's very pretty, albeit a bit young, but…"

She let the statement hang in the air, and he couldn't help but smile. Maybe the good detective wasn't quite as platonic toward him as he'd feared. In fact, judging by the blush staining her cheeks, he might actually have a shot at making it through coffee without it ending in his face.

He laid the folder on the table then steepled his fingers under his chin. "She's a good ten years younger, if you must know. She's—"

"Damn it, Deke. Don't you ever come around here during business hours?" A man bustled into the room, apron smeared with grease. "You nearly gave Stace a heart —" He cut off as his gaze landed on Caitlyn, tripping a step before seemingly pulling himself together. He glanced at Deacon, a sly smile capturing his lips as he stopped next to the table. "Sorry. Didn't realize you had company." He held out his hand. "Trevor. Trevor Reynolds."

Caitlyn shook it. "Caitlyn Decker."

Trevor held her hand for a few more moments before shaking his head. "I've got to hand it to you, buddy. Your taste in women just vastly improved." He leaned toward her. "You're way out of his league."

Caitlyn laughed, that delightful blush deepening.

Deacon grinned. "Perhaps, I should be more precise. This is *Detective* Caitlyn Decker." Deacon nodded at Trevor. "Sorry, I forgot to mention that part to Stacy. The good detective here is allowing me to join her investigation. We needed a quiet place to go over some files, and Stacy does make the best damn java in town."

Trevor rolled his eyes. "You just like to take advantage of your relationship." He thumbed at Deke. "Bastard knows his little sister wouldn't turn him down, even if she is stressed out about opening in an hour."

Caitlyn's eyes widened, her gaze swinging from the closed door over to Deke. "Sister?"

Deke shrugged it off. "Technically, step-sister. My mom remarried a few years after my father died, but...I never did see it that way. Blood doesn't make you family."

A brilliant smile lit up her face. "No. It doesn't."

Trevor straightened. "Colleagues, huh? That makes way more sense. No way a lady as fine as yourself would shack up with this lackey. Have you tried his coffee? It's biochemical warfare."

"I like it strong."

"There's a difference between strong and being classified as paint thinner." Trevor avoided Deacon's slap. "You guys hungry? I could whip something up for you."

Caitlyn waved it off, touching the back of her hand to her mouth. "No, thanks. Thinking I won't be eating for a while after this morning."

"Sounds like you two had a tough go, already. I'll leave you to your coffee and your...work." Trevor gave Deke a swat on the back before ambling into the kitchen.

Caitlyn eyed him from beneath the rim of her mug. "Clever. You wanted to see how I'd react. What assumptions I'd make. Perhaps you're as ingenious as I've heard."

He shrugged. "Not sure what you're implying? I thought you'd assume she was my sister." He grinned. "Though, you look noticeably more relaxed now that you *know* she is."

"Again, you're a jackass." She took another long swig, seemingly savoring the moment before placing the mug off to her right. She laced her fingers together as she stared at him. "So...are you going to let me look at those notes, or are we just going to stare at the folder? You said it has evidence that links this to some old cases."

Some of the tension from the alley returned, destroying the easy atmosphere he'd been enjoying. He sighed inwardly. Work always seemed to have a way of bleeding through—staining everything with a hint of darkness. No reason to think this wasn't going to be business as usual.

He nodded, taking a moment to stare at the beige offering. He couldn't remember how many times he'd gone through his father's reports. Tried to find something —anything—to lead him in the right direction before finally admitting his father might have been wrong. That the stress had gotten to the man and driven him over the edge. Sharing this information with Caitlyn... It made everything intimately real. As if he was seeing the world in color after living in a multitude of grays.

Caitlyn stared at the folder, finally lifting her gaze to him. "Deacon? You okay?"

He released a slow breath, trying to look confident but knowing he hadn't pulled it off. "I guess I just never thought I'd actually show this to anyone. Everyone thought my father was..."

She placed her fingers on top of his, giving his a light squeeze. "Crazy?"

"That was on a good day." He carded his other hand through his hair. "Before I open this, and we go down this road, I need to know one thing."

She glanced at the folder again, snagging her lip for a moment as she worried it between her teeth before nodding. "What's that?"

He leaned forward, pushing the file closer to her. "Do you believe in monsters?"

# CHAPTER THREE

Caitlyn stared at Deke, watching his lips twitch as his gaze never left hers, his fingers warm beneath her touch. His eyes had darkened slightly, a hint of gunmetal gray mixed in with the brilliant blue. She swallowed against the sudden dry feeling in her throat, his last word ringing inside her head. Monsters? She drew her brows together. God, she obviously needed more sleep. Now she was hearing things.

She released a slow breath, glancing at the folder before looking up at him. "Did you say, monsters?"

One eye narrowed slightly, his nostrils flaring as he exhaled. "Just... Humor me. Do you?"

She frowned. "I'm not sure I understand the question. When you say monsters, are we talking psychopaths or..."

"Or..."

"You mean *real* monsters? Like Bigfoot or the Bogeyman?"

"I mean like vampires. Werewolves. Demons. Things

we've all heard about, but no one in their right mind would actually believe exist."

She leaned back, wondering if she should pull her hand away. Hell, if she should make a run for the door while she still had a chance. He was serious. She could tell by the firm press of his lips, his increased breath. The way his hand trembled ever so slightly beneath hers, or how his gaze never faltered as he stared at her, obviously waiting for her answer.

Cait wet her lips, trying to think of something—anything—remotely intelligent to say only to grunt. "You're serious."

She hadn't phrased it as a question, and he didn't do more than give her a guarded nod.

She pushed a hand through her hair, pulling some wisps free from her tie. "Monsters. Honestly, I hadn't given it much thought."

He sighed, reclining in his chair as his hand eased free of hers. "You think I'm crazy for even mentioning it."

"I didn't say that." She snorted. "What the hell's going on?"

"Let's just say that whether or not you have an open mind is crucial to solving those old murders. This ongoing case."

"So, if I see a victim with a couple of puncture wounds on their neck and don't immediately reach for a wooden stake hidden in my pocket, I'm what? The crazy one? Not competent enough to work this damn case with you?" She huffed out her next breath when he just sat there, still watching her. "Fine. The truth?"

He didn't do anything other than nod, again.

"Do I think there might be things out there we don't understand? Sure. I've had the odd…experience. But I'm not sure I would use the term monster."

A hint of a smile quirked his lips as he leaned closer. "What kind of experiences?"

She shook her head, laughing. "You know, this wasn't what I was expecting when I suggested we grab some coffee and chat."

"You say that like surprises are bad things."

"Trust me. Where my life's concerned, they generally are." She leaned all the way back in her chair as she took another sip of her coffee. "If you must know, I believe in ghosts."

He smiled, and her damn stomach dropped as her breath stalled in her chest. Christ, but he was handsome, the hint of vulnerability making him more so. "So, you've seen a ghost?"

She grabbed her napkin and tossed it at him. "Why am I sounding like the crazy person in this conversation?"

"I never said I thought you were crazy. I asked if you've seen a ghost."

"God, Deke. Just tell me what the hell's going on."

"Again, just humor me. Please, Caitlyn." The pleading tone in his voice tugged at her heart.

"Okay. Yes, I've seen a ghost. Shortly after my parents were killed…" She cleared her throat when the words seemed to catch on something. "Let's just say, some very strange things happened for a while. Things would move, there'd be odd cold spots. And…"

He arched a brow when she just let the thought fade. "And?"

She met his gaze and held it. "I'd hear voices. *Their* voices. And no, it wasn't my damn mind trying to 'deal' with their death, as the doctors used to say."

"Just voices?"

"Fuck, you don't quit, do you?" She clenched her jaw, wondering if this was part of some cosmic joke. "I saw my mother, okay? Full-fledged, hovering over my damn bed. More than once. She used to appear as a warning...when there was someone in my foster house I needed to be *concerned* about." She shook her head, feeling strangely drained. "I swear she saved my life more than a few times. Got me to leave some very bad places while I still had the chance."

His expression sobered, a hushed curse drifting between them. "Damn, I didn't mean to—"

"Forget it. Bad shit happens. Period. I survived. Turned out pretty normal, though talking to you has me questioning that." She tapped the corner of the folder. "So, am I 'open minded' enough to see the file? Or do I have to go have an encounter with some alien or that guy with the sign over on Fourth Street?" She leaned in. "It says he can save my soul."

"We might very well need his help before this is over." He pushed the folder toward her, laying his hand over hers when she grabbed it. "Just remember...there's really no coming back from this."

"Something tells me I crossed that bridge when I agreed to have coffee with you."

He chuckled, reclining in his chair as he sipped his drink, looking remarkably calm considering he'd insisted on knowing whether she believed in bloody monsters before she could examine the damn file. A shiver crawled down her back, the inklings of fear chilling her. She stilled the tremors in her hands as she took a deep breath then opened the folder, sighing at the graphic photo that greeted her. Even in black and white, there was no mistaking the pools of blood or the way the victim's neck had been sliced open, the wound disturbingly similar to what she'd witnessed in the alley.

Cait flipped to the next one, examining the various angles the forensics technician had taken. Zoomed shots of the neck and torso, showing the extent of damage. Warning bells echoed inside her head as she continued, each scene an eerie reflection of the previous one. Even when the images changed to color, the accounts more in-depth, it didn't alter the fact that the murders looked connected.

She pushed her fingertips into her forehead, staring at the last photo. The man wasn't quite the same as the other victims. He lacked the steroid-like muscles and seemed older, though still obviously athletic. His death appeared more rushed—lacking some of the wounds along the torso, though there wasn't a shortage of blood splattered across what appeared to be a room in an old abandoned house or barn. But there was no missing the blood-stained badge tossed on top of the body. The familiar curve of the man's jaw.

She swallowed past the lump in her throat, blinking back the burning feeling in her eyes as she gathered the courage to gaze up at Deacon. His lips were pursed into a fine line, his face a stony facade. The muscle in his jaw fluttered as he repeatedly clenched his teeth together, his hands fisted on top of the table.

Caitlyn reached for him, wondering if he'd pull away, relieved when he relaxed his fingers, allowing her to cup them in hers. She took a deep breath, glancing one last time at the photo. "God, I'm so sorry."

That muscle in his jaw pulsed again, regret flickering in his eyes before he seemed to push down any emotional response—nothing but cold determination staring back at her. He gave her a quirk of his lips, nodding at the image. "Not exactly the kind of last memories a kid wants of his father, but..." He paused as if drawing on some inner strength. "I found a way to give his death purpose."

"It's why you became a federal agent. Following in his footsteps."

He snorted. "It's hardly an original concept. How many cops are on the force because of family? This kind of life... it's either in your blood, or it's not."

"But you didn't sign up just to carry on his legacy. You've been waiting for a chance to solve his case. For whoever..." She held up her other hand. "Or whatever killed him and these other victims to surface, again."

He arched a brow. "So you believe me when I say they're all connected?"

"Hard to argue with the evidence. These crime scene photos..." She whistled. "Christ, it's like looking at the same one, over and over, only with different bodies, in different locations. The way the throat's been slashed, the extensive mutilation to the torso... Just flipping through these images suggests a serial situation. I can't believe the bureau back-burnered this."

"The first case was forty years old. Even with it being a serial situation, there's only so much anyone can do without new cases. Then, when it started happening again, no one wanted to believe it was the same person. Like you said, what sixty-year-old person could kill guys that strong?" He speared his fingers through his hair. "They all thought my dad was crazy for suggesting it. That it was a copycat at best."

Cait slid a glance toward the photos, sighing.

He groaned, shaking his head as he leaned farther forward. "You agree with them. You think it's the work of a copycat, too."

"Deke—"

"Don't. If nothing else, you've always been honest with me, and I've always respected that. Don't start lying to my face now."

She snorted. "You know, for a smart guy, you're pretty damn dense. I never said I didn't believe you. I'm just not willing to rule anything out. I'd like to go through the notes in detail. Study the other evidence I've barely glanced at. Generally, investigators hold back certain aspects of the crimes to help weed out copycat killings. I'd like to see how identical these new killings are in terms of following the same pattern. Including all the nuances the first set of deaths had."

"I've already done that. More times than I can count."

"I realize that, but..." She gave him a genuine smile, hoping he'd see her sincerity. "We're partners, right? I need to know everything you do. And I need to see it with fresh eyes. Ones not colored by—"

"Grief? Revenge?"

"I was going to say conclusions." She gave his hands one more squeeze then let go, missing the warmth of his touch, the rough calluses that had moved beneath the pads of her fingers. "You've been studying these for so long, it'd be next to impossible to see them as anything other than what you've already decided. So...let me go through everything. I promise I'll keep an open mind." She winked at him. "I'll even keep a tub of salt on hand, just in case."

"Wench."

"Hey...there's obviously something unusual going on here. There's no doubt in my mind the cases are linked, but... Other than the lengthy amount of time between the sets of killings, the photos scream psycho to me. There's no bite marks, no gaping claw wounds—nothing that says it's a monster rather than a man."

The muscle in his temple jumped. "Read the medical examiner's reports. Focus on the close up shots of the heads. Then tell me this is just a 'routine' serial killer. Some eighty-year-old guy hopped out on PCP or steroids."

A chill skated down her spine. God, Deacon looked lethal.

She nodded. "I promise I'll go through everything in meticulous detail, right down to brand of underwear each victim wore. Let's just rule out some creepy family pact before we start crying wolf. Literally."

"I don't think it's actually a werewolf, but..." He nodded, though it appeared slightly forced. "Suppose I can't ask for more than that."

"Well, when you say it with such enthusiasm..."

His expression relaxed. "You're right. You didn't run out of here screaming or call a team to hustle my ass off to some psychiatric ward..." He smirked at her. "You didn't secretly call anyone, did you?"

She hid her smile. "Not yet."

"Then, I'll consider this a victory of sorts."

"Good." She thumbed through a few more pages, pausing on some notes. The handwriting was meticulous, as if the person had wanted to make sure someone else could read their findings.

Deke sighed. "My dad had disturbingly neat printing for a guy, let alone a fed. I swear mine looks like someone sneezed while trying to scribble."

She twisted the man's service photo, staring at a familiar set of eyes, an almost identical jawline. Deacon's father had been just as ruggedly handsome as his son, the same devilish sparkle in the man's gaze, and she had no doubt Deacon was more like his father than just in looks.

She sighed. Knowing Deacon had suffered a similar loss to hers—hell, one far more brutal than she'd experienced—only heightened her awareness of him. And she didn't need another reason to feel connected to the man. To have her heart race or her mouth go suddenly dry whenever he was close. She already reacted to him on a level that made her question her sanity—she didn't want to deepen that reaction.

He nudged her hand. "You okay?"

She met his gaze, cursing the sudden fluttering in her stomach, then pointed at his father's service picture. "You look like him. Same eyes. Same jaw."

He glanced at the photo. "My mom used to stare at me sometimes and just start crying. Said I could have been his twin brother."

She bit her lip. Christ, why the hell did she keep bringing sad shit up?

"Stop." He shook a finger at her. "He's been dead twenty years. Sure, I want to find whatever killed him, but... I can talk about him without you worrying you're crossing some kind of emotional baggage line. Besides, my mother also used to say I was just as damn stubborn and twice the pain in the ass he was."

"Well, she got those last two traits right. And, for the record, he was exceedingly handsome."

His mouth lifted into a roguish smile. "You think I'm exceedingly handsome?"

"I said your father was—"

"And that I looked like him, which translates into you thinking *I'm* exceedingly handsome, as well."

"Is it too late to change my mind about your current mental health?"

"Afraid so." He motioned to the file. "So, what's our next move, partner?"

God, just that one word made her pulse kick up. She eased back, glad the tension had lessened, despite the way her heart pounded inside her chest. "I have to go back to the precinct. Fill out some lovely reports, then head home for a few hours of troubled sleep before starting the whole process over again. Figured you could meet me at the office tonight? Around seven? We'll…talk."

He inhaled. "Oh, two words men fear more than any other."

"Jackass. Can I keep the folder? I promise to take really good care of it. I'd just like to go through all of it—"

"Without me staring over your shoulder."

"It'll carry more weight if I come to the same conclusions on my own. And it's just for today. I'll return it tonight." She held up three fingers. "Scout's honor."

"Take your time. I have digital copies at home…just in case."

"Of course you do." She cursed when her phone

beeped, before glancing at it. "Shit, that's work. Captain Rankin probably wondered where the hell I wandered off to." She stood, taking one last sip of coffee, allowing the warm liquid to soothe her nerves.

"Shall I get that to go for you? You mentioned something about it being better than sex. Wouldn't want to make you stop before you're...finished."

"If only. I'll survive." She grabbed the folder, tucking it inside her purse. "So, do you need a note saying you're allowed to stay over? That you're going to play nice in the sandbox with all the other children?" She arched her brow. "Share your toys?"

His jaw clenched, the blue of his eyes darkening again. "Hoping I don't have to share with everyone. Truman's not really my type."

"I'll see what I can do." She took a step then stopped. "Seriously, do you want me to call the bureau? Give them the official all's well?"

He waved off her concern. "Thanks, but...I think I'm good. I'll take a rain check if my boss thinks I've gone off the deep end."

"Pretty sure the man already fears that." She shifted her feet, knowing she had to leave but strangely wanting to stay. Enjoy his company a bit longer before the real world intruded. "Thanks for the coffee and for letting me keep the file. I guess I'll see you tonight."

"It's a date."

The words skittered along her flesh, leaving a wake of goosebumps behind. God, what she wouldn't give for that to be true.

Caitlyn nodded, somehow managing not to embarrass herself as she returned to her vehicle, settling the manila folder on the passenger seat. She started her car then paused as she stared at the file. While she wasn't quite sure about monsters, she couldn't deny the connection. Which meant her "routine" case had just gotten complicated.

# CHAPTER FOUR

Deacon turned into the precinct parking lot, tucking his Wrangler between two squad cars. Caitlyn had parked a few spaces to his left, her hair blowing about her face as she walked over to meet him, scanning the area before stopping beside his vehicle. She leaned against one of the police cars, watching him exit his Jeep. A deep furrow creased her brow as she exhaled, her agitation palpable.

He arched a brow as he shut his door, following her gaze, wondering what the hell she was searching for before nudging her. "Hey, everything okay?"

An irritated huff rumbled free as she crossed her arms over her chest. "What took you so long?"

"I drove as fast as I could without breaking the sound barrier. Besides, you said to meet you here at seven. It's only three-thirty. I'd just gotten about an hour's worth of sleep. What's so urgent it couldn't wait until your shift?"

She rolled her shoulders, doing one more survey of the lot before moving in closer. Her breath ruffled the edge of his collar, the sweet scent of her perfume filling his senses. "There's a…situation."

He tilted his head to the side, wishing he could just stand there, breathing her in for the foreseeable future. "Situation?"

"My captain called. Summoned my ass down here. The man told me to use the speed limits as a minimum, which means he's extra pissy."

Deke frowned. "And I rushed here, as well, because…"

"Because he also told me to see that you were here by the time I arrived."

"Me? Did he tell you why?"

"Of course not. That would ruin the 'surprise'."

She made air quote with her hands, and he couldn't help but chuckle. God, she was adorable when she got angry.

She tapped the pavement, glaring at him. "Don't see how this is funny, G-man. We're both obviously in some sort of shit."

Deke did his best to school his features as he reached up and tucked a stray lock of hair behind her ear. The silky strands brushed against his skin, and he wanted nothing more than to grab the mass and hold her head tight as he tasted her perfectly pouting lips.

Instead, he offered her a small smile. "He probably just wants to check in…make sure I'm going to play nice with you."

"Ya think? Then why the hell is your boss here, too?" She nodded when his mouth gaped open slightly. "Oh, I'm not shitting you. Thankfully, Truman called as soon as Captain Rankin hung up. The man wanted to give me a bit of a warning. Said your director waltzed into Rankin's office a couple of hours ago and they'd been...discussing our partnership ever since."

Deacon carded his hand through his hair. This wasn't exactly going as planned. "Shit."

"I think it's a bit past shit." She blew out a rough breath. "Just do me a favor? Follow my lead, and for fuck's sake, let me do the talking."

He opened his mouth to answer, but she was already spinning, her boots clicking on the asphalt as she headed for the main doors. He cursed under his breath, darting after her. She'd left her hair down, the long, auburn waves bouncing wildly about her shoulders as she jogged up the front steps, her displeasure marked in the rigid line of her back. The way she merely nodded when a fellow officer held the door for her.

Deacon thanked the man, striding up beside her as she reached the stairs. "Wouldn't you prefer to take the elevator? Give yourself some time to calm down."

"I hate elevators, and I don't want to calm down. I think better when I'm edgy."

"So you're more of a 'dark side of the force' kinda girl."

She looked at him over her shoulder as she reefed open the stairwell door. "Really? *Star Wars* references now?"

"It's never a wrong time for a *Star Wars* reference."

A hint of a smile quirked her mouth. "Damn, but you're something else. I just haven't decided what, yet." She started up the stairs, her pace noticeably slower. "Anything I should know about your director before I go toe-to-toe with the man?"

"He's...focused."

She snorted. "In other words, he doesn't subscribe to

unorthodox methods and is most likely the last person who'd ever consider the existence of anything…supernatural."

"He definitely doesn't believe in shades of gray."

"This just keeps getting better."

Deacon snagged her arm, stopping her as she reached the fourth floor. She glanced at where his fingers wrapped around her biceps, moistening her lips as if they'd suddenly gone dry.

He held her gaze, moving in until their bodies were nearly touching. "I'm not the kind of guy who lets others take the fall for me. If Assistant Director Jamieson is looking for someone to crucify over our arrangement, I'm not about to offer you up as tribute."

"And I thought I was the only one who spent far too much time watching movies. Just…do as I said. Follow my lead and let me—"

"Do the talking. Yes, I remember. I'm just not sure it's a wise idea."

"Trust me. It's better than the alternative."

"Which is?"

"You marching in there declaring our prime suspect is a vampire. Or wraith, or…something equally unbelievable." She placed a finger over his lips, stopping him from replying. "This isn't me saying I think you're nuts. Quite the contrary, actually, but… Shit, Deke, just trust me, okay?"

He nodded, instantly missing the press of her finger the moment she lifted it off, turning back toward the closed door. He grazed his hand over his mouth, the remembered feel of her skin against his making him shiver. Damn, the woman was dangerous. He just wished it made him want to distance himself instead of longing to grab ahold and never let go.

She motioned him to follow as she exited the stairwell, winding her way down a few corridors before turning right. More than a dozen cops milled around the open room, pockets of workstations scattered around the space. She headed for a man sitting near one of the far windows, stacks of files piled across his desk.

David Truman looked up as she neared, a smug grin tilting his lips. He glanced at Deke, reclining in his chair until it rested on the two back legs. "Bet you wish you'd taken me up on my offer. It'd be my ass about to get reamed instead of yours."

Deke eyed Cait. "Truman offered to take the case? Would have thought with the note, the violence of the kill…"

Caitlyn sighed. "That I'd what? Be too fragile to handle it?"

Deke chuckled. "That you'd recognize a train wreck about to happen when it pops up."

Her gaze swept the length of him then crawled up to his face again. Her lips lifted into a wicked smile. "Some things are worth the risk." She turned her attention back to the other man. "Rankin say anything else I should know about before I go in there?"

"He's come out three times already to see if you'd arrived. I think that says more than words."

She grimaced. "Great. Guess we shouldn't keep the man waiting. Thanks for the head's up. I appreciate it."

David shrugged. "Can't win the pool if I don't try and rig it, now can I?"

"You started a pool?" She waved her hand in the air,

cutting off any reply. "Forget I asked. I'm not even sure why I'm surprised."

She drew herself up, squaring her shoulders before glancing back. "You ready?"

She didn't wait for Deke's answer, striding forward with purpose. He had to hand it to her—if she was nervous about the meeting, she sure didn't show it. Between her lifted chin and the firm set of her shoulders, she radiated confidence, and his damn chest hurt as his dick seemed to push against his fly.

He gave himself a mental shake. Now wasn't the time to think about anything other than avoiding getting suspended—or worse, getting Caitlyn suspended.

The thought cooled the heat burning just beneath his flesh as he followed her to another door. He'd play along —see how the situation unraveled. But she had a hard lesson ahead of her if she thought, for one moment, he'd toss her under the bus. He'd made his choice when he'd decided to crash her crime scene—exaggerate the truth slightly in the hopes she'd let him tag along. He wouldn't jeopardize her career for his own selfish needs. He respected her too much to do that. There was also the pesky little problem of his undeniable attraction to her.

She hadn't even knocked before the door opened, Captain Rankin filling the doorway. He glanced at Deacon, clenching his jaw as he seemed to size up Deke before motioning the two of them inside. Caitlyn walked forward, moving off to her left until she reached the captain's desk. She nodded for Deke to join her, facing back the way they'd entered.

Rankin shut the door, joining another man standing in the far corner. Though his back was turned, Deke knew the guy's silhouette. The hard line of his torso, and the way he fisted his hands at his side. Assistant Director Jamieson stood a few inches taller than Rankin, his hair a stark blond compared to the other man's brown. But when Jamieson finally turned around, he wore the same, intense expression as the captain, only his unrest was completely focused on Deacon. Deke held the man's gaze, determined not to back down when Caitlyn took a small step forward, drawing both men's attention.

She nodded at Jamieson, then faced her boss. "Captain."

The man frowned. "Have a seat, Detective Decker."

Her lips quirked. "Actually, I've discovered it's generally best to stand in your office."

Jamieson grinned then sobered, once again glaring at Deacon.

Captain Rankin shook his head. "That sense of humor of yours is just as apt to get you into more trouble than out of it."

She cocked her head slightly. "I didn't realize I'd done anything wrong, sir."

"That so? Did you think the Assistant Director of the Bureau's Violent Crimes Unit just stopped by to buy me a cup of coffee? Which reminds me…Peter Jamieson, this is Caitlyn Decker. One of my finer officers, though I suppose in this instance, that remains to be seen."

Caitlyn shook Jamieson's hand, her face still a mask of fortitude. "Sir."

Jamieson glanced at Deacon then focused on Caitlyn. "I understand you were an asset in a joint venture several months back."

"The Morris case."

"Quite the arsenal of evidence you and Agent McGraw gathered. A refreshing change when our two departments work well together."

"Cats and dogs have been known to tolerate each other, sir."

"On occasion, I suppose."

"It's really not that farfetched. Agent McGraw has a very impressive record. I believe he has the highest conviction rate in his division, which is why I've asked him to partner up with me on my new case. That is why you're here, right?" She turned to Rankin. "I was going to make it official tonight when I started my shift, but it looks like you two gentlemen have beat me to the punch." She shifted her attention back to Jamieson. "I appreciate the bureau's eagerness to lend me such a valuable resource. I imagine you have plenty of your own cases piled up."

Jamieson's eyes narrowed as his mouth pulled tight. "You asked Agent McGraw to join you?"

"Yes, sir. Is that a problem?"

"I was under the impression McGraw all but begged you to be part of the investigation. Showed up at your crime scene this morning ready to pounce, despite the fact he's been warned about pursuing this particular... endeavor."

Caitlyn glanced at him, giving him a small shake of her head before smiling at the other two men. "Are you referring to those other unsolved files? The ones with identical homicides that suggest we have a serial killer on our hands?"

Jamieson arched a brow as he crossed his arms over

his chest. "I didn't realize you were privy to that... information."

"I wasn't, until Agent McGraw was kind enough to lend me the files, seeing as I believe the cases are connected."

"Then how did you know to call Agent McGraw in the first place?"

"It was obvious when I arrived at the scene that this wasn't the perpetrator's first offence. The violence of the attack, the way the body had been left out in the open, as if the killer wanted it found, the note...there's no way this was victim zero. But there hasn't been anything remotely like this in the area before—at least not through police channels. That kind of cryptic message would have been the talk of the town. So I took a chance and asked Agent McGraw if he'd come out and have a look. Let me know if it resembled anything the bureau was working on. You know the rest."

Jamieson glanced at Deacon, a smug smile lifting his lips. "So you're saying your partnership has nothing to do with the fact Agent Thomas McGraw, Deacon's father, led the investigation in the previous cases twenty years ago?"

Caitlyn sighed, genuine compassion coloring her eyes. "Look, I get that this might be a sensitive subject around the bureau—"

"Sensitive? An agent was killed the last time these sort of serial murders happened in the city. And his findings did little to ease that sting."

She nodded. "You think Deacon's father was...under a lot of stress."

"If that's your politically correct way of saying the man

had lost it, yes. And it made the bureau look less than stellar back then."

Deacon stepped forward. "I'd have thought the bureau would be more interested in capturing a serial offender than whether or not their reputation got a bit tarnished."

Jamieson matched Deke's movement, closing the distance until Rankin stepped between them.

He palmed Jamieson's chest. "Easy now. We're all on the same team, so to speak."

Caitlyn gave Deke a stern look, silently telling him to stand down as she faced his boss. "Director Jamieson—"

Jamieson held Deke's gaze. "Assistant Director."

She grinned. "I realize that the details of the previous cases are unusual." She held up her hand, motioning that she wasn't finished. "But that doesn't alter the fact that these cases *are* connected. While I'm still waiting for the medical examiner to send me her findings, everything suggests that the murder in the alley is the thirteenth in a very long line of killings."

Jamieson huffed. "That would make the guy–"

"Around eighty years old. Yes, I'm aware of the hurdles surrounding these murders. But it doesn't change the evidence, which clearly suggests Deacon's father was right. That it's the same killer. Now, I'm not sure how that's possible. Perhaps it's a family pact of some sort, and that's how they're able to duplicate the murders down to identical markings found on each of the victim's heads, making it appear to be the work of the original perpetrator. Or a ritual carried out by members of some kind of cult that only crops up every few decades. But there's no doubt in my mind this is just the beginning of what could be a very bloody and very public killing spree.

One that will be in the spotlight far more than any of the previous incidents."

Jamieson chuckled. "I've got to hand it to you, Detective. You certainly know how to talk the talk. I'm just not sure Agent McGraw is the best person to have working with you on this, considering the history."

"On the contrary, he knows these cases better than anyone. He can anticipate how the killer thinks, where he might strike next. He's created profiles of our next set of victims and has maps of where the killer will most likely attack. With all due respect, sir, we'll have five more bodies cluttering up the morgue if Deacon isn't in on this. I'll be floundering, at best, on my own."

Rankin looked at Jamieson. "Seems my detective has her mind set. And the woman's incredibly stubborn."

Jamieson held up his hands. "Fine. I'll authorize the joint venture. See you have all the resources we can offer at your disposal. Just do me a favor?"

She nodded.

"Don't let the man talk to any reporters. He tends to let his passion speak for him. And Deacon...I want regular reports on what's happening. No more rogue actions, like showing up at her crime scene uninvited while telling me you're taking a personal day." He waved his hands this time. "I know. The good detective has covered for you. And I won't question her integrity. For some reason, she seems to have an unhealthy respect for your abilities and has put both her job and her ass on the line. I suggest you don't let her down."

Deacon managed to keep his expression fixed. "Understood, sir."

"Good." He extended his hand to Caitlyn again. "Tread

carefully, Detective Decker. Cases like these have a way of biting you in the ass." He made his way to the door, stopping at the threshold. "And if you ever get tired of working on this side of the badge, give me a call. The bureau could use someone who exhibits your amount of grace under pressure."

Rankin scoffed. "Did you seriously just try to steal my best detective?"

"Damn straight I did." He gave a curt nod. "Captain."

The man left, the sudden void in the small office nearly suffocating.

Rankin whistled as he leaned his butt against the edge of his desk. "The man's right. You certainly know how to put on a show, Caitlyn."

She grinned. "I wasn't lying. I do need Deacon on this case."

"I'm not questioning that. What I *am* questioning is how you two went about it. We both know you didn't call the man from the scene. Truman already told me McGraw merely showed up."

"I probably would have called him. Does that help?"

The other man snorted. "Just...be careful. It's not only this department's reputation on the line. You're carrying the weight of the Federal Bureau of Investigation and those two previous unsolved files. This kind of case can ruin a career."

"I'm more concerned with preventing five more deaths than whether I get a bad review. But I'll keep that thought in mind." She motioned to the door. "Can we go now?"

"If you wait another five minutes, Truman won't win the pool."

She laughed. "I think I can live with him winning." She headed for the door then spun. "Thanks."

"Don't make me eat my words, Detective. You either, Special Agent. I'll take it personally if anything happens to her while she's in your care."

Deacon smiled at Caitlyn's hushed curse. "I'll see to it she doesn't get a scratch."

"I'll hold you to that. And I'll let Truman and the others know you'll be setting your own hours for a while...day. Night. Both, if I'm correct." Rankin grinned. "And I usually am. But I'll make sure you get paged if anything crops up that could be directly connected to this case."

She nodded her thanks as Deacon joined her, following her out into the main area. Truman did an exaggerated fist pump as they walked over to her desk, openly gloating over his apparent victory.

Caitlyn sighed. "He's going to hold that over my head for weeks, the bastard." She crossed her arms, staring up on him. "You told them you were taking a personal day?"

Deke shrugged. "I needed to see that scene. And I knew Jamieson wouldn't let me anywhere near it, so..."

"So you made up some lame ass story. Then proceeded to accept my offer of partnership, knowing full well your boss would flip his lid when he found out."

"I was kind of hoping it'd be later. So much so that he'd be unable to do anything about it without jeopardizing the entire undertaking. Guess the grapevine's quicker than I realized." He nudged her foot with his. "You didn't have to cover for me. I was more than prepared to accept the consequences of inviting myself to your crime scene."

"And have Jamieson suspend you? Or worse? No way. Besides, I wasn't lying. I really do need you on this case with me."

He arched a brow. "You want another cup of Stacy's coffee, don't you?"

Her smiled faded as she scanned the room before settling on his face as she leaned in close. Her scent surrounded him again, but it was the intense look she flashed him that stole his breath.

She held his gaze, her eyes narrowing. "What I want is for you to level with me. What's killing these people, because based on what I read in the ME's report—it's not human."

# CHAPTER FIVE

Caitlyn stared up at Deke, her heart racing, her breath nearly wheezing in and out as she tried to remain calm. But damn…how was she supposed to remain calm after everything she'd read in the reports? That's the real reason she was edgy. Knowing she'd have to lie to her boss until she had some kind of tangible grasp on what she was dealing with. She groaned inwardly. The chances of this case having anything remotely tangible was a pipe dream at best.

Deacon tensed, his gaze sweeping the precinct before returning to her. Disbelief flashed in his eyes before he swallowed, his neck bobbing with the action. She made herself move back. Being that close to him distracted her. Made her mind focus on him—on his scent, his voice, the way his fingers felt as they brushed against her skin, however innocent—instead of the case. And she needed all her attention on the murder. *Murders*. Shit.

She raked her hand through her hair, hoping he couldn't see the way it trembled as she gathered her composure. "Let's go grab coffee. We need to talk someplace we don't have to worry about who's listening."

"Afraid they'll cart you away?"

"Damn straight. Hell, I'm half considering just driving myself there. Save everyone the trouble of watching me slowly descend into madness, because what's in these files..." She shook her head, staring into his far too blue eyes. "It's madness."

"Stacy's is only ten minutes from here. It *is* open for business, but I'm certain she or Trevor could find us a private booth. Intimate, even."

She punched him lightly in the shoulder. "I'm not trying to seduce you. Quiet will suffice."

He flashed her a roguish smile, leaning in close. "Have you ever stopped long enough to consider maybe I'm the one who wants to seduce you?"

Her breath hitched at his words, his exhalation feathering across her neck before he pulled back, motioning to the stairwell again. She drew a shaky breath, hating that he could probably see the blush on her cheeks and throat as it disappeared down the vee of her top. She made her way back outside, heading for her car. She clicked the remote, startling a bit when Deke opened the passenger door.

She paused, glancing at his vehicle before opening her door and sliding in. "Aren't you going to meet me there?"

"And miss watching you squirm for ten minutes while you try to figure out which one of us is actually insane? Not a chance." He motioned up the street. "Besides, there won't be much parking."

She sighed, backing up then pulling out, following his directions as she wove through traffic. Though she was itching to corner him regarding the reports she'd read a dozen times, she couldn't quite bring herself to broach the subject during the drive. Whether it was the nonstop traffic or the fact the air inside the cab seemed thinner than usual, making it feel as if she couldn't quite catch her breath, she wasn't sure. All she knew was that she needed space. To distance herself from the spicy scent of his cologne or the way he seemed to dominate the small area, making it exceedingly hard to focus on anything other than his steady breathing or how his hands looked stronger and bigger than she'd noticed before. The kind of hands that could hold her limbs as he pounded into her against a wall.

Heat crept up her neck and into her cheeks as she turned at the next intersection, releasing a relieved breath when the restaurant appeared at the next set of lights. If she'd known the man was serious, and that he'd spend the entire trip over simply staring at her, she would have kicked his ass out of her car. Instead, she'd done exactly what he'd suggested—squirmed while wondering which one of them would be carted off first.

Deacon chuckled as she pulled into the rear parking lot, shoving her vehicle into first. "You're not crazy. Trust me."

"Trusting you is the reason I'm questioning my sanity." She shook her head. "Let's just go inside, find a quiet corner where we can focus on the case, and talk."

Deacon waved her forward, still smiling. Tension strained her shoulders as she made her way inside. This wasn't how she'd pictured her first evening working with Deke would turn out, and she wasn't sure if she was relieved he hadn't been lying to her, or scared shitless about what they were going to discuss, because the reality of it...

Deke chuckled. "Would you stop running it all over inside your head until we get settled? You're only going to make yourself feel more uncertain."

She stopped, turning to face him. "How the hell do you know I'm obsessing over it?"

"Sweetheart, if your back got any stiffer you wouldn't be able to walk. Besides, I'm more than familiar with what you're feeling. The disbelief. The shock...the fear that maybe I just pulled you inside my own delusional dream. Can't tell you how many times I've been standing in your shoes. Just try to relax until we go through it." He brushed a finger along her cheek. "You're not alone in this. Promise."

"Great, so they'll give us his and hers straightjackets. That's very comforting."

He winked. "Just think of the things we could do inside that padded room."

"Don't you take anything seriously?"

His smile faltered slightly. "We're about to discuss how some...*thing* killed my father. Pretty sure some levity is in order before we start."

She sighed then gave him a shove. "You sure your sister won't mind us crashing her restaurant unannounced? Again?"

"Are you mad? The girl adores me."

"So...it's a crap shoot. Could go either way."

His smile flourished again. "Why do you think I brought you with me? I needed a bodyguard."

"Who says I wouldn't help her kick your ass?"

He leaned in, his breath feathering across her cheek. "Who says I wouldn't let you?"

Her breath stalled as the temperature in the room seemed to skyrocket. She forced herself to swallow, praying Deke wouldn't notice her reaction as she spun, waving at the dining area. "So...do we just sit or—"

"Deacon?"

Caitlyn turned toward the woman's voice, grinning when Stacy gave Deke a playful swat on his chest. Her affection for the man was obvious, and Cait's stomach tightened. She'd been seventeen before she'd had any kind of connection remotely close to theirs, and she didn't like the pang of jealousy that burned beneath her skin.

Stacy snorted when Deke asked for a secluded table, eyeing Cait suspiciously. The woman appeared to consider the issue, then motioned for them to follow her. She wove her way to the far end of the room, stopping beside a small booth tucked into a corner. "It's not your usual table, dear brother. The one that affords you the best view of all the exits and other kinds of spy-like crap. But it's quiet, and no one will bother you."

Deke laughed. "It's not crap to want to know what your options are should something unexpected happen."

Stacy arched a brow as she palmed her hips. "You do realize you're the only one who sees the world that way, right? Who believes everyone is out to get them? And what makes it crazy is you seem to think we're all the insane ones for not sharing your paranoia."

"I believe the word you're searching for is realism."

"Just...try to refrain from frisking everyone who comes through the door. I'm trying to make a living here."

"I'll do my best to behave. Which reminds me... I

promised Caitlyn another cup of your amazing coffee. Can I go help myself to a pot and some mugs?"

"You know where to find everything."

Deke gave his sister a peck on the cheek, then headed for the kitchen. Caitlyn couldn't help but watch him cross the room, his large stride eating up the distance. Even merely walking the man oozed strength and determination, and she had a bad feeling he'd willingly cross a few lines if it meant getting his father's killer.

"He's...unique, isn't he?"

Cait glanced over at Stacy, somewhat confused by the woman's words. "He's an excellent agent."

Stacy laughed. "Agent, right. This is another 'work' date?"

"It's a joint case. Deacon merely thought this would be a good place to go through the files. In private."

"So the fact he's never brought another colleague through that door, let alone twice in the same day..."

Cait forced herself to swallow, hoping to ease her suddenly parched throat as she schooled her features. "We're not—"

"He likes you, Cait. And not as a detective."

"I'm sure you're just reading more into this than there is."

Stacy grinned. "What do you know...you like him, too."

"Stacy..."

The woman waved her hand. "Just...tread lightly. I know he comes across as if he's bulletproof, but the truth is... He rarely gives anyone a chance to really get to know him. But something tells me he wants to let you."

"I'll keep that in mind."

"Good, because I take my role as protective little sister very seriously."

Caitlyn grinned. "I'll wear my Kevlar vest when we come here...just in case."

Stacy nodded, taking a few steps away before spinning toward Cait again. "You two make a cute couple, in case you were wondering. And you certainly bring out the best in him. I haven't seen him smile or laugh this much in years."

She turned, heading toward the kitchen before Cait could respond. Deke passed the woman halfway through the dining area, dodging his sister's mock punch as he returned to their booth. He placed the coffee pot and mugs in the center of the table, pouring Cait a cup before finally sitting.

He nodded toward the mug. "Might be best if you get your fix in, first, in case you decide to go for those matching straightjackets."

She picked up the cup up. "How did you know how I take it?"

"I'm a fed."

"You called Truman, didn't you?"

"Actually, I just paid attention this morning." He took a sip of his, looking at her across the top of his cup. "Is that so surprising?"

She smiled. "Considering I, also, paid attention... you take yours black with, I believe, three sugars. But then you are a bit on the sour side, so..."

He grinned as he set the mug down, the easy symmetry of his face making her heart race. Damn, but the man made her insides turn to jelly.

Deke sighed as he leaned back in his chair. "I hate to change the subject, but..."

She nodded. "But, we need to talk. About the case."

"About why you seem to have jumped on board my crazy train. So...what did you discover that changed your mind? You seemed fairly certain this morning that you'd find a reasonable solution—that family pact thing you'd been grasping onto."

"Can you blame me for wanting a logical explanation? Seriously, the alternative—"

"Was crazy?"

"I was going to say seemed impossible. Or unlikely. But now..."

She leaned back in her chair, staring at him. Some of the tension had eased from his shoulders though she could tell he was still wary. Unsure if he'd like what she had to say. Good. She didn't like it, either. In fact, it made her stomach tighten and her chest constrict. Though, that could just be sitting across from him.

She groaned inwardly at the thought. She needed to get her damn head on straight. "Anyway, I decided to go through a few of the notes. I'll admit, at first glance, there wasn't anything that struck me as supernatural. Sure, the killings are were violent and feel felt like overkill, but...it didn't scream monster."

Deke's mouth curled into a knowing grin. "Let me guess. You were puzzled by the markings around the head."

Her breath hitched. "Yes. How..." She shook her head at his knowing smile. "Initially, they looked like bruises, mostly likely from the killer holding the skull firmly during the fight or maybe shortly after. But when I took one of the newer photos and examined it under magnification…what appear to be fingerprints aren't fingerprints at all. It's almost as if the perp's fingertips were covered in barbs somehow. The bruising was caused by a series of tiny puncture wounds that resemble the overall shape of a print."

Deke nodded. "So, I'm guessing you turned to the medical examiner's reports next."

"Have you been spying on me?"

He had the good grace to shake his head. "Sorry. Occupational hazard. Like I said this morning… I've gone over the evidence more times than I'd like to admit. Please, carry on."

She took a sip of her coffee, hoping it'd settle her nerves, distract her from the look on Deacon's face—as if she'd just given him a glimmer of hope when he'd lost all of his. "Unfortunately, the report didn't answer my questions. Seems the ME couldn't tell exactly what the markings were and left it as inconclusive but mostly likely irregular blood pooling. That seemed odd to me, so I read through the rest of the doctor's findings. That's where things…"

Christ, how did she say that's when she'd realized Deke hadn't been lying? That something was killing these people and she wasn't convinced it was human? She jumped when Deke's hand grazed hers.

He gave her fingers a gentle squeeze. "I'm not going to think what you tell me is crazy. I'm the one who dragged you down the rabbit hole, remember? Just tell me what you found disturbing."

Cait glanced at where he held her, wishing the innocent contact didn't soothe the fears she'd been reeling with all day. "What's disturbing is that all of the people... all of them...died instantly."

"I hear that expression every day. Hell, my mom and I were told those very words regarding my father. As if knowing his death hadn't been dragged out was supposed to ease the pain somehow. Lessen the blow. I assure you, it didn't."

She gave his fingers a squeeze back. "That's what I thought initially, as well. Instantaneous death usually refers to the victim losing consciousness immediately with the trauma being significant enough to stop the heart within seconds, leading to brain death shortly after. But it's not an accurate account of what really goes on inside the body. Our cells don't all just stop functioning at the same time. It takes hours for the body to truly die. That's how coroners can determine time of death among other things. But in these murders..." She raked her hand through her hair. "Damn it, everything inside them stopped working. Just...stopped. All at once."

"And you didn't just brush it off as an anomaly?"

"In every case? Hell, no. Besides, I got a second opinion." She held up her hand when his mouth gaped open. "Relax. I didn't go showing your files off to some random person. I had Riley take a look at just the sections in the ME's report that were troubling. He said it wasn't possible. That either the doctors in the cases recorded their findings wrong, or..."

"Or it was as if the person's life force was literally sucked out of them, killing everything at once. As if someone just flicked a switch and the person was gone." He leaned in closer, still holding her one hand. "Who's Riley?"

Caitlyn sighed. Deke must really have her tied in knots if she let Riley's name slip without realizing it.

Deke arched a brow. "Hmm, perhaps you weren't being honest when you mentioned you didn't have a bed partner."

"What?" Cait laughed. "God, no." She cringed when Deke merely stared at her. "Shit. I really need more sleep. Fine. Riley is my brother, okay? Well, technically, he's my adopted brother, or I guess I'm his adopted sister through foster care. He also happens to be a brilliant trauma surgeon over at Harborview. When those reports seemed off, I paid him a visit—had him read just those few sections, in case I was interpreting them wrong. Medical jargon was never really my forte, but he agreed. When I pressed him for some sort of answer, he just shrugged and said if he had to guess, he'd say their very souls had been sucked out of them." She matched Deke's previous motion as she leaned toward him. "And Riley isn't the religious type, so for him to say that, even if he was joking, is huge."

She let the rest of the words just fade. Damn, but this meeting was getting worse by the second. Now, she was starting to think she really was crazy.

Deacon held her gaze for what felt like forever before easing back in his seat. "I didn't know you'd been in foster care, or that you had a brother as a result of it."

"That's your takeaway on this? That I have a guy out there I consider my brother?"

"I already knew the rest, sweetheart. And yes, I find it odd you've never mentioned him before. We spent a lot of time together during the Morris case."

"Mostly talking about safe subjects, like favorite

movies and the weather. You never told me you had a sister, either."

"True. I guess I just assumed—after what you'd mentioned to me this morning about your foster experiences—that you hadn't made any lasting connections."

She shrugged. "I didn't start living with him and his dad until I was seventeen. And to be honest, I hadn't planned on staying more than the time it took to recover. But—"

Deke frowned. "Recover?"

She cringed. Shit, this wasn't the time or place for *that* conversation. Though, truth be told, there wasn't a good time or place to talk about that part of her life.

Deke sighed. "Based on the way you're reacting, I'm thinking there's a story behind it. Care to share?"

"Not something I like to talk about."

"I see. What about his father? Do you still keep in touch?"

"Joe? He died a couple of years ago. Riley took it pretty hard. The jerk has made it his mission to save everyone, even if it isn't possible. We check in with each other a couple of times a week. He works a lot."

"Sounds like someone I know."

"Yeah. You. Now can we get off the awkward subject of my life and back to this case? Do you know what's killing these people?"

Deacon thumbed his cup, shaking his head. "Not a clue. Based on the previous two sprees, our 'killer' appears to attack every seven to ten days until it's made half a dozen kills, then simply disappears. Why it only stayed gone twenty years this time instead of forty, I don't know."

"Or maybe it didn't. Maybe there are six other deaths that never got connected."

"You've seen the crime scenes firsthand. You know that kind of killing wouldn't go unnoticed."

"Maybe our killer didn't butcher every victim? Or the deaths were attributed to something else? The notes could have gotten lost or stolen. Might be worth checking out. The more data we have, the better we can predict where and when it'll strike next."

"You sure you still want to be my partner? After everything we've talked about?"

"I don't scare easily. There's a lot more going on here than some sick family killing pact. Exactly what it is, I'm not sure, but you've definitely got my attention. Just...do me a favor and don't go telling my boss we're chasing some kind of soul-sucking vampire or whatever. Best we try to keep this investigation within the realm of the believable for the sake of appearances. But if you've got any idea how to proceed, I'm all ears."

"I promise I'll hide my wooden stake. As for where to begin... My father made a connection with a woman who claimed to be a Wiccan during his investigation. That's a—"

"White witch. One who practices healing spells and the like. I'm familiar with the term. Did she give him any leads?"

"There isn't much documented, at least, not in these files. I think my father was trying to keep it out of the official record. All I have is a name. Beverly Howard. I checked after you left. She owns the Harvest Moon

Apothecary Shop over on the east side. Not too far from here, maybe fifteen minutes. I was thinking we might pay her a visit. See what she told my father that he didn't think belonged in a bureau dossier. If you're game?"

She tossed him her keys. "It'll save us time if you drive. But can I get the coffee to go this time? Something tells me I'll need it."

"Of course. Wouldn't want you to go without finishing twice in the same day."

"Jackass."

"Oh, there's that pet name again. Gives me goosebumps." He stood, offering her his hand. "Come on. We'll get you an extra-large coffee to go. I just suggest you drink it before we get to Ms. Howard's place. Her testimony might sour your stomach."

# CHAPTER SIX

Deke parked alongside the curb, staring at the small bungalow across the street. A wooden sign hung on a metal post, the hinges creaking in the light breeze, the word *apothecary* carved into the surface beside a tribal art drawing of a full moon. He glanced at the folder wedged against the console, wondering if the tight feeling in his gut was anticipation or fear. If he was honest with himself, he never really thought he'd ever be in this position—investigating his father's death with the full blessing of the bureau. He assumed it'd be a venture he tackled on his own—after work or on his days off—without the aid of any official backing. Just knowing he didn't have to hide his involvement...

He released a shaky breath. He needed to pull himself together, preferably before Caitlyn saw through his damn facade. And she would. The woman seemed to have a knack for reading what he tried to hide, and the last thing he needed was her questioning his ability to have her back. She'd already gone out on a limb for him—risked her job, likely her life—and he couldn't let her down before they'd even started.

A hand landed on his shoulder and he turned, nothing but the vibrant green of her eyes filling his view. Small lines creased the edges as she squinted slightly, looking at him as if she wasn't sure whether to punch him or kiss him. His dick jumped at the thought. Damn, but the woman was going to be the death of him. And all they'd shared were a couple of cups of coffee and some small talk disguised as business.

She gave him a reassuring smile. "You okay?"

He wanted to joke, brush away her worries like he always did, but something about the way she watched him, concern flashing in her eyes, made lying impossible. Instead, he gave her hand a pat. "This is just...surreal, I suppose. After hiding the fact I've been trying to make any sort of leeway on this case since forever, to actually be investigating it—legitimately, even if not with the full blessing of my boss—it's..."

He didn't finish. Didn't know what to say. How to verbalize the whirlwind of emotions churning in his gut without sounding like a complete wuss.

Caitlyn sighed, lifting her hand before grazing her thumb along his cheek, leaving it against his skin long enough to make it tingle before dropping her hand. "We're going to find out what killed your dad. What's lurking in the shadows. No matter how long it takes." She shifted over, cracking open her door then glancing at him across her shoulder. "And I'd be worried if this wasn't a bit overwhelming for you. I just hope you realize you don't always have to be ten feet tall and bulletproof. I can deflect a few bullets myself."

He chuckled as the tension bled away before following her out. He shook his head as she rounded to his side of the car. "So, you're telling me I'm partnered with Wonder Woman?"

"If only I had that damn lasso of truth. Now, *that* would come in handy."

"Funny, I was picturing you in that outfit…" His words morphed into a grunt as she punched him lightly in the chest. "Point noted." He waved toward the house. "After you."

She struck off toward the pathway leading to the shop, her hips swaying hypnotically as she moved. Deke forced himself to focus on the door, on anything but how good her ass looked in her pants as they climbed the few short steps up to the porch. Caitlyn motioned to the doorbell, a sly grin on her face.

He pushed the button, glancing over at her. "You could have rung the doorbell. We're partners, remember?"

"I have my reasons for allowing you this privilege."

"Such as?"

"First, courtesy. You've been waiting a long time to launch an official investigation into your dad's death, and I'm the last person who'd steal this moment from you."

"And second? Because there's got to be a second if you said first."

Her grin widened as footsteps sounded beyond the door. "Second, I'd prefer you to be the first line of defense in case this person turns out to be our soul-sucking monster."

"Wench." He ignored her snicker as the door slivered open, a woman's face filling the small space. "Beverly Howard?"

She nodded. "I'm sorry, but I'm closed on Sundays."

Deke palmed the door when she went to close it. "We're not here to buy anything, ma'am." He held up his badge. "I'm Special Agent McGraw. This is Detective Decker. We were hoping we could talk to you about some old cases we're looking into."

The woman stared at the badge, glancing from it to him then back before her eyes rounded, one hand lifting to her mouth. "You...you're Deacon. Thomas' son." She opened the door wider. "I don't know how I didn't see it right away. You're the spitting image of your father." Her expression fell. "I was sorry to hear about his death. Thomas was a good man who tried very hard to tackle something he really didn't understand. But I suppose that's why you're here? The old cases you mentioned?" She snorted. "I saw that a young man was murdered on the news. I thought the details sounded eerily familiar. You're here to tell me it's back, aren't you?"

Deacon glanced at Cait, but she had the same doe-eyed expression he suspected he did.

Beverly sighed. "Where are my manners? Please, come in. I'll fix you both some iced tea."

Deacon inched forward. "That's not necessary, ma'am."

"Beverly, please. And trust me...by the expressions on both of your faces, what you really need are a few shots of bourbon, but since I'm fairly certain you won't drink while on duty...the tea will have to do." She motioned to the hallway. "The parlor is down the hall, second door on the left. I'll be right in with the tea. Feel free to look around."

She shooed them into the large space, disappearing

down the corridor. Glasses clinked in the distance, a faint humming sound drifting through the air.

Caitlyn walked around the room, stopping at a series of photos on a shelf. A young man smiled at the camera, a flash of red in his eyes spoiling the otherwise stunning picture. The guy looked in his early twenties, his similar jaw suggesting he must have been Beverly's son.

"Call me crazy, but the woman's got family portraits right next to... Shit, I don't even know what this stuff is." She lifted one of the containers, staring at the odd yellow liquid inside. "I can't pronounce half the names on these bottles. I think they might be Latin, or Greek or...alien, though I'm pretty sure this one translates into 'eye of newt'."

Deke scoffed at her. "You agreed this was a good place to start. And that you'd keep an open mind."

"And I still do. Still am, it's just..." She scanned the room again as she replaced the bottle. "I'm just having a hard time believing I'm standing here, about to ask some poor woman if she believes in monsters. Hell, if she knows the kind we're chasing."

"No need to worry, Detective. I'm a firm believer in the paranormal."

Caitlyn spun as Beverly entered the room, a small tray balanced in her hands. There'd been no hesitation in her voice, no slight waver of pitch indicating the woman was at all fazed by Caitlyn's statement, the fact of which both intrigued and worried Deke. Obviously, his father had come here for a reason, though Deke wasn't sure if he was really prepared for some of the answers. What if he discovered his dad had been as crazy as everyone had thought, and that the solution was nothing more than some kind of weird drug the perpetrator gave his victims that accounted for the odd findings?

Beverly sighed. "I realize this kind of...discussion doesn't come easily for most people. Folks tend to have a hard time believing what they've never seen. But I assure you...there're things out there no one wants to admit are real. Creatures straight out of horror books. It's a shame my son's not here. He's had his share of encounters. He might have come across as more credible in your eyes, being closer to your age."

Cait waved her hands. "I sorry. I didn't mean to imply anything."

Beverly merely laughed, turning to Deke as she placed the tray on a small coffee table. "No apologies necessary. In fact, Thomas was every bit as skeptical as the next person, until he saw it. After that..." She shrugged. "Let's just say he stopped by more than a few times in the hope of gathering enough information to kill it. I'm just sorry he didn't. When he died and the killings stopped...I assumed he'd managed to put an end to it before passing on."

Deke took a sip of the drink, hoping the cool liquid would ease the dry feeling in his throat before he drew a deep breath. "So, you know what it is we're hunting? What's killing these people?"

Beverly sighed, taking a seat in a chair opposite them as she sipped her own drink. The ice clinked against the glass as she set it on the table. "Not exactly. Thomas wasn't able to provide enough information for me to narrow it down to just one creature."

Caitlyn held up her hand, her eyes wide, a hint of panic in their depths. "Perhaps we should start with what information Deacon's father did share with you. See if we have anything new to add and go from there."

Beverly nodded, rising then heading over to a large bookshelf. She thumbed through a few volumes before removing a large leather tome. She walked over to the counter near the far wall, laying the book down before shuffling through the pages, stopping at an odd-looking drawing. She tapped the page. "I started with this one."

Deke looked over her shoulder. "What is it?"

"The common term is soul vampire."

"Vampire?" Caitlyn moved in beside him. "As in… vampire-vampire?"

Beverly gave them both a sympathetic smile. "I understand this must be hard for you to process—"

"Hard?" Caitlyn raked a hand back through her hair, pacing across the room before spinning. "You're seriously telling us that the stories, the lore…it's all true? Vampires? Werewolves?"

Beverly merely nodded. "I realize that Hollywood has portrayed all these creatures as everything from monsters to sex symbols. I personally believe the truth is somewhere in the middle. A mixture of human and non-human traits. After all, if they were completely irresistible, there wouldn't be any regular people left, and if they were all bloodthirsty, relentless monsters, there'd been more murders like the ones you're investigating."

Caitlyn held up her hand. "Trust me. There's plenty. I see it every day, which is why…" She waved her hand at the book. "This is…difficult." She looked at Deke. "I know. Open mind and I'm trying. I know what I read in those reports, what Riley confirmed, it's just…" She sighed. "I'm feeling a bit out of my element."

Deke walked over to her, giving in to the urge to brush his thumb along her jaw. "You're here. That's what counts."

A shiver worked through her, and he couldn't help but wonder if it was the situation or them. She looked over at Beverly. "You said there was more than one possibility?"

Beverly nodded, seemingly unfazed by Cait's lack of conviction. "A few more." She flipped to another page. "There's a banshee. It's a kind of ghost that scares its victims, causing their death before feeding off the soul, though I'm not sure if it'd leave the kind of carnage Thomas mentioned. Or this..." She held up the book, showing off a distorted creature. "You'd know it as a wraith. It literally sucks out the soul of a person, much like the vampire. There are other entities that also feed on souls, but Thomas had said the creature touched its victims and that the death was instantaneous. That makes these three your top contenders, unless it's something I've never read up on."

Cait arched a brow. "Since when do ghosts touch people?"

"Oh, honey, ghosts might well be the most dangerous of all. They have more power than folks want to believe, and are incredibly hard to dispatch."

Cait's face paled before she turned, seemingly interested in a book on Beverly's shelf. Deke sighed, knowing the woman's words had cut deep, especially after Cait had confessed to seeing her mother's ghost. Believing that it'd saved her.

He touched her arm. "Cait—"

Her phone blared, making her jump. She gave him a token smile before answering it as she secluded herself to the far side of the room. Deke sighed, carding his fingers through his hair. The last thing he wanted was to awaken unwanted memories for her. Despite the fierce bravado she wore around her like a shield, he had a gnawing feeling her time in foster care still ate at her—like a festering wound only she could see.

Footsteps sounded beside him as Beverly held out a folder. "I'd prepared this for your father, but he never came back. I kept it in case…" She crossed her arms after he took it. "I'm afraid there's not much else I can do for you. I do have some herbs that might offer you both some protection. Feel free to come back if you think you discover anything new that might help me narrow down what's out there. Hunting." She leaned in closer. "I'm glad you're not alone in this. That's what it looks for. People it considers vulnerable. I begged Thomas to confide in someone else, but…" She glanced away as Caitlyn returned, shoving her phone back in her pocket.

She released a weary breath, fluttering the wisps of hair around her face. "That was the coroner. I'd asked her to call me once she'd completed the autopsy. Seems our latest vic had the same anomalies. Strange bruising around the temples, readings that suggest the body merely shut down all at once. Officially, the findings related to the marks and the anomalies will be inconclusive, which won't really matter seeing as cause of death will be ruled exsanguination. Unofficially, she's recording it as some kind of weird side effect from a drug that must dissipate quickly. Says it most likely distorts the normal readings. Allows our perp to mask the actual time of death—give him an edge. I guess that's easier to believe than…"

"Than monsters sucking out people's souls."

"Honestly, yeah." She visibly drew herself up. "I'll have Riley look at the report once I pick it up, just to be sure, but...I think it's a safe bet that whatever this is, it's back. And I doubt it'll stop until it's claimed another five victims." She extended her hand to the other woman, handing Beverly a card. "Thank you for taking the time to talk with us. If you think of anything else that can help, please give me call. Any time, day or night."

Beverly smiled, tucking the card in a pocket as she walked them to the entrance. The woman watched them until they'd climbed into Cait's vehicle, before finally closing the door.

Deke stared at the folder, wondering if they'd both lost their minds when Cait's cell blared again. He glanced over at her, listening to her side of the conversation.

"What? Where?" She jotted something down on the outside of the folder. "No, don't send any other units. I'm on my way." She snorted into the phone. "It's a joint case with the bureau. I've got Agent McGraw riding with me for the next little while. He's more than enough backup. I'll be fine." She glanced at him, giving him a wink. "The man's a pain in the ass, but he's a good marksman." She chuckled when he gave her a playful shove. "I'll check in once we survey the site."

She hung up. "Seems there's been a report of an attempted abduction several blocks from our crime scene. Guy fits the killer's preferred type. The intended victim said the perp took off—headed for some warehouse. You game to go have a look around?"

"Show me the way. Though you should know...I left my silver bullets in my other pants."

She huffed, holding up the address. "I think we'll be okay with normal lead ones. But maybe we can find a wooden stake, just in case."

"You're going to hate having to eat those words when this turns out to be a damn soul-sucking vampire."

"Right." She glanced at the house, then the folder. "Let's just be ready for anything. And who knows, maybe we'll get lucky, and it'll just be some drugged-up psycho with a knife."

"Sweetheart, you really need to get out more."

He pulled into the street, heart kicking against his ribs. God, he hoped she was right because the alternative might just get them killed.

# CHAPTER SEVEN

"Looks like we're here."

Caitlyn stared at the warehouse as Deke parked the car, cutting off the engine. The sudden loss of background noise sent a shiver down her spine, leaving a rash of bumps in its wake. Dark shadows shrouded the door, dulling the gray metal. The place looked deserted.

She glanced at her partner. "I have to say, Deke. You pick the nicest places."

He grinned, winking at her. "Just wait until we go on a real date...I'll find somewhere even creepier for you."

"Well, when you make promises like that..." She exited the car, looking around the area. "Looks like our victim decided to bugger off. That's unfortunate. Would have helped to have gotten another perspective on what tried to grab him." She drew a deep breath. The lingering stench of garbage with a hint of urine curled around her, and she pressed the back of her hand over her mouth. "Does every potential hideout always have to smell so damn bad?"

"Hides the underlying scent of evil."

She glanced at him over the top of the vehicle. "It's most likely nothing. You know that, right?"

He nodded, rounding the vehicle as he headed for the door. "Nothing. Right. Just a deserted warehouse in a high crime district a few blocks from where a man got shredded. I'm sure it's all unicorns and rainbows." He knocked on the door. "Seattle police. We'd like to talk to whoever's inside."

Deke tried the handle when no one answered. The door swung inward, the hinges creaking loudly. He looked back at her. "Got a bad feeling about this." He took a step inside. "Seattle PD."

Cait followed him in, motioning that she'd stay right as he inched his way down a dark corridor. The wedge of light from the open door quickly dimmed, shrouding the last half of the hallway into black. She lowered one hand to her belt, removing a small flashlight. Grasping it in her palm, she braced her gun across her arm as she swept the area with both, looking over at Deacon. He'd copied her approach, the muzzle of his Glock just visible above the beam of light.

She sighed. She didn't generally draw her weapon when there hadn't been an overt threat, but...damn, Deke was right. Something felt off, and she'd spent too many years relying on her instincts to deny them now. Something clattered in the distance, followed by the soft padding of footfalls.

Deke glanced over at her, motioning her closer. "Sounds like we're not alone, after all." He kept his voice low, preventing it from carrying.

Cait shook her head as they stopped at an adjoining

door, leaning in so she could whisper. "You don't have to be smug just because you were right. Though, there's nothing, yet, to suggest it's anything other than some creepy-ass *human*."

"Good thing we didn't order anything at Stacy's because you're going to be full eating that pride of yours."

She gave him a glare, nodding when he grabbed the handle then looked at her. He smiled, dropping her stomach, before counting to three. The room ghosted into view as he reached zero and threw open the door, darting to the left after he'd crossed the threshold. A series of grease-smeared windows lined one wall, the dull light creating patches of gray amidst the dark. A number of pillars broke up the open space, some abandoned car chassis scattered throughout the room casting odd shadows across the floor.

Deke motioned to the right, angling with her as he continued toward the far side of the building. A few more doors lined the other walls, and Cait knew they'd have to search every room before they'd be able to rule this out as a dead end.

A loud thump near the back corner halted their progress. Deacon swung his flashlight toward the area, but the beam barely lifted the dark shadows, leaving most of the room still layered with black. She nodded when he motioned toward it, slowly picking his way diagonally across the warehouse. A hint of sulfur teased her senses, and she lunged at Deke, pulling him to a halt. He arched a brow in question.

She scanned the area, wishing they weren't standing in a relatively open section. "Do you smell that?"

"You mean the touch of rotten eggs? Yeah, it started over by the far wall before we cut across."

"Could suggest we have a gas leak on our hands. If that's true, and we fire off a round…"

"We could go up like roman candles."

"Might be best if we backtrack—call in the fire trucks and let those guys have a look around before we do something we'll regret."

Deacon's expression fell. He obviously didn't want to leave until they'd cleared the warehouse of anything other than a prank call. He sighed, glancing back the way they'd come when something scuffed the floor in the corner they'd been heading for.

Caitlyn cursed under her breath, nodding toward it. If there was a person hiding in the shadows, they couldn't in good conscience leave with the possible threat of a leak. She countered Deke's movements, ensuring he was covered as he inched forward, his flashlight eating up the darkness. He swung the beam around the area, illuminating a few rusty pieces of metal before angling toward a large barrel snugged close to the wall, catching a hint of movement.

Deke firmed his stance, giving her a quick, sideways glance. "Seattle PD."

A grunt rumbled across the space, followed by a flash of red eyes in the light.

Deke flicked the beam toward them. "Game's over. Come out from behind the barrel with your hands up."

Something akin to a growl lit the air.

Deke frowned, sparing her a quick glance. "Easy, buddy. We just want to make sure you get out of here okay. We think there might be a gas leak, so just stay calm, and we'll have a short chat once we're all safe. No need for this to turn ugly."

Another low, throaty noise drifted to them. "I don't like guns." The voice sounded raw, as if the guy hadn't spoken in some time.

Deke frowned. "We'll put them away once we're certain you're not a threat."

Those eyes seemed to flash red again in the flicker of the beam of light, his face and body still mostly hidden behind the barrel. The guy's gaze seemed to travel between the two of them before focusing on Deacon. "I don't think you came prepared, did you?"

Deacon coughed. "Excuse me?"

"No one ever does."

There was a moment of eerie silence when everything felt as if it'd frozen in place before the air around them strummed. A blur of red preceded the attack as the guy virtually appeared in front of them, his teeth flashing white against the darkness. His skin rippled, distorting upwards as the bit of flesh visible in the flashlight bleached a pale blue, taking on a leathery appearance. The stench she'd smelled earlier billowed around her—a surge of energy propelling her backwards.

Cait's chest constricted around her next breath as she flew through the air, impacting the floor several yards back. She slid to a halt, pain pulsing through her body. A series of hollow pops echoed through the warehouse, a volley of guttural cries drowning them out. Someone shouted close by, the man's voice lost to the loud ringing in her ears. Glass clinked in the distance, then nothing. She groaned, wondering if they'd somehow set off a small explosion, when Deacon's face appeared above her.

He grabbed one arm, yanking her to her feet before twisting her against his side, shouldering some of her weight as he started leading them back the way they'd come. She groaned again when a fiery ache ignited in her ribs, pulsing to the beat of her heart.

She swatted Deke. "I can run on my own."

He didn't let go, still moving them forward. "Your side's bleeding, along with a gash across your head. And that's not even taking into account you're most likely seeing double."

"I'm bleeding?" Fuzziness swam across her vision, and she tripped a step before Deke managed to juggle his hold. She frowned. "But how?"

"Like I fucking know. One minute, I'm asking that perp to come out, the next, he's transformed into... some...*thing*. God, when he struck you..." His face paled. "Never seen someone fly through the air like that. Not from a single swing. Thought the bastard had killed you."

She frowned. She didn't remember any of that.

Deacon grunted, kicking the adjoining door open as he barreled them through. "I shot its ass four times point blank, but all it did was piss it off. And when I moved in front of it, the bastard grabbed me by the neck. Fucking thing lifted me clear off the ground with one arm. I swear it stuck its fingers through my chest."

She glanced at his shirt, hissing out a breath at the red patches staining the front. "Deacon—"

"I'll live."

"How is it we're both still breathing if the bullets didn't hurt it?"

"Again, no fucking clue. It had me—put its other damn hand on my head just like..." His voice faded into a rough grunt as he maneuvered them through the front doors and over to her car. "Then it just shrieked, like it was in pain, dropped me and vanished. Last thing I saw was a black blur crashing through that window." He opened the passenger door, all but shoving her inside. "Which is why we're getting the hell out of here."

"We can't just leave. We need to call it in. Get a team out here. Maybe it left some evidence behind."

"Like hell we can't." He closed her door, quickly getting in the other side. Fresh blood soaked his shirt, the marks growing larger. He turned to look at her. "Whatever we encountered in there wasn't human. Christ, I was there and I don't know what the hell that was." He motioned to her injuries. "How are we going to explain this? Because I'm pretty damn sure if you tell your captain we just got attacked by some kind of supernatural creature, we'll both be sent off to the psychiatric ward. Or were you planning on lying to him?"

"And say what? That we got jumped by some armed psycho that managed to injure a cop and a fed?" She shook her head. "I don't want to lie. It only leads to more until we'll somehow talk ourselves into a corner. But at the same time—"

"No buts. If there's evidence to be found, it's probably all over our damn clothes. We'll have a thorough examination of everything once we're safe. Though I'm certain there's enough of our blood on the floor of that warehouse to put us in the spotlight if we bring anyone out here. Might be best if we didn't have our teams look into it until we have answers. The kind others might believe." He sighed, brushing his finger along her jaw. "You're bleeding. Fuck, we're both bleeding. We'll go back to my place, lick our damn wounds and..." He shook his head. "I don't even know what's next, but we'll do something."

Caitlyn stared back at the warehouse, her resolve slowly fading. "You're right. If I call it in and make up some lame-ass story, I'll be taken off the case. You right along with me. Better we keep this to ourselves until we have an idea what we're dealing with. What, exactly, hurt it and how we might gain the upper hand. Until then...I'll let dispatch know we checked it out but didn't find anything useful. There's no reason for them to send another unit out, so...we'll just pray no one decides to swab any blood splatter in there and run DNA tests on it."

Deacon merely nodded, spinning the vehicle around before heading out. Cait called in her report, sounding relatively convincing as she claimed the warehouse had been a bust. Then she bought them some time by saying they were checking out other buildings in the area. While not exactly the truth, it beat the lie she'd have had to concoct if she'd called in their confrontation with...

She let the thought fade. Her head hurt far too much to try and puzzle anything else out. Instead, she stared out the window as Deke wove through traffic, heading southwest. They travelled in silence, nothing but the drone of the pavement beneath the tires sounding inside the car. The steady hum scratched at what was left of her sanity until she finally turned to Deacon as the man pulled into driveway.

Cait looked outside, staring at the small bungalow as it appeared amidst some tall trees. The property was large for the area, the house hidden mostly from view. Deacon stopped in front of a set of garage doors, turning off the car before twisting toward her. He gave her a stunning smile, which tilted the scenery even more.

He waved at the stone pathway off to the right. "Home, sweet, home. You feel well enough to walk by yourself?"

"Do you really want me to have to kick your ass just to prove a point?"

He chuckled. "I'll take that as a yes."

He opened the door, frowning when she tripped out of hers, going to one knee on the driveway. She clenched her jaw, pushing upright—using her door for balance as she reached in and grabbed her purse. Deacon stopped next to her, brow raised in challenge as he offered her his hand.

She scoffed. "You've lost more blood than I have."

"Wasn't me who got tossed across the damn warehouse like a rag doll, sweetheart." He tapped his head. "I'm not seeing double. Or is it triple now?" He held up one hand. "How many fingers?"

She glared at him. "Seriously?"

"That hard?"

"Two…on each of your three hands."

He laughed this time. "Damn, you are a piece of work." He shuffled up beside her. "Humor me."

She wrapped her arm around his shoulders, biting back a groan as each step pulsed pain through her temples and into her ribs. He juggled some keys, opening the door then maneuvering them through, using his foot to kick it closed. He motioned for her to drop her purse then headed down a hall to a doorway at the back. It wasn't until they'd walked halfway through that she realized it must have been his bedroom. A king sized bed took up much of the space, a scattering of masculine furniture neatly placed around the area. He opened an adjoining door, leading her into a large washroom. He stopped next to the counter, waiting until she'd steadied herself before releasing her.

Deke knelt next to her, rummaging through a cupboard then standing and placing a first aid kit beside her. He opened it, nodding at her shirt. "You might as well just strip that off...let me have a look at how badly you're hurt. See if it's something that'll need more than some skin adhesive and tape."

Cait sighed. Going to the hospital wasn't really an option. "I'm positive it won't."

"I see you're as stubborn about your well-being as you are about everything else. Your shirt."

She stuck her tongue out at him, fisting the hem before slowly lifting the cotton over her head. She hissed out a breath as it tugged against the wound on her side, reigniting the pain that had just started to lessen. Her hands shook as she placed the garment on the counter, finally getting a look at her side.

Deacon cursed. "Shit, one strike and it fucking clawed your skin to shreds." He gently probed her ribcage. "Two of the four gouges are really deep. Thinking I need to take you to the clinic, after all."

"No." She glared at him when he huffed. "I just reported that our little recon tour was a bust. If the captain finds out we had to go to the clinic..." She shook her head. "Trust me, it won't end well for either of us."

"Watching you bleed to death isn't an option. My damn job's not worth that." He mumbled under his breath when she shook her head. "At least call Riley. I'm assuming the man would patch you up, off the record. He is your brother, right?"

"He's more of a by-the-book kind of guy than most, but..." She sighed. "Just glue and tape it. I'll be okay."

"Of course you will. Give me your phone."

"Deacon."

"Either give me your phone, or I'll dial nine-one-one on mine."

She scowled, handing over her cell. He merely raised a brow until she unlocked it, letting it fall into his palm. He touched the screen, thumbing his way through the contacts before holding the unit up to his ear.

He held her gaze, as if daring her to challenge him, before drawing himself up. "No, actually, Riley, this is her partner, Deacon McGraw, now before—" His eyes darted to the side as Riley's voice echoed over the speaker. "Easy. She's okay, it's just...we ran into a bit of trouble, and she could use a few stitches, but she's too stubborn to go to the clinic. Don't suppose you'd drop by? Have a look?" He nodded, rattling off his address before handing her back her phone. "He said he'll be here in fifteen minutes. Thinking he might break a few speed laws in order to accomplish that, but seeing as you're his sister...we'll let that slide."

"I don't need Riley's level of expertise. Hell, if you'd just move, I'd tape the damn cuts myself."

"Which is exactly why I called him." Deke stepped into her personal space, his body mere inches from hers. "Would you stop worrying about being some badass superhero chick for one moment and let me assure myself you're okay? Christ, when it attacked..."

His hand landed on her waist on her other side, his

fingers hot against her skin. He didn't make a move, simply stood there, his forehead nearly touching hers, his fingers flexing and releasing against her flesh. The spicy scent of his cologne teased her senses, but it was tainted with the underlying hints of sulfur and blood.

Cait forced herself to look up, meeting his gaze while he watched her, his nostrils flaring as his tongue swept across his lips. She inhaled when the tip brushed against her mouth, a ghosted taste of the man lingering on her flesh. A hushed curse preceded the kiss, the gentle caress of his mouth on hers pulling her under. She closed her eyes on a sigh, the soft sound muffled between them. Fingers wove through the hair gathered behind her head as he dipped forward, slightly deepening his possession.

Caitlyn hummed as his tongue slid inside her mouth, playfully dancing across hers. A subtle hint of Stacy's coffee mixed with a heady flavor that was unmistakably Deacon. Masculine with a touch of spice that seemed to ignite every nerve ending between her mouth and her groin. Her skin tingled, arcs of awareness fluttering her stomach as she raised her hands to his chest, leaning into his embrace.

He stiffened, the fingers in her hair clenching before he must have forcibly relaxed them. But he didn't fully crush the groan as he broke the kiss, resting his forehead on hers.

"Shit." Cait lowered her hand, shoving against him. "Damn it, I know you're in pain. Hell, I feel your muscles bunched beneath my hands."

He cracked a smile, the slightly smug tilt so fitting with his character. "Did you ever stop to consider I'm tense because I finally have you in my arms?"

"Liar. Show me your chest."

Deacon chuckled as he took a step back. "Why, Detective, I didn't know you wanted to move this quickly. Though I suppose since you've already removed your shirt..."

His voice morphed into a grunt when she swatted his shoulder.

"Nice try, but I'm not that easily swayed." She motioned to the patches of blood on his shirt. "Nor am I blind. And I'm betting your injuries are worse."

"They're not." He held up his hand. "Trust me. They can't be worse than those bloody claw marks. Which reminds me..." He grabbed a package out of the first aid kit, ripping it open before handing it to her. "Hold this over the wounds until your brother gets here. Might stop the bleeding by that time."

"Is this how you typically react after you kiss a lady? Because, damn, I see why you're not in a relationship. You change gears so fast, even my head's spinning."

"Your head's spinning because you likely have one hell of a concussion." Deke smirked. "And I hadn't actually planned on kissing you."

"Again, if this is your usual seduction..."

He chuckled. "Wench. I meant, I hadn't planned on kissing you, yet. Not until after you were all stitched together, and I knew it wasn't the blood loss making you accidentally fall into my arms."

"Trust me. No amount of blood loss would make me do anything of the sort. I'm not overly trusting when it comes to guys..." She stopped. Damn, had it sounded as telling as she'd thought?

Deke frowned. "Something tells me there's a story

behind that. Probably tied to how you came to have a brother. But, I can see it's making you uncomfortable just thinking about it, so..."

"And you've successfully changed the subject. How did you put it earlier? Your shirt?"

A devilish gleam lit up his face as he grabbed the hem. "I'm starting to think you're only interested in my body, sweetheart, and not my mind."

"You are such an ass."

He winked at her, the fucker, then gently eased his shirt over his head. She didn't miss the way his stomach flexed in pain as parts of the fabric stuck against his skin before finally letting go, the sticky sound of his blood separating from his flesh making her stomach clench. He tossed the garment on the floor, seemingly indifferent to where it landed before releasing a shuddering breath.

Cait stared at the gaping wounds and thought her damn legs might buckle. She reached for him, softly trailing her fingers above the holes, wondering how he'd had the strength to practically carry her out of the warehouse. "Fuck, Deacon."

He layered his hand over hers, gaining her attention. "While I love the thought of that, Riley will be here far too quickly for that to happen."

"Don't you take anything seriously?"

"It's a few cuts. I'll heal."

"Cuts? It looks like that bastard stuck his fingers into your chest." She tried to slide her hand up, cursing when he simply held it still against his pec. Instead, she used her other, tracing a path down the side of his face. "It left behind a few of those odd marks. Christ, it nearly—"

He cut her off with a quick, hard kiss, dropping a

second on her nose when she furrowed her brow. "I'm fine. Honest. Now hold that damn bandage against your side while you wait for Riley. I'll tend to my wounds—"

"You'll sit your ass down once Riley gets here and let him fix you, is what you'll do. I'm not the only one who's being stubborn." She poked his shoulder. "That's not up for debate, by the way."

"Caitlyn—"

"Don't even try to sweet talk me. I'm immune." She reached for his chest, thumbing the pendant hanging against his skin. "A cross. Didn't take you for the religious type."

He gave her a small, half smile. "It was my dad's. Haven't taken it off since his partner gave it to me that night."

Her chest constricted around a lump. "Shit, I'm sorry."

"Are you going to apologize every time you inadvertently bring up my father? Because it's going to get exhausting for you."

"I just..." She grinned. "You are definitely one of a kind. And I was going to say, you got some blood on your necklace. You might—" She jumped with someone pounded on his front door. "And, there's Riley." She tried not to pout when Deke released her hand, instantly missing the warmth of his skin. She turned, tripping her way to the door, stopping just before opening it as she turned to glance back at him. "Riley can be...you'll see, just... Try not to let him scare you off."

"I just went a few rounds with something out of a horror book. I don't scare that easily. You'd best remember that. Now, let the man in."

# CHAPTER EIGHT

Deacon did his best to appear imposing as Caitlyn opened the door, sighing at the man standing on Deacon's porch. The guy seemed far too young to be a doctor—more like a damn model if Deke was being honest—sporting sandy blond hair tousled about his head, and easy, symmetrical features that Deke was sure attracted the ladies. And the guy looked as if he spent an equal amount of time in the gym, the fabric of his shirt hugging the muscles bunching beneath.

Riley's gaze dropped to Caitlyn's side, his temple jumping as he clenched his jaw in obvious anger. He gently pushed past her, giving Deke a sideways glare before spinning to face his sister. "Goddamn it, Cait. What the fuck did you do? And why the hell didn't you go straight to the hospital?"

To her credit, Caitlyn barely gave her brother more than a shrug as she eased past him. "Occupational hazard, dear brother. And it's not that bad. Hell, you haven't even seen the wounds, yet. You're jumping to conclusions."

"Am I? So the blood seeping through the bandage? That gash on your forehead?" He huffed, cupping her elbow as he led her over to a chair beside Deke's kitchen table. "I don't need to see the wound to know you shouldn't have wasted the time it took to drive here." He looked glanced over at Deke. "You don't look much better, though I'd have thought you'd have had better sense than her. Insisted you both get proper, medical attention."

Deke tried to cross his arms over his chest, hissing when the motion burned his flesh. "I didn't have time to see how much damage there was. I'd hoped what I had in my kit would be enough."

"Then you're obviously as reckless as she is. And whatever happened to partners having each other's back?" He shook a finger at Cait. "Where the hell is Truman? I thought he teamed up with you on cases? That guy isn't nearly as careless as you and your new *partner* seem to be."

Cait gave the man a punch in the chest. "Don't. Don't you dare stand there and judge when you don't even know the story. Especially when I wouldn't even be sitting here if it weren't for Deacon. The man risked his ass to save mine. And if you must know, this is a joint case with the bureau."

Riley's gaze swung to Deke. "You're a fed?"

Deke smirked. "Well, when you say it like that..."

The man mumbled something under his breath, focusing back on his sister. He motioned to Deke without actually looking at him. "Sit down before you give yourself a concussion by falling. I'll deal with you, next."

Deke pulled out the chair beside him, watching Riley work. The man didn't seem fazed by the raw edges of the wounds or the way Caitlyn twitched every time he touched her. Though, Deke supposed Riley wouldn't be good at what he did if he shied away because his actions were uncomfortable.

Riley shook his head as he readied a needle. "I'll freeze the area. You'll need stitches for a couple of those gouges. Thankfully, it looks far worse than it really is, not that it isn't serious."

Cait closed her eyes as the man poked sections of her side. "Damn, can't you do that without making me see double?"

"You're seeing double because you have a concussion. Don't think I didn't notice that. And I'm hoping the pain will make you take better care next time, though it hasn't seemed to work, yet." Riley eased back, the expression on his face suggesting he wasn't quite as unaffected as Deke had thought. "You up-to-date on your tetanus?"

"You know for a fact you gave me a shot a few months back when I got nicked by that knife."

"You mean when some punk kid stabbed you."

"He got the raw end of the deal, as I recall."

Riley glanced over at Deke. "What about you, G-man?"

Deke sighed at the raw tone in Riley's voice. The man obviously didn't approve of Deacon's career choice. "I'm fine. Had a shot less than a year ago."

Riley just kept shaking his head as he turned to face Deke this time. "Which confirms that you're just as reckless as my sister." He motioned to Deke's chest. "It'll take a few minutes for Cait's side to freeze before I can stitch it, so...let's have a look." He shuffled over, poking Deke's skin close to the holes. "Do I even want to know what you two went up against? Because it wasn't a knife.

In fact, I'm not sure what did this, but if I had to guess, I'd say it looks more like an animal attack."

Deacon glanced at Cait, noting the way she shook her head as she motioned to her brother. "It's part of an ongoing investigation, so I'm not really at liberty to say—"

"Save the bullshit. I get more than my fair share from her. All of which means, you're both trying to hide this from your supervisors, right?" He met Deke's gaze. "That's the real reason you didn't go to the clinic? You don't want anyone to know you got hurt."

Deke sighed, wincing when the man smeared something on his wounds. "Cait's right. You need to work on your bedside manner."

Riley arched a brow. "Thinking it's proportionate to the amount of information you're both giving me."

"Fair enough. And for the record, I would have taken her to the hospital if you hadn't agreed to come over, whether they reported it back to my boss or not."

Riley studied him for a moment then shrugged. "Since it isn't a bullet wound, no one is obliged to report anything. And seeing as you're both law enforcement, I reckon you know whether it needs to go higher up your food chain." He got out some Sterie Strips. "While the holes are deep, the bleeding's stopped and they aren't that wide. Thinking it's wise to just tape them together, if you're okay with that. Allow the wounds to drain if needed. The strips should hold well enough, as long as you aren't planning on going a few more rounds with your attacker for a few days."

"That wasn't the plan, but..."

"But you'd jump right back in if need be. God, you really are just like her. Fine, I'll leave a roll behind so you can re-tape it if it loosens, or should I say *when* it loosens. Hers, too."

Deke nodded as the man worked. He had to hand it to Cait's brother, the guy was skilled. He'd had his fair share of lacerations, and he'd never had anyone do quite as good a job patching him together.

Riley straightened once he was finished, plastering a few bandages across Deke's chest. He looked at his face, reaching up and tilting his head over. "You've got something embedded in one of these odd bruises." He dug through his bag, removing some angled tweezers. "Hold still."

Deke held his breath as the man tugged against his skin. A sharp pain burned through his defenses, and Deke couldn't quite crush the loud grunt as the other man yanked something out. "Shit. I swear that hurt more than when it grabbed me."

Riley arched a brow as he held up the tweezers, a small, black object grasped between the ends. "It?"

Deke ran a hand through his hair, avoiding his temple. "Just...do you know what that is?"

"Looks like a barb of some sort. Honestly, I'm not sure." He rummaged around in his bag again, removing a small container. He twisted the lid open with one hand before dropping the barb inside. He capped it, handing it back to Deacon. "I'm assuming you'll want to run some tests on that? DNA or something."

"Something."

Riley snorted. "Why am I not surprised by that answer? And if you're testing shit, you might want to have a closer look at that cross around your neck. Looks like there's some skin burned onto the surface, though not sure how that's possible. There's blood, too, though it could be yours."

"Will do." Deke unclipped the necklace, thanking Riley when the man handed him a spare glove to put it in.

Riley waited until Deke had placed the glove on the table before he leaned forward, once again examining Deke's head. "Why the hell does this look familiar?" He glanced over at Cait, the lines around his eyes deepening. "Fuck. It's the same pattern as in those files you asked me to go over. The same discoloration, weird puncture marks. It's tied to those unsolved murders, isn't it? Damn it, sis, did you two confront the psycho responsible for those? Without backup?"

Cait rested a hand on his shoulder. "Easy, Riley."

"Don't tell me to take it easy when I'm still stitching you up."

Her expression softened, and Deke got a glimpse of the sister beneath the cop. "We're both fine. Sure, a bit roughed up, but thanks to you, we're okay. And to be honest, we're not sure what we're up against here, which is why I insisted we didn't go to the hospital. We need to keep this in-house until we know what we're dealing with. There's no sense getting everyone worked up until we have some evidence to go along with our claims."

"Which is cop speak for 'fuck off'. Yeah, I'm familiar with it since I'm stuck with having you as my pain-in-the-ass little sister."

"It could be worse."

"How's that?"

"Your big brother could be an overly protective doctor."

He stared at her for a moment then laughed. "You

know, I'm still not sure if Dad was brilliant or insane when he insisted you stay with us after you'd been assaulted. Might never figure it out."

Deke frowned at the man's words, chancing a glance at Cait. Though she gave Riley a playful swat while calling him a jerk, there was no mistaking the tension in her shoulders or the sadness in her eyes. He'd been right. She had more secrets hiding in her past, and he had a bad feeling they were the reason she drove herself as hard as she did. As if she always had something to prove—someone to best.

Riley snorted, threading his needle as he motioned for her to lean over more. "You could have taken more backup."

She shrugged. "Deacon's my backup."

"The guy's sporting nearly as many wounds as you are. Thinking you needed more than one guy."

"What I need are people I trust. Deke's one of the few that fit that description besides you."

Riley paused, swinging his gaze over to Deacon. His eyes widened a bit as he seemed to study every inch of Deacon. The other man appeared to give himself a shake then returned to his work. "Not everyone's out to hurt you, sis. You know that, right?"

She glanced at Deke. "All I know is that trust is earned, and Deacon has mine."

"There really is no reasoning with you. I'm just not sure if it's because you're a cop or a chick."

"That's detective to you, Doc."

He laughed again, tying off one line then starting on another. "Nearly done. You'll both need a shot of antibiotics, and you'll have to change the bandages daily for the next few days. Let me know if it starts to look or feel infected."

"We'll be model patients. Promise."

"Now that would be a nice surprise." Riley cut off the last stitch then placed a layer of gauze over her side. "Okay, both of you drop your pants so we can get the shots out of the way before I look at your head."

Deke scoffed. "Seriously? Can't you just stab us in the arm?"

"You suddenly shy?" He tapped on a syringe. "I'm the doctor, and I said drop 'em."

Deacon gave Cait a glare then lowered his pants enough to expose half his ass. Riley merely wiped some alcohol on a swath of flesh then injected him, seemingly oblivious to his hushed curse. The man repeated the procedure on Cait then settled again as he motioned to her head.

She took her seat, wincing when he probed the slice along her hairline. "It's not that bad. Just stings a bit."

"Thankfully, it's not too deep. I'll just use the adhesive. God forbid I tape on any strips that will announce you were less than perfect out there."

"See, we do understand each other."

"Fat chance." He moved back once he'd finished, surveying his work. "Now, for that concussion you obviously have..." He waved his hand, cutting off any reply. "I know. Taking time off isn't an option. Starting to think it's never an option with you. Just...be careful. Try not to hit your head again, and if you have any other symptoms, call me. Immediately. I mean that." He glanced at Deke. "Keep an eye on her. She should rest, but I'm not that naive. And for God's sake don't let her put herself in a position she needs to use her damn gun for a couple of days."

Deke looked over at her, smiling. "I'll see to it... personally."

Riley groaned. "Don't bang her head on the damn bed, either, if you two go a few rounds between the sheets in the near future."

Cait slapped her brother. Hard. "Damn it, Riley. Why do you say shit like that?"

He tsked, packing up his supplies. "Like I don't feel the tension between you two. Please. Besides, it's my job, as your doctor, and your brother, to make sure your G-man boyfriend doesn't risk your safety for some hot sex."

Cait palmed her face. "And he just keeps on talking. Making it worse."

Riley leaned in and dropped a kiss on the top of her head. "Love you, brat."

She gazed up at him. "Love you more, jerk."

He headed for the door. "Okay, I'm gone. I'll keep this little fix job between us should anyone ask. Don't make me sorry for doing it."

"Hey, jerk?" She gave the man a brilliant smile when he glanced back at her. "Thanks. I appreciate you coming over to patch me up, again. Oh, and I have another report I'd like you to look at. Same as the others. Can I send it over later?"

"We both know you will whether I say yes or no, so..." He nodded at Deke. "Take care of my little sister."

Cait huffed as Riley left, shaking her head. "The man's a menace."

Deacon eased back in his chair as the door slammed

shut, finally skipping his gaze over to Cait. "So, that's Riley?"

Cait smiled. "I know. He's...intense."

"Probably because he loves his sister. And because this isn't the first time the man's stitched you up. Couldn't help but hear that remark about getting stabbed a couple of months ago? Don't recall you mentioning it in passing."

"Some kid landed a lucky strike while I was dealing with another perp. Trust me. It wasn't bad as far as knife wounds go. I'd know. And it's not the kind of subject that comes up when discussing possible crossover cases."

He furrowed his brow. Had she just insinuated she'd been stabbed before? He pushed away the irritating question, reminding himself to ask again later. When his damn fingers didn't itch to touch just a fraction of her skin.

"Guess that's my problem. I haven't been asking the important questions." He shuffled forward until his knees brushed hers as he sat next to her. "Don't suppose the blood loss will make you more willing to tell me how Riley came to be your brother? I'm pretty damn sure that's where every other story begins."

She snorted. "The amount of blood loss required for *that* conversation would mean I'm dead. I'd suggest you ply me with alcohol, but I don't think either of us are in the condition to drink right now."

"Never was the kind of man to use liquid courage. I much prefer this..."

He leaned forward, gently cupping the back of her head as his mouth molded over hers. She inhaled, her lips tense beneath him for a moment before they softened, one hand lifting to curl around his neck. Her mouth parted on a contented hum, and he used the opportunity to tangle his tongue with hers. Her nails flexed against his scalp, adding a slight sting that made his heart race. He grabbed hold of her chair, scraping it toward him in one, jerky motion until he could smooth his hand along her spine and tug her flush against him. Her breasts crushed against his chest, the hard buds making his gut clench in anticipation. He needed to feel those nubs against his tongue.

He released her, nipping his way along her throat, sucking at the sensitive hollow at the base of her neck. She mumbled something that sounded like his name, though it came out as more of a strangled moan. He smiled against her skin, continuing his path until her reached the edge of her bra. It wasn't fancy or lacy, more of a sports design, but damn if it didn't make him want to tear it off. He nuzzled her breast, gently biting her nipple through the fabric.

"Just take the damn thing off, already."

He chuckled. "You sound positively desperate."

"Wasn't my cock notched against my hip a moment ago."

He moved back until he was even with her face again. "Touché. Though I think I deserve a medal for keeping that at bay while your brother was here. Took a year's worth of control."

She grinned. "So lose it."

He clenched his jaw. Fuck, didn't she realize how close to the edge he really was? Between encountering that... thing. Then watching her get tossed across the warehouse, wondering if he'd let her down the first chance she'd needed his help... His body was primed.

She sighed, drawing her thumb along his jaw. "You're not the only one feeling a bit...raw. But if you're not into this—"

He kissed her. Hard. Demanding her full surrender as he tasted every inch of her mouth, one hand landing on her breast, his palm rubbing the hard peak as she moaned into his mouth. He snagged her bottom lip once he'd pulled back, sucking on it before letting her go.

He tsked her. "Not into this? For the record, if I were any more 'into this' I'd already have finished. Wanting you isn't the question, it's whether this should happen when we're both obviously still coming down from the adrenaline rush." He released her breast to tuck some hair behind her ear. "I don't want you as a side effect of a botched investigation. I want you so damn hungry for me, the real me, that you can't see straight."

Her breath hitched, some of the green in her eyes disappearing beneath the black. She moistened her lips, biting at the bottom one before quirking her mouth at the side. "I'm already seeing double."

He grinned. "While that's the result I'm hoping for, I can't shake the feeling it's due to that pesky concussion you have, not because of desire."

"So the fact my panties have been wet since Stacy's?"

"Fuck."

"You keep promising..."

He took her mouth again, tilting her head back to deepen the kiss. She used her other hand to grab the side of his pants and yank him closer, wedging his dick against her mound.

The throaty hum that vibrated free from her chest damn near had him humping against her. Shit, she set him on fire. And all she'd done was kiss him. Tempt him with words. God help him once he got her stripped down, his tongue on her cleft.

Cait copied his previous action, mouthing his neck as she moved to his collarbone. She licked her way over then back, moving up to nip at his jaw. She smiled at the raspy whisper of her name. "Does that mean I've got your attention?"

"Oh, sweetheart. You're about to get *all* of my attention. For the next few hours."

Her lips parted on a soft hum, her gaze drifting down his body. "Hours, huh?"

"Are you seriously questioning my stamina?" He sucked one of her fingers into his mouth, drawing on it before letting it pop free. "That kind of sass can't go unanswered."

He stood, taking her with him. She gasped as he pulled her against his body, his hand connecting sharply with her ass. Her breath held, her head tilting back slightly as he squeezed the firm muscle, rubbing his erection across her mound. She arched into him the best she could, another luscious moan slipping free.

"Hell, yeah. The only question is whether or not we make it all the way back to my bedroom."

A stunning smile lit up her face as she fisted his pants, working to loosen his buckle. She'd just opened the metal clasp and pushed the button through the hole when blaring music broke through the sensuous atmosphere. Cait stiffened, her gaze drifting over to her purse heaped on the floor by his front door.

Deke bit at the corded muscle in her neck. "They can call back."

She inhaled when he licked the shell of her ear. "What if it's work?"

"I think we've already put in a day's worth, don't you?"

"Yes, but…"

The music cut off. She relaxed a bit, threading one hand through his hair as he used his hand to lift her breast free of her bra before bathing the taut peak with a series of quick flicks. A tremble raced through her, her fingers tightening against his scalp.

He laved the bud again, slowly sucking it into his mouth when another blast of music cut through the air. He jumped this time, cursing as he reached into his back pocket. He glanced at the screen, sighing in disappointment. "It's Truman. How the hell did the man get my number?"

Cait blinked, as if her mind was playing catch up. She frowned, then shrugged. "I'm sure Rankin gave it to him. He said he'd have us paged if something turned up that might be connected to our case."

Deke bit back another curse, swiping his finger across the smooth surface. "McGraw."

"Where the hell is Cait? She didn't pick up her cell."

"Good evening to you, too, Truman. And Cait's fine. She was just using the facilities. Left her purse behind by accident, I'm sure."

"Cait? Forget her phone? If you say so."

"Can I help you?"

The man muttered something, yelling at someone else before breathing into the line. "We've got a body. Not too far from the other. I'll text you the address. You guys should come and take a look."

Deacon frowned. "Are you sure it's connected? Our guy tends to stick to a schedule, and it's a good five days ahead of that. Haven't had an instance where he's deviated, yet."

"Well, guess he's switching things up for you because there's no doubt it's your guy. The body..." Truman coughed. "Christ, it's bad. And there's another note. Not as creepy as the other one, but it's a sure indication this one's yours."

Deacon carded his hand through his hair, suddenly aware Cait had moved back, her arms now crossed over her chest. "We'll be there shortly."

"I'll be waiting."

Deke disconnected the line, shoving the cell back in his pocket. "Seems we have another body."

She nodded. "I heard. A bit early for our killer, isn't it?"

"Yeah. Nearly a week early."

"Think we had something to do with that?"

"I don't know, but..." He swept his gaze the length of her body. "The timing couldn't have been any worse."

"Maybe it's a sign."

"A sign? About what?"

She toed the floor, looking slightly lost. "That we shouldn't mix business with pleasure."

"Fuck that." He forced himself to take a soothing breath. After the day they'd had, the last thing either of them needed was to have him talk out of his ass. "This is a temporary inconvenience, nothing more. Unless you've changed your mind." He held up a finger, stopping her from answering. "Don't say anything. Like I said, we're both a bit too close to the edge. Let's just do our jobs, and we'll revisit this once we've both cooled off a bit."

She didn't say anything just turned. She took a few steps toward the door before cursing under her breath then glancing back at him. "I just remembered. My damn shirt got shredded, and I don't have a spare in the car. Don't suppose you have something I could borrow? Something Truman won't immediately guess came from your closet?"

"I'll grab you something, but anything I have is going to be big on you, sweetheart. I don't make a habit out of having women's clothes just lying around. But I'll look for something small."

He headed toward his bedroom again, irritation stiffening his back. Not only had he possibly ruined his one chance with Cait, but it seemed their little showdown might have just changed the very essence of their case.

# CHAPTER NINE

Caitlyn sat in the car, watching the city fade past the window, trying to ignore the fiery ache in her side. She'd given Deke the keys again, content to use the short drive to the scene as a way of gathering back her control. Praying everyone at the site didn't instantly deduce that she'd made a play for her new partner. Of course, his oversized, button-up shirt didn't help hide that, but it beat her blood-soaked, torn one. And she could always tell Truman she'd gotten grease or something on hers at the warehouse. That Deke's home had been closer to stop at. Anything, but the truth.

She sighed. Deke had been right about one thing— adrenaline had definitely still been coursing through her veins when she'd all but begged him to fuck her. And it'd done a decent job of masking the pain. But now... Every damn breath tugged against the stitches, and she had a steady beat in her temples that continuously shifted the scenery. Though neither of those compared to the tumbling feeling in her gut. The one that warned her she'd stepped way outside her comfort zone. That this potential relationship with Deacon was far more dangerous than going up against that creature, especially when she already felt as if she'd fallen for the guy. The way he'd reacted to her injuries—it was as if they'd hurt him more than her—not to mention trying to get between her and that thing... She had no doubts he would have given his life for hers, and while a part of her brushed it off as the lawman in him, another part couldn't quite shake the look on his face. The way he'd pulled her close just for the sheer pleasure of holding her. Then she'd leaned in and...

And she'd fucking crossed a line. Taken his lips with hers, rubbed herself against him. If Truman hadn't called, she'd be writhing beneath Deke right now, feeling him fill her, rasping his name as he pounded into her, finally banishing the empty feeling she'd had since her parents had died.

Brakes squeaked in the background, drawing her out of her thoughts. She blinked, finally realizing Deke had stopped. Red and blue lights reflected in the growing darkness, lines of yellow tape off in the distance.

Cait drew a deep breath, cursing the hint of spicy man that filled her senses. God, he smelled good enough to eat. A flutter of need snaked through her core, and she reached for the door when he snagged her other elbow. She glanced over at him, breath catching at the sight. Eyes narrowed, mouth drawn into a tight line— there was no mistaking he wasn't pleased about something.

He arched an eyebrow, looking far too cocky for his own good. "Out with it."

She furrowed her brow, regretting the motion when her vision blurred. "Out with what?"

"Seriously? You just spent twenty minutes staring out the window without saying a single word. In all the time we've known each other, I've never seen you go more than a couple of minutes without starting up a conversation about something. So, spill."

Twenty minutes? Had it really been that long since she'd stumbled into the car?

She forced herself to swallow past the lump in her throat, giving him a token smile. "I guess I got lost in thought."

"About how big of a mistake you nearly made back at my house."

It wasn't a question, and the ounce of truth to it made her flinch.

She released a weary breath. "I never said that."

"Sweetheart, I've seen that look on your face more times than I care to admit. Usually staring back at me in the mirror after a regrettable one-night stand. You just don't want to say it out loud. So you're doing what most people do—letting it fade. You hope by not bringing it up, we'll both just pretend as if I didn't have my tongue down your throat less than an hour ago, or that I wasn't a few moments away from stripping you bare and tasting your release." He fisted his hands in his lap, a deep flush coloring his cheeks. "Well, fuck that. If you want me to bugger off, you're going to have to say it to my face."

Her mouth gaped open, an odd ringing sounding in her head. She stared at him for several heartbeats before her brain seemed to process all his words.

Cait crossed her arms over her chest, wincing as it

pulled against her stitches. "Is that what you think? That I regret what happened but don't have the balls to tell you?"

"That would be the logical conclusion."

"Screw logic." She clenched her jaw, praying she wasn't setting herself up for an even bigger fall. "Did it ever occur to you that I'm feeling just a bit flustered? That you've got so tied up in knots, I'm not sure whether to kick your ass or get your name tattooed across mine?" She raked her hand through her hair. "I'm not good at letting people in. Haven't been since my parents died and I learned the hard way that most people only want what they can take from you. What benefits them. You're the first guy that's made me re-examine my beliefs in that area, and frankly, I'm not exactly sure what to make of it. That, coupled with the fact my head feels as if it's going to explode if I turn wrong, might be the reason I was able to stare out the damn window while you sat there, brooding. And apparently trying to read my mind, which you sucked at."

Deacon's mouth quirked, a hushed snort rumbling from his chest. "Are you always this direct?"

"Are you always going to assume the worst?"

"You're not the only one questioning your beliefs. Like you said earlier, there's a reason I'm not in a relationship. Why I'm *never* in a relationship."

She sighed, easing back in the chair. "Fine, you want honesty? Am I a bit freaked out over basically throwing myself at you? Yes."

His expression softened. "You didn't—"

"Let me finish. Do I have conflicting feelings? Sure. My head is telling me to run like I always do, but my heart…

Damn, even now I'm fighting with whether to punch you for being a jerk or kiss you because I can't get your taste out my mind."

The smile that lifted Deke's mouth flipped her stomach. The guy was simply too handsome when he looked at her like that.

He leaned forward, softly stroking his thumb along her jaw. "Why do I have the feeling I'll never win an argument with you?"

"Do men ever win arguments?"

"Wench."

"I wouldn't be this…"

He chuckled when she paused, obviously aware she was trying to pick her words carefully. "Scared?"

"Terrified, actually, if I didn't really care about you, or where this is going. And if that means there's going to be the odd, awkward silence while I try to wrap my head around the fact you're not like every other guy I've ever met, then so be it."

"Guess we'll just have to hold each other's hands through it." He closed the last bit of distance, his mouth an inch away. "Now, before we get out of this car and the real world intrudes, I'm going to kiss you one more time. And no, I don't give a fuck if anyone sees us."

He slid his hand all the way back, cupping her head when his lips closed over hers. His spicy scent filled her senses as he dipped his tongue into her mouth, tangling it around hers as if they were still back at his house. He didn't rush, didn't seem to care that there were a dozen cops mulling around as he lingered until her lungs burned before finally easing back.

He dropped another peck on her nose, brushing off any

hint of moisture with his thumb. "Damn, but you're dangerous. Ready?"

"Other than being wet...again?" She laughed at his rough intake of breath. "Is it wrong I'm kind of hoping this isn't our guy, but just a run-of-the-mill psycho?"

"You and me, both." He grinned, then frowned as she swayed getting out the car. He shut his door, leaning against the side as he nodded at her. "You sure your head's up for this? Don't think I missed the part where you said it felt as if it was going to explode."

"I'm fine."

"Liar." He glanced at the taped off scene farther up the alley. "I can handle this one solo."

"And when Truman asks where I am..."

"Please. You're not the only one who can cover for their partner."

"Thanks, but I'm fine. Really."

He snorted when she took a stumbling step before catching her balance on the hood of the car. She stuck her tongue out at him, enjoying the way his gaze seemed to linger on her mouth before finally lifting to her eyes. He shook his head, joining her at the front as he motioned toward the scene. Her pulse quickened when he dropped his hand to the small of her back, seemingly directing her through the throng of onlookers before ducking beneath the tape. Though the action was innocent enough, she didn't miss the way his thumb drew small circles across her shirt, or how her body cooled the instant he removed his hand.

Truman glanced up as they approached, his gaze running the length of Caitlyn's body. "Nice of you two to show up. I was starting to think I'd interrupted something." He snickered when she flipped him off. "Is that a new shirt? What happened, you wreck yours, or is Agent McGraw exerting a visible show of ownership?"

Caitlyn hitched out a hip as she crossed her arms. "So, we're talking personal lives, now? Great. How's Clare?"

He snorted. "Straight for the jugular. Well played. And *that* is obviously not going as well as the two of you. I swear I felt the heat from that kiss all the way over here."

Deacon took a calculated step forward, his back stiff, hands fisting and releasing at his sides.

Truman laughed this time, waving the man off. "Easy, slugger. I'm just teasing." He nudged Cait. "Guy's touchy. You must really have him by the balls." He grunted when she punched him in the shoulder. "Does he know about your violent tendencies?" He dodged her next one. "Fine. I'll stop." His grin faded as he pointed to the laceration Riley had glued shut. "What the hell happened to your head?"

"Lost my balance. Now can we get to why we're here? It's been a long-ass day, already."

"And you want to get back to playing tag with the fed."

"Does the word douche mean anything to you, Truman?"

"Oh, if only I had a buck for every time I've been called that. Be one rich son of a bitch. As for the job…" He blew out a rough breath. "I think the body speaks for itself." He turned, bending down to remove the body bag someone had tossed over the corpse. "I wasn't sure how long it'd take you two to get here, and it feels like rain, so… thought I'd preserve what I could of the crime scene."

Cait nodded, sighing when he yanked off the plastic off, revealing what looked like the remains of an animal kill. Chunks of flesh and bone were scattered across the pavement, blood spattered in every direction. "Christ."

Dave nodded. "Thought you might think that. Whoever did this must have been seeing red. I've never seen this much rage in a kill before. Damn disconcerting if you ask me."

Deacon knelt beside the body, using the cap of a pen to turn the white sheet toward him. He stared at the offering, cursing slightly before glancing up at her.

Cait cringed inwardly. "Just tell me what it says."

Deke nodded. *"Be careful what you wish for. You just might get it. He did."*

"Well, that doesn't sound encouraging."

"Definitely more to the point than previous notes." He stood, frowning. "Not sure I like all the deviations."

"You think this might be a copycat?"

He seemed to mull the idea over. "Thinking that's an even worse scenario. Guess we'll have to wait for the ME's report. See if there's other ways to connect them. Suppose we can't rule out that possibility until we have more information." He turned to Truman. "Any other evidence? Witnesses?"

Dave snorted. "Right, like the guy who's doing this would leave a witness. And what you see is what you get. CSI is on their way, as is the coroner." He paused when his phone rang, glancing at the screen. "Shit, gotta take this. I'll be right back. Forensics should be here any time."

Deacon followed the man's progression over to a more secluded area of the alleyway before bending low again. He reached into a back pocket, removing a glove before slipping it on. He tilted the victim's head off to one side, leaning over what was left of the body.

Cait moved in closer. She got halfway onto one knee before pain shot through her head, spinning the landscape. She managed to grab Deke's shoulder before she fell, electing to straighten.

Deke snagged her wrist, holding tight until she looked at him. "Damn it, Cait, you said you were fine."

"I am..." She huffed when he motioned toward where her hand gripped his shoulder. "Okay, my balance is a bit off, and I'll admit, I'll be happy to sit down, but...I can last a bit longer. You see something?"

"We really need to work on that stubborn streak of yours. And it looks like there's a couple of barbs in his head."

"You mean like the one Riley pulled out of yours?"

"Exactly like that." Deke scanned the area, then pinched one between his fingers, quickly removing it. He turned his glove inside out, tying it off to keep the small object from slipping out.

"You're stealing evidence, now?"

He took her hand, then rose, stuffing the glove in his pocket before shifting her hand grip to his waist. "There's still two more embedded in the guy's skin. I just want a chance to compare the two. See if there are any differences. I can get us access to the bureau's lab. Once you're done seeing double, that is."

"Jackass."

He grinned. "And I thought we could pay Beverly another visit. Maybe if we show her that barb she might be able to narrow down what we're chasing."

Cait raked her hand through her hair, grimacing when the motion rolled her stomach. "That's not a bad idea. It's not that late. We could probably catch her before—"

Deke silenced her with a firm finger across her lips. "All you're doing tonight is sleeping. And even then, I'm going to have to wake you every few hours, just to be safe."

"I'm fine."

"Bullshit." He shook his head. "I wasn't asking. God forbid your big brother found out I'd left you alone when you were still displaying symptoms. Unless you want me to call him and have him stay by your side?"

"Jesus, you're as paranoid as Riley is."

"You introduced Deacon to Riley? Either Deacon's brave or he's nuts."

She jumped as Truman's voice sounded behind her, placing a hand on her chest as she spun, nearly falling over. Deke caught her arm before she'd done more then shuffle sideways, bracing her weight until she steadied herself.

"Damn it, Truman, don't scare me like that." She eased her hand away from Deacon, instantly missing the connection. "And yes, Deke had the unfortunate pleasure of meeting Riley early tonight."

Dave whistled. "And none of his limbs got broken? Damn, I swear your brother would crack a guy's arm knowing he could set it, especially considering how much he hates feds." He frowned. "Wait a minute. The shirt, the mark on your head. The way you're tripping over yourself... Shit. What the hell did you do? I thought dispatch said you didn't find anything at that warehouse?"

She groaned. "Nothing that we can report. And I'm fine. Just banged my head."

"Right. Because you call your brother every time you do something trivial."

"Truman..."

"Fine. Pretend I don't know you gave yourself a concussion. Just do us all a favor and let Deacon take you home. You look like shit, and there's really nothing else you can do right now. You've both been on the job nearly twenty-four hours straight, seeing as the captain called you in early. Pick this up tomorrow. I'll make sure any reports get put on your desk. And I'll personally call if anything turns up that can't wait. Promise."

She wanted to protest, but her heart just wasn't in it. "Thanks." She started toward the car, glancing at him over her shoulder. "You won't mention anything to Rankin, will you?"

Dave smiled. "Which part? Where you obviously lied about that warehouse, or how you're playing *extra* nice with your new partner?" He laughed this time. "Your secrets are safe with me. Now, go home. And don't poke your head around until it's back on straight."

"This is going to cost me, isn't it?"

"Hell yeah. Oh, and Agent McGraw?"

She paused as Deacon turned toward Dave.

Dave nodded at her. "I consider Caitlyn a friend. And I don't like it when anyone hurts my friends. So you'd best be good to her."

She mumbled a curse, flipping Truman off again as she allowed Deke to help her back to the car, praying it didn't *look* as if he was helping her back to the car, especially when the ME's truck pulled up beside hers. She gave the woman a nod, sliding into the seat before she fell in. Deacon rounded the vehicle, stopping to chat with the doctor, instantly drawing her attention away from Cait.

Caitlyn sighed as she settled in the seat. She wasn't

sure what put her on edge more—that the killer was altering his MO, or that Deacon had just promised to spend the night with her. The door chimed as he opened the driver's side and got in, giving her one of his gut-wrenching smiles.

She closed her eyes. No contest. It was Deacon.

# CHAPTER TEN

Five days. That's how long it'd been since Deacon had hauled Caitlyn's ass out of the warehouse, praying whatever they'd encountered didn't launch another attack, and they still weren't any closer to identifying what the creature was than when they'd started. Even with new evidence to scour over, they'd come up with absolutely nothing. A fact that was slowly driving him insane.

He glanced across the desk at Caitlyn, watching as she scanned through more files, her mouth quirking as she went. Who was he kidding? She was the prime source of his frustration. After finally leaving the crime scene the other night, he'd driven her home, only to discover her big brother sitting on her porch, waiting for her. He'd muttered something about her stubbornness, then had unceremoniously shooed Deacon away—announcing he'd be staying with her until he was satisfied her concussion wasn't going to have any unwanted effects. And it'd been that way every night since. The man was like a damn guard dog.

Of course, Deacon had recognized the guy's actions for what they really were—a way of distancing Caitlyn from him. Deacon just wasn't certain why. Though Truman had mentioned something about Riley hating feds, it felt as if the man's reasons ran deeper. As if Caitlyn's attraction and seeming trust in Deacon challenged Riley's position somehow. Either way, it meant Deacon hadn't garnered any private time with her since. And he couldn't stop from wondering if she'd been blowing him off, after all. If she'd called Riley as a way of doing exactly what Deacon had claimed—letting their feelings quietly fade.

A wadded up paper hit his shoulder, drawing his attention. Caitlyn arched a brow as she eased back in her chair, a smile playing across her lips. At least, she looked better. The laceration on her forehead had healed into little more than a thin, red line, and she no longer walked as if something was stabbing her in the ribs with every step. The only silver lining in the whole mess.

Her smile faltered. "You okay?"

"You were the one who threw the paper at me."

"Because you were staring off into space—looking as if you'd just lost your best friend." She leaned forward, a loud creak from her chair fraying at his nerves. "What's up?"

He schooled his features. The last thing he needed was for her to know how far he'd fallen for her already, or that the distance was killing him. "You mean other than it's been five days, and we don't have a single lead? Nothing. Everything keeps coming back 'inconclusive'. How is that even an option? Shouldn't your lab be able to source out if it's even human DNA that makes up that damn barb? Or the blood and residue from my cross?"

She tensed, glancing around the station before standing and crossing around to his side of the desk. She leaned against the edge, her leg brushing his. "You might want to keep that last part to yourself until we have some evidence that doesn't make us both look batshit crazy."

He clenched his jaw at the rush of heat the simple contact pulsed through his body. Fuck, he was a goner. He reclined in the chair, gazing up at her. "Do you really think I care what anyone thinks of me?"

"I know you don't, but we don't want to get kicked off of this assignment before we've stopped our barbed friend from killing another four people. And after that last attack, nothing is predictable anymore." She blew out a weary breath. "I keep expecting the next dead body to get called in any second, which is pissing me the hell off. We're supposed to be stopping this...thing. Not sitting here, waiting for it to strike on the off chance it leaves us a clue. We already have clues. We just don't know what to do with them. How they help us."

Deacon smiled.

Caitlyn glared at him. "What the hell are you smiling at?"

"You. You're damn cute when you get angry."

She snorted. "Jackass."

He pushed to his feet, enjoying the way her breath hitched as her gaze swept the length of him. Distance or not, there was no doubt in his mind she was still attracted to him. The way she sucked in her lower lip for a moment, worrying it before letting it go. Or how the green in her eyes wasn't quite as noticeable as it was before.

He leaned in a bit. "Then let's get the hell out of here."

"And go where?"

He glanced at his watch. "It's early. We could go back to Beverly's. Her shop is bound to be open."

"Beverly's? Why? We already went there...twice. All she did was stare at that barb and the residue on your necklace as if she was seeing a damn ghost then mumbled something about having given us all the information she could. She wouldn't even touch them. And if she'd shooed us out of her house any faster, I'd have gotten another damn concussion. That second time she didn't even let us in the door." Caitlyn shook her head. "The woman's scared. Not that I can blame her. Couldn't help but notice her son was in the next room. The guy fits the type this thing goes after. The woman is probably worried that we're drawing too much attention to her. We can't risk her family like that. We need to figure this out, ourselves."

"We've been mulling everything over for nearly a week. Haven't made any significant strides forward yet."

"Why didn't it kill us?"

Though she'd kept her voice down, Deke still gave the room the once over, ensuring no one was even glancing their way. "Maybe because I put four bullets in it."

"Generally, I'd say yes, but...you said it grabbed you as if you hadn't even wounded it. So what happened that made it turn tail?"

He dipped his hand into his collar, grabbing his cross and easing it over his shirt. "It's got to be because it touched this."

"I agree. But was it the cross or the silver that hurt it? And why didn't Beverly confirm either of those? Surely it must be a common thing. Don't werewolves react to silver?"

"Why do I sound crazy for not knowing the definitive

answer on that last question? As for the rest…I don't know. You just said you thought she was scared. That could be enough of a reason. Maybe it's both. Or neither. I searched my dad's notes. There's nothing in there about sensitivity to holy objects or things made out of silver. And if it is affected by crosses, wouldn't they have to be blessed by a priest or something? You know I'm not religious, so…is it merely the object? Or the faith of the person wearing it?"

Caitlyn groaned, allowing her head to tilt back. "Every time we think we might have an answer, all we get are a dozen more questions. Never thought I'd wish for a normal, damn psychopath as a suspect."

"Can't have everything, sweetheart."

She smiled, some of the tension easing at the simple endearment. "I think we both know where we need to go next."

He sighed. He knew it'd eventually come to that. "You want to go back to that warehouse."

"It's our only tangible lead."

"It's also where we nearly died."

"I know. Trust me, I know. And there's a reason I haven't suggested it before now."

"Probably because you knew I don't really want to take you back there. Hell, *I* don't really want to go back. Not when we don't know how to fight it. And as much as I want to catch this thing, I'll be damned if I sacrifice you in the process. I've already lost someone I care about to this creature. Sure as shit not adding you to the mix."

Her gaze softened. "That's very sweet. But I'm not fragile, despite my dismal attempt at holding my own during our last encounter."

"You were totally badass."

"So...it's settled. We'll go back." She leaned in closer. "I even brought a silver knife, just in case. And a cross. They're in the car. Figured it couldn't hurt."

He chuckled. "You are something else, Caitlyn Decker. Fine. We'll go back, but if there's even a hint that thing is hiding in there—"

"We'll bug out as fast as possible. Tails between our legs and everything."

He simply shook his head, following her out to her car. They'd been taking hers most days, though they'd traded off driving. He liked that she didn't feel the need to always be in control. That she trusted him enough to give him that token gesture. Of course, it had made him wonder if she'd extend that privilege into the bedroom. If she'd enjoy surrendering to him.

He grinned when she tossed him the keys, jumping in the passenger side. He slipped in, adjusting the seat before pulling into traffic. Music played in the background as he drove toward the warehouse, occasionally glancing at her.

He waited until they'd gotten a few minutes into the journey before nudging her. "So, is Riley still hanging out? Ensuring I don't give you another concussion?"

She huffed. "The man's a damn pain in the ass. I finally told him if he showed up again, I'd let my gun do the talking." She sighed, looking over at him. "Is that what's been bothering you? You still think I regretted trying to get in your pants? That I've been having Riley run interference for me?"

He coughed. "Well, I wouldn't have put it that way,

but…let's just say the timing did make me wonder. Just a bit."

"I thought I told you I didn't regret anything?"

"You also said you weren't good at letting people in."

She nodded, staring out the window again. "I'm not. But for some strange reason, I don't want to shut you out. Not sure if it's a wise decision, but…and since I'm no longer seeing double…" She arched a brow. "Maybe you'd like to come over tonight? I promise I won't let my brother anywhere near the door."

"Or maybe I'll just take you back to my place again, to avoid any chance of a confrontation."

"Oh, a rebel. I like that." She sighed when her phone rang. "Decker."

A voice sounded on the other end, too muffled for Deacon to make out. Cait toyed with her lip as she listened, the unconscious action more than endearing.

"Whereabouts?" She pulled out a notepad from inside her jacket, jotting something down. "We're heading in the opposite direction, checking out another lead. I'll call Truman and have him secure the area until we can get there."

She hit a few buttons, waiting until another voice echoed over the phone. "Hey, where are you?" She paused. "Dispatch just called. They got a report of some remains over at that old factory on Harbor Street. I'm texting you the address as we speak. I don't think it's connected to our case, but…" She nodded at something he must have said. "We're just running down another possible lead. Do you think you could head over? Don't go in, just keep anyone out until we get there. We'll search the premises together."

She snorted. "Yes, I'll buy you coffee for the rest of the week as compensation for babysitting the crime scene for me." A smile lifted the corners of her mouth. "Thanks, Truman. I owe you. Just promise me you'll wait, okay?"

She removed the cell, glancing over at him. "Remind me to text Truman when we leave, so he doesn't get antsy and venture in by himself."

"Asking him to hold off until we get there was a smart move."

"It didn't sound like something this creature would be involved in, but I'd rather err on the safe side. I just hope he waits for us. He's been distracted lately. He's having personal issues. And he's stubborn. Thinks he's bulletproof."

"I can see why you two get along. You're a lot alike."

"Smartass."

He smiled, chuckling when she started singing along to the music, seemingly careless to fact he was there. He wove through traffic, secretly wishing he could extend the drive just to enjoy her company but aware Dave wouldn't wait forever. She sighed as they pulled into the same abandoned parking lot, glancing over at him when he stopped.

She shook her head. "Looks just as damn creepy as before."

He turned off the engine then twisted in the seat to face her. "You don't have to go in. I can take a quick peek around by myself."

"After everything I just said to Truman, do you seriously think I'd let you go in there alone?"

"It was worth trying." He smiled when she pulled a

sheath and a cross out from her glove box. "You weren't joking."

"Hell no. I just hope one of these works if it's waiting for us." She opened the door then looked over at him, offering him the knife. "You should be armed with something other than your sharp wit."

"You sure you want to carry that cross and give up the knife?"

"I'm not too proud to admit you're stronger than me. And probably have more training with knives than I do. Though, I'm pretty damn good at dodging them."

Heat burned beneath his skin as he pushed open his door, looking at her across the top of the car. "Did I hear you wrong, or did you just confirm that the knife attack a couple months ago wasn't your first? Because you virtually said as much before, but I'd hoped I was wrong. That I was reading too much into your words. But that was definitely a veiled comment."

She didn't even flinch, merely shrugging one shoulder. "Ancient history."

"Christ." He closed the door, meeting her in front of the vehicle. "We'll table that discussion for another time because I know these aren't the right circumstances for *that* kind of conversation."

"Trust me. There really aren't any right ones."

He grinned. "Oh, I don't know. You tucked in my arms, your natural defenses weakened after a few hours of lovemaking..." He grunted when she swatted him in the chest. "What?"

"Now's not the time to talk to me like that, either. I need to be focused on the task at hand, not how much I'd like you to bend me over the front of my car."

"Fuck, sweetheart."

"There you go again, making promises you haven't kept yet."

"Wench. Challenge accepted. But first…" He motioned to the warehouse. "You sure about this? No harm in admitting this is outside of your pay grade."

"It's outside of my damn comprehension. But, yeah… we need to see if there's something inside that might help us figure out how to catch this bastard."

He simply nodded, heading for the door. He didn't bother knocking, just turned the handle and pushed the door inward. He glanced at Cait. "I don't remember if we closed it when we left."

"Me, either. You were basically carrying me."

He gave her a small smile. "Wasn't about to pass up a chance to have you in my arms. Though it could mean our friend came back."

She held out the cross. "Then let's find out what makes him bleed."

Deke sighed. The girl had balls to spare. He just hoped they both measured up. He picked his way down the hallway, listening for any hint of movement beyond. But all that registered was the pounding throb of his pulse in his head. He paused when they reached the next door, using hand signals to convey his instructions. Cait nodded, immediately dodging right when he swung the door inward. It looked like it had the last time, shadows blanketing most of the area. He flicked on his flashlight, swinging the beam around a bit before walking forward. He didn't angle as far over this time, choosing to head for where they'd encountered the guy—the creature.

Deke stopped just shy of the containers, scanning the

far wall. "That's where it escaped. Just jumped right through that window as if it was nothing."

Cait scanned the floor with her flashlight. "Looks like most of the glass went out with it, as expected. We can check the ground outside once we're done in here. See if there's any useful DNA evidence on any of the pieces."

"Great. More inconclusive readings."

"They might, at least, be able to confirm it came from the same source."

"Right." He focused the light on the ground in front of him, where dark droplets splattered across the concrete. He bent over, running his finger across one of the spots. "Blood."

Cait knelt beside him. "Yours, mine or its?"

"Thinking your blood's over there, where I picked you up. And I was off to the left when it got ahold of me, so..."

"So the damn thing bleeds. Which means we can kill it."

"Isn't that what everyone says in those horror movies right before they die?"

He dodged her slap as he reached into his back pocket, removing a small zippered pouch. He opened it, retrieving a swab. "We can have forensics test it. Maybe this sample will be more conclusive than the stuff off of my cross." He put the swab in the container and shoved everything back into the pouch and into his pocket. "The guy was standing behind those barrels. It's a good a place as any to start."

She didn't reply, just headed over, scrounging around. Time ticked by as they systematically searched the area, moving on to other sections of the warehouse.

Thirty minutes had passed before Deacon finally held up his hand. "There's nothing else here."

Cait frowned. "While I'm not surprised, I am disappointed. Not sure what move to make next."

"Let's go rendezvous with Truman. Confirm that site isn't part of our investigation then we'll get these samples to the lab. Maybe we'll end up catching a break."

"Right, because luck's been on our side so far."

"Buzzkill. We'll just snag some of those glass chips..."

Cait nudged him when he just let his voice drift off. "What?"

He motioned her to wait, inhaling again. Though it was faint, he detected a hint of sulfur. "Do you smell that?"

She took a few deep breaths, twisting her head before nodding. "Sulfur. But not nearly as strong as last time."

"I swear it wasn't there a minute ago...shit!"

He dove at her, bowling her out of the way a moment before a figure landed on the floor next to them, the loud thud sending a chill down his spine. Deke spun, gaining his feet as the creature turned to face him, any semblance of humanity long gone. Hollow eyes stared back at him, its face more like aged leather than skin. Long arms hung on either side, its fingers trailing into thin daggers. It bobbed its head, seemingly appearing in front of him in the space of a heartbeat. It reached for his temple, those barbs covering the pads of its fingers.

Deke swiped at it, catching the tip of the knife along its ribcage. Dark liquid bubbled up along the line, making a strange hissing sound before staining the end of his blade. The creature howled, knocking the damn weapon out if his hand as it grabbed him and flung him across the warehouse. He hit hard, pain sparking through his shoulders and back as he skidded to a halt. A strange ringing sounded in his head, the scenery washing into muted shades of gray.

Cait's voice lit the air, and he shook off the fuzziness, pushing onto his hands and knees when an ungodly howl pierced the air. He managed to focus just as the creature stumbled backwards, palming its chest where blood seeped between its fingers. It growled, knocking Cait down then racing past them, stopping at the same window it'd jumped through previously.

An angry snare echoed through the room as it glanced back at them. "You never should have come looking for me. This won't end well."

Its voice resonated through the large space, the eerie tone a distinct reminder the thing wasn't human before it tossed something on the floor then disappeared.

Deke staggered to his feet, blinking as his vision tilted. Colors bled into each other as he waited for the scenery to stabilize, finally managing to trip his way over to Cait. She accepted his hand, dusting off her clothes as she gained her feet.

He cupped her chin, making her meet his gaze. "Are you okay? Did it hurt you?"

"I'm fine. You definitely took the worst of it." She grazed her thumb along his jaw. "You've got a damn lump on your temple."

"I'll live. All it did was toss me. But that knife hurt it."

"I know. I managed to pick it up and slice it before it bowled me over. I only wish I'd had the chance to see if the cross worked, too."

"Thinking we lucked out as it was…again."

She pointed to the window. "Did you hear it speak? Or was that my imagination?"

"Wish it were. Then I'd be able to forget that sound. Like bloody nails on a chalkboard only with syllables."

"I don't think it likes us."

"Ya think?" He winced as he touched the lump she'd mentioned. Great, now he'd be the one seeing double.

Cait tsked, gently pulling away his hand. "Don't touch that until I can clean it up." She motioned to the window. "Did you see what it threw at us?"

"Sorry, I was too busy getting my ass handed to me."

Deke walked across the room, vision still a bit blurry as he bent over. Something glinted off the diffused light from the broken window. He cursed under his breath, fumbling with his flashlight until he managed to center the beam on the patch of flooring. He froze, breath lodged tight, heart thrashing.

"What is it?"

He turned as Cait stopped beside him, grabbing her by the shoulders. "Don't."

"Don't what? What the hell is it?"

"Just...let me check things out before you jump to conclusions." He groaned inwardly as she pulled free of his embrace, lighting up the offering on the floor.

"Is that a detective's shield...oh my God."

"Cait."

"It can't be. It just can't."

"Cait!"

But she was already racing toward the door, juggling her phone as she went. Truman's name echoed through the open space, but Deke knew she hadn't gotten an answer.

# CHAPTER ELEVEN

"Damnit, Caitlyn, I know you're in there." Deacon banged on the door. Again. "Either open the damn door, or I'll kick it in."

He waited, heat burning beneath his skin as he listened to the silence beyond the door. He'd give her one more minute before he broke the fucking thing down. Muffled footsteps sounded from within the house before the lock tumbled over with a resounding click. More footsteps padded away from the door, then nothing.

Deke reached for the handle, sighing when it twisted within his grasp. He entered, getting his first look at the inside of Caitlyn's house—though he'd certainly spent enough time staring at the outside, wishing he could follow her in. Modest furniture with a few black and white photos gracing the walls—it was refreshingly comfortable. Not quite the sterile environment he'd anticipated, especially after all he'd inadvertently learned about her childhood over the past week. For some reason, he'd envisioned gray walls with black accessories, and the punches of color and personal items made him smile.

He glanced at the small side table in the entranceway, cursing at the photo tipped against the wall. Though Caitlyn's smile dominated the image, it was the man standing next to her that drew his attention.

Deke stared at the floor. He still couldn't believe it. Couldn't wrap his head around the fact Dave was dead. That the factory had been some sort of decoy, and Dave had walked headlong into an ambush. Hell, Truman wasn't even the creature's preferred type. But if Deacon's suspicions were correct, the damn thing had been targeting them, and Dave had accidentally stepped into its crosshairs.

Guilt weighed heavy on Deke's shoulders as he kicked off his boots, making his way into the main room. Caitlyn had sequestered herself onto the end of the couch, whiskey bottle half empty on the coffee table, a fresh shot sitting in front of her while an empty glass sat next to hers. She didn't speak, merely poured another drink before shoving it toward him.

He walked over to her, lifting her legs off the cushions as he sat next to her. Her breath hitched at the seemingly innocent contact, her muscles stiffening until he placed her legs over his thighs, absently giving one calf a squeeze before taking the drink. He offered a mock toast then downed the rest of the brown liquid in a single gulp. Soothing heat burned along his throat and into his gut, finally settling it. He grabbed the bottle and poured himself another, topping hers off. A tentative smile tugged at his lips as he gazed over at her.

He motioned to the liquor. "And here I thought you'd be in the corner, drowning away the guilt."

She glanced at the far end of the room, shrugging. "The floor's harder than shit. I prefer to self-loathe in comfort, if it's all the same to you."

He sighed, taking a swig of his shot. "That's kind of the point. Dave's death wasn't your fault."

Caitlyn's chin quivered for a moment before she visibly steeled herself. "The hell it wasn't."

"Caitlyn—"

"Truman was at that damn warehouse because of me. Because I'd asked him to do me a favor." She looked pointedly at him, chin quivering again. "Because I was too busy to go over there, first, instead of searching that damn warehouse again. I never should have told him to go. I knew he wouldn't wait for us."

"He was a trained officer."

"But he wasn't a match for..." she waved her hand in the air, "...this. Whatever this fucking thing is."

Deacon drew in a deep breath, trying to gauge his best line of reasoning. Though he suspected she wasn't looking for excuses. For a way out. What she needed was to put all that energy into something else. Something raw. Primitive.

His dick pulsed at the thought, and he silently willed the damn thing to back off. First, he needed to get her to understand nothing could have saved her friend. Then...

He reached for her, lifting her chin with a single finger. "We had no way of knowing that call was a ruse to get us over there. We thought we were the ones taking the risk. And even you can't be two places at once."

He took another swig, contemplating just drinking

straight from the bottle. "Had I suspected, for one moment, Dave would truly be in danger, I would have dragged both our asses over there the second that call came in. Everything pointed to our location, not his. We should have been the ones battling for our lives again. Hell, I fit the profile of the creature's victim type, not Dave. He never should have been a possible target." He released a weary breath. "Which means *I* screwed up. *I* missed something. If you need to blame someone, I've got shoulders to spare."

She sighed, placing her drink on the table as she curled her legs beneath her. "I don't blame you, Deacon. Truman was my responsibility. I sent him in blind. If I'd given him more information—what to expect—"

"Right!" Deacon laughed, but not because the situation was funny. "Because folks are so eager to believe that supernatural creatures are running amok. I mean, it only took, what…having that thing damn near kill both of us before you truly believed. I'm sure Dave would have embraced the knowledge with nothing more than your assurances."

She glared at him.

He shook his head. "Sorry. The last thing you need is me acting like a petulant ass. It's just… We still don't know what we're up against. This…thing…it's behaving differently. Not only was Dave not physically similar to the other fourteen victims, he's also the first body we've found without one of those crazy notes. It attacked him in the middle of the damn day at a location that's way outside what I suspect is its home range. None of it makes sense."

"That's because it's not following its old habits,

anymore. Not since we confronted it at that warehouse and changed the balance of power."

"I guess we know what it meant when it spoke to us the other day. It's made this personal."

Caitlyn leaned toward him, taking his hand in hers. "It was personal when it killed your father. Now...now it's getting cocky, which will be its downfall. We'll figure it out. And we won't stop until we nail its ass."

He nodded, lifting her hand to his mouth before dropping a kiss on the back. "That's my girl." He motioned to the whiskey. "Another?"

She glanced at the bottle, her expression falling. "It's not helping."

"Did you really think you could drown the pain?"

"Every guy I ever dated didn't seem to have any problems drinking anything and anyone out of their heads."

"That's because they were douches. I have to say, for a woman of your intelligence, your taste in men could use an overhaul."

She snorted. "So, the fact I've fallen so hard for you, means... Shit." She covered her mouth, stumbling to her feet, trying to break his hold when he grabbed her to stop her from falling on her face. "I...forget I said that. It's the whiskey talking."

He smiled, holding her still as he closed the distance. "Oh, my dear Caitlyn. Alcohol can be blamed for a number of ill-conceived ideas, but it doesn't make people lie. Quite the contrary. Besides, we've been dancing around our attraction all week. It's hardly shocking news."

"I realize that, but I didn't mean it the way it sounded."

"And how did it sound? Like you're interested in more than a quick fuck against the wall? That you care? A lot?"

She closed her eyes, glancing upwards as if praying for divine intervention. "Deacon…"

"You're not the only one who cares far more than they ever have. Do you really think I make a habit out of checking up on my colleagues? Please, I'm the king of giving people their space. Yet, here I am, standing in your living room, thankful I didn't have to break down the damn door just to make sure you were okay. Because I would have—broken it down. Besides, this isn't the first time we've been in this situation. Though that does present a problem."

She lowered her head, meeting his gaze again as she seemed to swallow with effort. "What's that?"

"Where we go from here, because sweetheart, I'm having a very hard time coming up with a single reason why I shouldn't pick you up and take you to bed."

She palmed his chest when he crowded her against the sofa. "Once we cross this line, there's no coming back."

"In that case, let's light the fucker up because I have absolutely no desire to go back to being nothing more than your colleague or part-time partner. I'd much prefer to be your boyfriend. Your lover. The man you intend on spending the foreseeable future with." He lowered his head until his mouth was even with hers. "Are we clear?"

She did one, slow sweep of her lower lip before giving him a ball-busting smile. "Crystal."

She tiptoed up, taking his mouth in hers as she wove her fingers through his hair. Deacon snaked his arm around her waist, tugging her tight against him. She moaned, leaning into him as he tilted her head, effectively deepening the kiss. The heady flavor of the whiskey filled his senses, tempered by the sweet heat he knew was her.

Their breath mixed when he finally eased up, keeping her close, their mouths an inch apart. He breathed her in, savoring the floral scent of her perfume and the hint of coconut in her hair. She blinked, the green in her eyes blending into black as she stared up at him, all pouty red lips and flushed skin.

He grinned. "Fuck, you're stunning."

Her nose crinkled as she laughed, the sound morphing into a moan when he claimed her mouth again, this kiss far more desperate than the last. He didn't ease into it, he conquered. Tangling his tongue roughly with hers as he slid his hand along the curve of her hip, digging his fingers into the firm muscles of her ass. She arched into him, notching his dick against her mound. Heat burned a path along his spine, threatening to unhinge him with simply the promise of more.

He broke the kiss, mouthing his way down her neck, tasting the soft hollow above her collarbone. Her head lolled back, her increased breath barely registering above the thrashing of his heart.

He nuzzled his way beneath her shirt, dropping a kiss on her shoulder. "God, it's all I can do not to rip off your fucking clothes, bend you over the damn couch and pound into you."

She pressed her lips together as if crushing a moan before smiling. "Nothing's stopping you."

He clenched his jaw. "It's our first time. I don't want to screw it up."

"And you think making me see stars will screw things up?"

*Shit. She wasn't making this easy.*

"I don't want you to think I'm only after the release. That you're simply a toy for me to play with when it suits me."

Her expression softened. "I think you made your intentions quite clear." She snagged his bottom lip, drawing on it before allowing it to slip free. "And just because we play, doesn't make it any less meaningful. Love's a contact sport. So, unless you're trying to tell me one hard fuck from behind will wear you out for the rest of the night, I'd say all's fair—"

Deacon tugged her closer, crushing her breasts against his chest. "Are you seriously challenging my virility, Detective?"

A devilish smile curled her lips. "Guess you'll have to prove me wrong, G-man."

"And it's going to take half the night. Now, I suggest you strip before I ruin your clothes. I'll count to ten."

Caitlyn's eyes widened as she took a stumbling step away, catching her balance on the back of the couch. She gazed at him, as if judging whether he'd go through with his claim.

He chuckled. "Do you honestly think I'm bluffing? One. Two. Three…" He inched closer.

"Fine." She grabbed the hem of her sweater, lifting it over her head before tossing it on the sofa. She shucked her pants next, kicking them toward the table, seemingly indifferent to where they landed. She'd just thumbed the top of her panties when he tsked at her.

"That's ten, sweetheart." He reached for her underwear, snagging the small elastic band holding the tiny triangle of fabric in place. "Wouldn't want you to think I'm not a man of my word."

He twisted the thin strap, snapping it in half. The material fell away, exposing half of her smooth skin to his gaze. His pulse kicked up, and he couldn't resist tearing the other side then allowing the fabric to fall from his grasp. It puddled on the floor, a small offering of white amidst the hardwood.

She inhaled, staring at the ruined panties before focusing on him. "I was getting to them."

"Really? Because I'm pretty damn sure you were testing me." He grinned. "Thinking I passed. Now, for the bra."

She swatted at his hand when he tried to grip the strap. "I like this one and good bras are damn hard to find."

"Then I suggest it joins the rest of your clothes. Quickly."

She huffed, but there was no mistaking the heat in her gaze or the hint of womanly musk surrounding them. Her hands trembled slightly as she reached between her breasts, twisting the clasp open. The sides separated, still clinging to her skin. She looked up at him, smiling. "Think you can take it from here without ruining it?"

He couldn't help but chuckle. "You are, without a doubt, the most unique, infuriating, and amazing woman I've ever met. You've definitely got me tied in knots, sweetheart."

He eased his hands to her shoulders, slowly brushing off the straps. They dropped to her elbows, pausing there until she shook her arms, finally freeing the cups from her breasts. The bra fell behind her, but all Deke registered was that he finally had her naked.

He swept his gaze over the length of her, grinning at her socked feet. Nearly naked. He stepped closer, trailing one hand up and down her arm, loving the rash of goosebumps that rose along her skin. "Like I said before. Fuck, you're stunning."

Her lips quirked. "I'd reply in kind, but...you're still fully dressed. And while I love a man in jeans and a tee as much as the next girl, I'm thinking it's about time I got a better look."

He snagged her wrists, holding them tight against his chest. "Not that I don't want you undressing me, and I promise to indulge you—eventually, you're forgetting the fact you stripped for a purpose. One that can't wait."

He pulled her flush against him, crushing his mouth to hers. She opened willingly, thrusting her tongue into his mouth when he retreated. She nipped at his lip when they finally parted, her breath rasping over his jaw. He shook his head, releasing his hold just long enough to wrap his arms around her waist and hike her up on his shoulder. She gasped, struggling a bit until he gave her ass a light tap.

She stilled, a muted moan lighting the air. God, the woman was going to be the death of him. Just thinking about putting her over his lap, watching her ass redden beneath his palm, had his dick pressing against his zipper, threatening to launch the tiny metal teeth across the room.

He moved around to the other side of the couch, placing her on her feet again before quickly spinning her. She grabbed the back of the sofa in what looked like an attempt to steady herself, fisting her hands around the gray fabric. He took a moment to admire the way her skin gleamed in the soft light from the lamp before placing one palm on her spine. He pressed forward, lowering her chest to the top of the cushions as he snaked his other hand around her waist, tugging her hips toward him. He gently kicked her feet apart, moving his upper hand to one of her wrists then locking it against her spine, effectively keeping her pinned.

He hummed, running his other fingers along her flesh, kneading the muscles in her back and ass. "Damn, sweetheart, I could stare at you like this all day. Your back flexing, your butt begging to be touched." He inhaled. "And I can smell your need. How wet are you?"

He dipped his hand between her thighs, trailing one finger the length of her cleft. "Fuck, you're soaking. Practically dripping down your thighs."

She moaned, tilting her hips upward as if seeking a firmer touch. "Don't think I missed how hard your cock was. I'm surprised it didn't tear through your zipper."

He laughed, giving her ass another whack, loving the way it shimmied from the contact, her skin flushing slightly. "True. But we're talking about you right now. And I can't help but wonder if I can fuck that sass right out of you."

"Doubt you could last long enough… Dear God."

Her head bowed forward as he pushed two fingers inside her pussy, using his thumb to rub her clit. She trembled, moaning his name as he plunged inside a second time.

He leaned over her, still pumping her sex as he nipped her shoulder. "God, I love the way you say my name. Like a fucking prayer. This first time…holding you to your word that you're as raw as I am. That you need the edge taken off just as much as I do. Now keep your arm behind your back, or I'll use my handcuffs."

Her pussy creamed at his words, and he damn near came in his pants.

He squeezed her wrist. "Hell yeah. I'm into that. And so much more, but for now…"

He released her arm, waiting to see if she'd obey his wishes or challenge him. Her fingers twitched, her gaze meeting his across her shoulder. She snagged her lower lip, body tensed as he continued to finger fuck her, brushing her clit with every thrust. She held firm for a few moments then closed her eyes as she met his next stroke.

Her visible surrender made his damn cock harden to the point of pain. He fumbled with his belt, finally managing to unbuckle it before unzipping his pants and lowering them over his hips. His dick tented the front of his boxers, a noticeable wet spot staining the dark fabric. He didn't bother stripping completely, merely freeing his shaft enough he'd be able to feel her ass bounce against his groin. Enjoy how her juices slicked his skin as she climaxed around him.

He cursed, wishing he could make love to her with nothing but flesh between them, but it was far too soon for *that* conversation. Instead, he snagged his wallet out of his back pocket, grabbing a condom from one of the folds. He held the packet with his teeth, tearing it open. Cait's body shivered at the sound of the foil crinkling, a fresh wash of arousal warming his fingers.

She managed to open her eyes, inhaling when her gaze landed on the tiny square in his hand. She looked as if she was going to say something, but only a desperate moan slipped free as he pinched her clit. "Damn, would you just fuck me already? I'm dying."

He swirled more juice around her nub, grinning at the way her hips bucked at the contact. "We're going to need to work on your patience, sweetheart. It's supposed to be about the journey."

"Do you know how long it's been? Screw the damn journey. I need…"

Her voice carried into a drawn out moan as he wedged the head of his cock at her sex, sinking just the tip inside her. Even through the thin barrier, her juice heated his shaft, making him acutely aware of every inch as he slowly joined with her. Her walls contracted around him, the firm pressure clawing at his control.

He reclaimed her wrist, moving his other hand up her spine to land in her hair. He buried his fingers in the silky mass, using his hold to tilt her head toward him. She moaned as he bottomed out, grinding his groin against her ass, feeling as if she'd locked him inside her.

Deke leaned forward, nipping at her shoulder muscle. "God, you're tight. Tight and hot and so fucking wet I wouldn't be surprised if you soaked my skin through the damn condom." He licked the shell of her ear, grinning at her hissed breath. "You ready to see stars?"

He straightened, dragging his cock through her quivering walls until just the head stayed snugged in her channel before thrusting back in, slapping his sac against her pussy. Her entire body shimmied from the impact, ruffling her hair about her shoulders. He tightened his fingers around more of the strands, pulling her head and shoulders back until her one hand was braced along the top of the couch. He released her wrist again, trapping that arm between her back and his abs as he palmed her chest, holding her tight.

"That's how I want you, sweetheart. Your body hard against me. Feeling you react to every thrust. Fuck…"

He pumped his hips, loving the throaty sounds she made every time he filled her. Her one hand landed on his arm, her nails digging into his skin as she pressed her head into his shoulder. Her pussy quivered, her breath coming in strangled pants.

"I know you're close. Shit, so am I." He lowered the hand on her hip until he reached her mound. "But I won't go over before you." He rubbed his finger across her clit, keeping time with each punishing stroke.

"Oh God." She arched within his embrace, pressing against his hold as if her body was trying to break apart. "So close, I'm…yes."

She drew out the word as she broke, flooding his cock with her release. The slick essence heated his shaft, taking him with her. He bowed his head against her spine, letting himself go. He pounded into her, knocking them both into the back of the couch as he chased the orgasm pooling in his sac, waiting for that last push. Cramps clenched his muscles, the unrelenting burn shaking his limbs until she exploded again, and he came.

Black dots flickered across his vision as it blurred at the edges, the immensity of his release stealing his breath. He managed to shout her name, or at least a version of it, as his cock emptied into the condom, draining his strength. He grabbed the sofa, using it to brace his weight as he focused on breathing. On not taking Caitlyn to the floor with him if his damn legs just gave out. She trembled within his arms with her head lolled against his shoulder, her chest pressing against his hand with every rapid inhalation.

Deacon closed his eyes, savoring the feel of her skin on his, in the few places it actually touched. Shit, he'd barely undressed. A wrong he intended on righting as soon as he could move without falling on his face.

Caitlyn whimpered as he gently eased free, not willing to do more than stand there, holding her. She seemed to share his mindset, not trying to break free of his embrace as time ticked away. It wasn't until she shivered from what he suspected was the cold that he snapped out enough to drop a kiss on cheek.

He nuzzled his neck, begrudgingly letting go. "Do me a favor and just stay here for a moment."

She managed a small nod, gripping the couch with both hands as he backed up, making his way to the washroom just off the hallway. He quickly disposed of the condom, rummaging around until he found a cloth. He took the time to clean himself then wet the cloth for her, making sure it was warm enough she wouldn't flinch. Then he headed back, stopping to lean against the wall at the sight of her. She was still braced against the couch, head low, breasts rising and falling as she seemed completely focused on breathing. The woman was gorgeous.

He ambled forward, gently folding her in his arms, her back pressed into his chest. She relaxed against him, her easy weight clenching his heart. God, he knew becoming lovers would strengthen his attraction, but he hadn't counted on falling like this. Not so soon, when he hadn't really cared for anyone ever before. But she'd broken through his defenses, daring him to give her everything. To trust her to return his love. He released a slow breath, distracting himself by lowering his hand and swirling the cloth across her flesh, cleaning her. She hummed, arching into his caress, and he suspected the simple act turned her on more than anything else. Which was exactly what he wanted. He could confess his feelings later. Right now he had another promise to keep.

He dipped his head forward, kissing her nape. "So, I'm going to go out on a limb and say you saw those stars you talked about."

She chuckled. "Still seeing them."

"Good, then I have a chance to do this properly before you come all the way down."

She glanced back at him. "Do what properly?"

"Make love to you. And this time, I won't stop until I've tasted every inch of your skin."

CHAPTER TWELVE

Deacon bent low, scooping Caitlyn into his arms before turning and heading for the hallway. She inhaled roughly as he shuffled her weight slightly when he reached the corridor, twisting so he didn't smack any part of her on the walls. He glanced at the doors, then her.

"Last on the left." She grinned. "Unless you were thinking of bending me over the counter next."

"Wench." He walked ahead, enjoying the simple pleasure of having her in his arms. He snorted when she tightened her hold around his neck, obviously trying to bridge some of her weight. "Please, I think I can carry you to the bedroom without pulling a muscle. Or do you think I'm that weak?"

"I don't think you're weak at all, it's just...I've never been carried before. At least, not by a lover."

"I'll say it again. Your previous taste in men was dismal. Thankfully, your new partner is a step up." He grinned when she swatted his chest, then paused when he reached the door to her bedroom. "Don't you like being carried?"

"That's the problem. I like it a bit too much. Feeling your muscles flex...afraid I've made that cleanup job you just did a wasted effort."

His jaw clenched, closing his eyes for a moment, before he shook his head. "You're determined to ruin my every attempt at making love to you without you being pinned to the wall or bent over the furniture, aren't you?"

"Sweetie, if what you did to me in the living room was wrong, don't ever make it right."

He sighed, kicking her door open then marching inside. He headed straight for the bed, placing her on the edge. "You are so much more than I bargained for. Should have guessed you'd be just as stubborn, just as damn reckless in bed as you are on the job."

"You make that sound like a bad thing."

"Hell no. I just thought a round of good sex might temper it a bit. Seems I didn't quite fuck the sass out of you, after all."

"I warned you that wasn't going to happen. Not easily. And it was far better than just good sex."

"Glad to hear. Though that first part sounded like another challenge. Luckily, I'm up for the task. Now, I believe you mentioned something about being wet."

She cupped his shoulder, stopping him from straightening. "Not so fast. I'm naked."

He chuckled. "I know."

"And you're still dressed. Hell, you pulled up your damn pants just to carry me in here. It's my turn."

"Never said I'd play fair, sweetheart. And you'll get your turn...eventually. Once I've taken the edge off."

A wicked smile curled her lips. "I thought that was why you bent me over the sofa?"

His dick hardened inside his jeans from her words, tenting the fabric slightly. He leaned forward, making her palm his chest in order to maintain her hold. "The sofa was so I could expend enough primal energy to allow us to play. But I'm still too raw to relinquish control just yet." He inhaled, allowing her scent to infuse his senses. "Besides, you smell good enough to eat."

She moaned into his mouth as he claimed her lips, taking them both backwards onto the bed. She snaked one of her hands around his neck as the other carded through his hair, anchoring him to her as she fisted the strands. He nipped at her bottom lip when they finally parted, continuing to kiss and lick down the side of her neck.

Rough exhalations followed every caress of her flesh until she arched against him. "Damn, Deacon. How do you make me so desperate with nothing more than your mouth on my skin? It doesn't seem fair."

"Fair's overrated." He moved lower, blowing a heated breath across one distended nipple. "And you're not the only one who's desperate." He shifted, pressing his cock against her leg. "You've got my balls going blue, again."

"Bring that up here, and I'll take care of the problem for you."

He tsked. "Dangerous. Tempting me like that, because there's nothing I'd like to watch more than you sucking me off."

"So what's stopping you?"

He raised his gaze to hers, noting the lust-blown pupils and flushed skin. "The fact that I need to taste you.

Have you unravel beneath me as you grind your pussy on my face...come all over my tongue."

Her breath hitched, her pupils dilating even further before she seemed to force herself to swallow. "Christ."

"Pretty sure he's got nothing to do with this."

"Jackass."

"If you want me to play with your ass, sweetheart. All you have to do is ask."

Her eyes closed on a moan, and Deke damn near came. God, the woman was going to kill him. And he knew he'd go willingly.

He nuzzled the underside of her breast. "Good to know. But we'll save that for another time. Can't use up all my tricks in the first few rounds. Not when I intend on spending the foreseeable future like this."

"Making me wait?"

He laughed. "Glad to see you still have your sense of humor. Relax, while I see if I can make you see stars again."

He kissed his way across her chest, stopping just shy of her nipple. It crinkled against her flesh, the hard nub more than inviting. He flicked his tongue across the tip, rewarded with a harsh exhale as her fingers flexed in his hair, adding a slight sting. He glanced up her torso, grinning at how she'd snagged her bottom lip, worrying it as if using the flesh to keep from screaming.

He licked her nipple, nodding when her teeth clamped tighter. "You can try and hold back, but I'll hear you scream my name before we're done."

Her gaze snagged his, determination shaping her expression. She looked as if she was going to argue the fact when he slipped her nipple into his mouth, sucking it hard against the roof of his mouth.

"Yes. So good." She arched against him, warm wet arousal coating his abs as he pinched her other bud. She grunted, squirming beneath him.

He laved each peak, kissing his way down her ribs. "You're so responsive. So beautiful. I love that I can get you going like this."

"Just don't stop."

He winked at her, suspecting it'd make more of the determined detective in her bleed through. "Would you arrest me if I did?"

"I'd fucking kick your ass, then handcuff you to my bed until you saw the error of your ways."

"Handcuffs?"

She sighed. "Please."

"Fine. But just imagining you bound with both our sets…"

Her head fell back into the mattress as a moan rumbled free from her chest. "Shit. You're going to kill me."

"Not quite."

He paused, staring at the red lines across her side. Fuck. He should have anticipated that the bastard wasn't just some creepy guy. Should have gotten in front of her before the creature had been given the opportunity to touch her. He moved his hand over the marks, tracing the scars with the pads of his fingers.

Caitlyn stiffened beneath him, pushing up onto her elbows. "You okay?"

"I hate that it hurt you. That I *let* it hurt you."

"You didn't let anything happen. It just did." She

scoffed at his frown. "Please. There's no way either of us could have guessed that the man wasn't human. Not really. He *looked* human. Shit, he spoke to us. He *sounded* human."

"I should have known. I've read my dad's notes so many times—"

"And I've read them once, too. There was nothing in there about what the creature looked like. Sounded like. I doubt your father even knew it could take the shape of a man before it attacked him." She nudged him with her knee. "Do you really want to have this discussion now? I'm practically dripping onto the sheets."

He closed his eyes, inhaling slowly before meeting her gaze. "And you claimed I'd be the one killing you." He grazed his fingers across her skin, only to stop again. A series of white lines crisscrossed her flesh by one hip, a deeper one down on her thigh. He arched a brow as he motioned to them. "I thought you said that punk just nicked you?"

She pursed her mouth, the heat he'd admired moments before fading into the background. "That's not from work. That kid caught me in the back."

A loud roar sounded in his head as he stared at the scars again, fire burning beneath his skin. "You got this while in foster care? This is why you ended up with Riley and Joe?"

Her chin quivered before she steeled her expression. "It's ancient history. Been out for over a decade. I'm fine."

"You're fucking incredible, but...fuck!" He took a few calming breaths, dropping a series of kisses across the lines. "I just hope the asshole is either dead or in jail because if I ever come across the motherfucker..."

Her expression softened as she shifted her weight to one elbow, reaching down to caress his jaw. "I think it's sweet you're being protective."

"Good. You'd best get accustomed to it, because it's not going to change anytime soon."

He did his best to push aside the anger. Just staring at how she'd furrowed her brow as her hands fisted in the blankets told him she wasn't ready to talk about it, but damn if he didn't want to know. Wanted her to trust him enough to confide in him—allow him to shoulder some of the pain that deepened the fine lines around her eyes and twitched her lips. While the scars were visible, he knew the worst of them were the ones she hid inside. He sighed, allowing his scowl to fade as he focused on the present. On replacing the bad memories with ones worth recalling.

He gave her an easy smile, drawing small circles on her skin as he glanced at her pussy, then back to her face. "Now, I believe I was on my way to seeing if you really are dripping on the sheets." He licked at her belly button, chuckling when her muscles contracted. "Ticklish?"

"If I say yes, you'll only torture me more."

"Which you just did." He dropped a wet kiss near her hip. "Not tonight. Promise. Besides, I'm feeling just as needy."

He mouthed his way to the top of her mound, loving how the smooth skin twitched beneath his lips. "So soft, sweetheart. I love that you shave. Let's me see every tiny reaction. Like this."

He teased the vee of her slit with the tip of his tongue, lapping at the juice covering her flesh. Sweet musk burst along his tongue, and he couldn't resist from delving lower—licking her from cleft to clit. Her thighs tightened around his shoulders for a moment, then opened wider, granting him more room.

He hummed against her tight nub, grinning when it fluttered against his tongue. "I knew you'd taste sweet. God, I could lick you for hours."

"I'm not going to last five minutes."

"Then I'll have to make the most of them." He eased one finger between her folds, sinking it slowly inside her. "So tight."

She tried to arch into his penetration, but he moved with her, keeping her from deepening it. She huffed, the sound morphing into another moan as he added a second finger, increasing the force of his stroke. "Yes."

"Fuck, what you do to me."

He withdrew then pumped back in, the wet sound spiking his need. He wanted to pound into her. Have that noise echo around him as he pushed her from one climax into another, crushing any remaining doubts she might harbor about their future together. It didn't matter that he'd never managed to make a relationship work before— all that mattered was Cait. Her body surrounding him, her voice whispering in his ear. He wanted to go to sleep with her in his arms every damn night and wake up the next morning the same way. He just wanted *her*. Any way. Every way.

"Deacon. Please, so close."

Her voice had him glancing up. She'd collapsed onto the mattress again, her fingers fisting the sheets as she writhed in pleasure. Every muscle seemed to contract in sequence, as the flush on her skin deepened. Her breath came in ragged pants, the last one hissing out when he crooked his fingers, rubbing the tips across her G-spot. Her back arched off the bed, as her hips tilted toward him.

"Now, God, yes." The last word became a strangled moan as her pussy began to quiver.

"Not, yet, sweetheart. Not without my face buried in your cleft."

She called his name, thrashing beneath his hold as he latched onto her clit and sucked the small nub into his mouth. She clenched her thighs around him, breath held before she broke, her cry sounding above his wet thrusts as warm arousal covered his fingers. He lapped at the slick essence, humming at the sweet flavor.

"You taste so damn good. Don't suppose you want to do that all over again?"

One hand landed in his hair, the noticeable shaking drawing his attention. He glanced up, staring into her glassy-eyed gaze as she beckoned him to her with nothing more than a look.

He stood, grabbing another condom out of his wallet before removing his pants and kicking them across the room. Her gaze never left his as he sheathed his cock, finally crawling over top of her. He snugged one arm around her waist, shuffling her back so she was fully reclined on the bed. He smiled as he lowered over her, taking her mouth in a sensuous kiss.

A muffled sob sounded between them, and she wrapped her arms around his neck when he finally released her—her tight grip keeping him dangerously close. Their breath mixed, the intimate position forcing him to see her. The real her. The woman who'd had his back in the warehouse. Who'd believed in him when everyone else thought he was crazy. Who'd given herself to him with nothing more than a whispered promise.

He wanted to close his eyes against the rush of emotions, but he couldn't. Couldn't break their connection when he sensed she needed it more than another release. More than words or actions.

He nuzzled her nose, dropping kisses along her jaw as he gathered her closer, cupping her shoulders as he slowly sank inside her. Wet, hot pressure engulfed his shaft, threatening to push him over after a single pass through her channel. He stopped fully seated, his balls resting against her ass, already covered in her previous release. Her head tilted back, the muscles in her neck cording as she moaned a hushed 'oh'.

He nipped at her chin, smiling down at her when she finally met his gaze. "Watch me."

Those green orbs misted over, the color darkening even more. She focused on him as he began to move, each thrust drawing another whimper from her. Her nails bit into the base of his neck as her body trembled within his embrace. He lowered more, pinning her to the bed with his forearms as he bridged his weight, smiling at her response. How her eyes rolled back slightly, her pussy creaming his shaft, when she inhaled, heels locking behind his tailbone.

"Are you close already, sweetheart?"

She took a few shuddering breaths, the last one rasping into another moan. "I need…" She didn't finish, her voice rising into a throaty version of his name. She spasmed around him, and he knew she'd orgasm with or without him.

He lifted up slightly, still keeping her tight to the bed,

as he pounded into her, all thoughts of control a distant memory. She met each punishing stroke, using her heels to angle him deeper. He finally pushed onto his hands, needing the added leverage to move faster—chase the release burning a path down his spine. She chanted his name, scratching at his back before gasping once, then tumbling over the edge. She contracted around him, squeezing his dick until he thought she'd locked him in place, before more fluid washed over his length, pushing him into a hard climax.

He grunted her name, jerking above her as he emptied into the condom, grinding his groin against hers. She held firm, fingers digging into his flesh, legs hugging his hips before her strength seemed to wane, and she went limp beneath him.

Deke followed her down, once against resting on his elbows as he fought to just breathe. Stop the scenery from spinning or the heat still billowing though his body from dragging him under. He tipped his forehead against hers, enjoying her muffled moans as she slowly descended, finally opening her eyes.

He smiled at her, lowering just enough to kiss her lips. She sighed, opening for him, tangling her tongue with his. He placed a soft peck on her nose once they'd parted, drinking in their combined scent.

He hummed. "Fuck, you're amazing."

She snorted. "You did all the work."

"I disagree, but...you can ride me next time." He thumbed the corner of her mouth. "And there *will* be a next time, just as soon as I recover. Christ, I swear I could sleep for a week."

"How about the night? Here with me."

"Did you think I was going to leave? Seriously, sweetheart. We need to work on your communication skills. I clearly told you I was in this for the long run. Last time I checked, that equated to more than a few tumbles between the sheets." He winked. "Or against the couch."

"Sweetie, if you make me come like you have, you can take me against anything in the house."

"Noted." He eased free, instantly missing the warm wet heat.

Caitlyn tightened her hold. "Don't go."

Though she'd barely whispered the two words, they hit him full force. He trailed his fingers along her jaw. "Not going anywhere. But I should clean up. Get a cloth for you."

"In a minute."

He nodded, quickly tying off the condom then wrapping it in some Kleenex she had on the small side table. He'd toss the damn thing out in a minute. Then he shuffled onto his back, gathering her against his chest. She burrowed into him, a contented sigh caressing his flesh.

He gave her a squeeze. "Better?"

Something akin to a sob bubbled free before she placed a kiss on his pec. "Much. Thanks."

"Don't have to thank me for holding you."

"For coming over tonight. For staying."

He smiled. "My pleasure, sweetheart. Now rest. I plan on keeping you to that promise just as soon as I can move my legs."

"My promise?"

"That counter in the kitchen has your ass written all over it."

# CHAPTER THIRTEEN

Caitlyn yawned, snuggling against Deacon as sunlight diffused through the room, the first rays chasing away the shadows. The steady rhythm of his heartbeat sounded in her head, the warmth of his body making it impossible to even consider moving. She glanced up at his face. Long, dark lashes rested against sun-kissed skin, his full lips twitching in his sleep. Only now, she saw more than just his rugged good looks. The muscles that flexed beneath her palms, even in his sleep. She saw the man.

A nervous quiver raced through her stomach. God, she was so far out of her element, she wasn't sure what move to make next. She'd never slept with a man she'd considered more than a temporary distraction. A friend with benefits or a guy she suspected would hang around for a week or two before deciding having a cop for a girlfriend wasn't quite the fantasy he'd imagined. Truth was—she'd never really cared. Not like this. Deacon had somehow skirted her usual defenses, leaving her to constantly readjust. But as quickly as she erected new walls, he scaled them. Or simply busted right through.

And she'd fallen for him. Hard. Fast. And so damn completely it scared her. What if he didn't feel the same? If he'd merely said what he thought she'd wanted to hear in the heat of the moment? If once this damn case was over, he'd walk away—leave without a second thought like almost every other man in her life? Other than Riley. But the big jerk didn't have a choice, did he?

"Either I'm the best lover you've ever had, or you're freaking out. Something tells me it's the latter, sweetheart."

She jumped, blinking to find Deacon grinning at her. Shit, she'd drifted off into her thoughts while staring at him, and he'd apparently woken to find her gawking at him. God only knew what expression had been on her face. She schooled her features, praying she'd pulled herself together enough to keep from blurting out the truth. From answering every question with a form of *I love you.*

Cait lifted her hand, drawing patterns along his chest with her nails. "I'm not freaking out."

He laughed. "You lie worth shit, you know that?" He leaned down, teasing her with a hint of his lips against hers. "It's okay. I'd probably be more concerned if you weren't all up in your head about last night."

"And why's that?"

"Because it means you care."

She swatted his chest. "Of course, I care."

"I meant as more than a friend, or your backup, or some guy you don't plan on seeing again. In fact, I think you're just realizing you've gotten yourself into a bona fide relationship, and you don't know whether to run screaming from the bed or pounce on top of me."

Her breath lodged in her chest at his words, finally escaping in a throaty rasp. The cocky jackass grinned at her reaction, looking far too smug for her liking.

She pushed onto one elbow, tapping him with a single finger on her other hand. "You think you've got me all figured out, don't you?"

He grabbed her finger, bringing her hand up to his mouth before sucking the digit inside, drawing on it as she longed to take his cock. "On the contrary. I'm just praying you feel the same as I do, because sweetheart... you've got me seeing double. This is new territory for me, too. But you're definitely worth getting burned over."

Some of the doubts in her head faded, the warm press of his skin against hers making the other reasons seem insignificant compared to the heat blossoming in her core. Or how just staring at him gave her a sense of peace she hadn't realized she'd been missing.

The tension in her shoulders eased, and she leaned forward, getting closer without actually touching him. "Are you always going to say the right thing? Because that could get really annoying."

He chuckled. "I promise I'll screw up on a regular basis."

"Better." She snagged her bottom lip, allowing her gaze to sweep down his body then back up. "Now, didn't you say something about pouncing?"

He reacted, wrapping his arms around her and twisting her over, effectively pinning her to the bed. He grinned smugly again when she tried to wriggle out from beneath him. "Yes, I did. And it turned out rather well, don't you think?"

"Damn it. It's my turn."

"I believe I said...eventually. Turns out, I'm not done playing, yet."

She huffed, fluttering the wisps of hair around her face. "How about I make you a deal?"

"I've got the upper hand here. Thinking I don't need any deals."

"Are you honestly telling me you don't want me to give you the best damn blowjob of your life?"

The muscle in his jaw clenched as his breathing roughened. "I'm listening."

"The shower. Steam billowing around us. Me on my knees. Your release painted across my chest."

His pupils dilated as he seemed to drag in air through his nose. "Or I can lick you dry then make love to you for an hour."

"Join me in the shower first, and you can pin me against any surface, bend me over any piece of furniture you want. For as long as you want. Hell, I'll plant my ass right back in this very position if that's your preference."

Deke levered up, resting back on his heels as if considering her proposal. "Not that I don't love blowjobs as much as the next guy, it's just..." His voice faded off, a hint of uncertainty tightening the lines around his eyes.

She pushed up, cupping his jaw. "You were right. I was freaking out a bit. I've just never had anyone actually hold true to a promise, other than Riley. Who I trusted not only to have my back, but to show up when I didn't even ask them to. And it's humbling to think I might have found a man who's more than worthy. Who somehow dodged my defenses without me even realizing." She thumbed the corner of his mouth. "I know you're not in this for a quick, hot fuck. Honest. So stop worrying that allowing me to please you is somehow taking advantage of me, and get your ass in the shower so I can finally run my tongue all over you."

He made a low, growling noise as he fisted his hands as if using the action to maintain control. He climbed off the bed, offering her his hand. "Can't argue with that." He tugged her against his body once she'd gained her feet. He smoothed his hand down her back and along the curve of her ass. "But once we're done, I plan on christening every damn room in this house. Then we'll move over to my place for good measure."

"Deal." She eased out of his embrace, swaying her hips as she headed for the bathroom, pausing to glance back at him. "If you think you can keep it up that long."

He darted after her, chasing her into the bathroom before pinning her against the counter. She opened for his tongue, battling for control before finally surrendering. Damn, but the man had a way of owning the very air she breathed until she felt no other recourse but to let him lead. The fact it made her wet was just a bonus.

He nipped at her bottom lip, shaking his head. "Still sassing me. And after that impromptu session in the kitchen in the middle of the night. I thought licking you on the counter until you screamed would have lessened your stubbornness just a bit."

"Afraid you'll have to keep trying, G-man."

"Is that a direct order, Detective?"

"If it'll get your ass inside that shower and your cock in my mouth quicker, then yes."

"Wench."

He pulled back, tapping her ass before shuffling over to the shower. He turned the taps, fiddling with them for a few moments before the spray kicked in. The patter of water filled the room, the air already growing heavy with the added moisture. He stepped inside, beckoning to her with a flick of his hand. She sidestepped to the cupboard, grabbing a couple of towels. They landed on the counter with a dull thud as she reached for him, twining her fingers through his as she stepped beneath the spray.

He backed up until he hit the wall, dragging her against him as he possessed her mouth again. His fingers dug into her hips, the hard ridge of his cock notched to one side.

He hummed, licking at her neck. "You just taste so damn good."

She smiled, easing away enough so she could palm his chest. "I can't wait until I can say the same thing."

She went to her knees, trusting him to deflect the water a bit as she scored her fingers down his ribs, avoiding the set of scars on his pecs. She couldn't think about how close she'd come to losing him. Not without blurting out just how far she'd fallen. Instead, she focused on his shaft. Thick, engorged, it hung level with the floor, the length wet from the spray. She brushed her fingers along the sides, applying enough pressure it didn't bob up toward his stomach. Deke's thighs flexed, and she couldn't help but smile.

This is how she wanted him. Strung tight. Hot. Wanting. Completely at her disposal. While she appreciated his determination to see to her pleasure, first, he needed to understand his meant just as much to her.

And there was no better way than making him shout her name as he came all over her chest.

She thumbed the tip, smearing a layer of pre-cum around the head. "Maybe I was wrong? Maybe you'll be able to keep up after all because I haven't even started, and you already look like you're ready to explode."

He speared his fingers through her hair, fisting the strands hard enough to add a slight bite. "I've been ready for months." He nudged her lips with the crown. "No teasing. I'm too far gone."

She thought about sassing him back, but something in the way he stared at her—a mixture of pure heat and uncertainty—wouldn't let the words form on her tongue. He was giving her control, but she sensed the true surrender ran much deeper. That it was his heart he was giving her, and not just his body.

She smiled up at him, licking the tip. Salty musk filled her senses, and she dipped down for another taste. Deke groaned, punching his hips forward. She didn't resist, opening her mouth and taking his length inside.

Deacon's fingers flexed against her scalp. "Fuck. Your mouth is just so damn hot. God, the pressure." He pulled back, slowly sinking inside again. "Christ, I'm going to come in record time. How you drive me crazy with want."

She didn't answer—didn't want to release him long enough to bother with words. Instead, she wrapped her fingers around the base of his shaft, keeping it aligned so he could move freely within her mouth. Then she used her other hand to massage his sac, taking time to rub the patch of skin just behind it. Deke's motion hitched, as he grunted in response.

Cait looked up at him, again. He tipped his head back,

the lines of his neck straining. She grinned inwardly, using her hold on him to temporarily stop his movements so she could take control. His breath hissed through his teeth as she pumped him in time with each downward stroke of her mouth, laving the bottom as she eased back, applying enough suction her damn jaw started to cramp. But she didn't care. She'd stay there for hours if that's what it took to push him over. To watch him give himself to her—make himself vulnerable for just a few moments as he climaxed all over her.

Deacon seemed at odds with the twist. It was obvious he wanted to fuck her mouth, but the expression on his face when their gazes clashed suggested he also wanted her to take him over. To make him surrender. She doubled her efforts, wanting nothing more than to hear her name bounce off the walls as he pulsed in her hand, his warm, wet seed coating her skin. Raspy grunts followed her next few strokes, and she knew he wasn't far off.

"Damn, sweetheart. I'm so close."

She slipped her other finger into her mouth, gathering some saliva before tracing it back behind his balls, sinking just the tip inside his ass. He stiffened, fingers clenching in her hair, legs shaking from the strain. She didn't stop, slowly working the digit inside until she grazed his prostrate. The single touch sent him off. All semblance of control snapped. He palmed her head, holding it still as he fucked her mouth. She let him set the pace, doing her best not to gag as he hit the back of her throat, the head of his cock flaring with each pass. But just knowing she'd pushed him past his limits empowered her. She firmed her grip, thinking she might just swallow his release, instead, when he shouted her name.

"Now. Fuck, I want to see my cum all over your chest."

She didn't fight it when he pulled out, still pumping his length as the head swelled, turning a dark purple shade before plastering a rope of white fluid across her skin. "Yes. More. Give me more."

She squeezed his length, rewarded with another splash across her breasts. Deacon stiffened, his cock jerking in her hand as he emptied another four spurts onto her flesh before he leaned into the wall, his gasping breath rising above the patter of water.

She grinned, bending forward to take his cock in her mouth again, wanting just a taste of him on her tongue. He groaned, shaking against her gentle assault as she worked him for a few more strokes before finally releasing him. She dropped a kiss on his hip, moving into his arms as he eased his fingers from her hair, wrapping them around her.

She hummed, licking his skin then nipping at his shoulder. "Something tells me you're not unhappy with our deal."

He chuckled. "Hell, no. I just hope I don't fall flat on my face when I try to walk." He thumbed her jaw. "Don't think any woman has made me come like that." His gaze dropped to her chest, a primal grin shaping his lips. "Fuck, I love seeing my release all over you. Marking you as mine."

"That's a bit Neanderthalish, don't you think?"

He simply shrugged. "You can take the man out of the cave, sweetheart, but..."

She shook her head. "Jackass."

"Well, it certainly was my ass. Never had anyone touch

me like that before." He winked at her. "Hoping it's not the last time you do."

"After witnessing how hard you come…definitely not."

He leaned in, taking her lips in a slow, wet kiss. Then he nodded at the spray. "Turn around. Let me wash you."

She spun within his arms, sighing when he swirled his hands across her body, leaving a trail of soapy suds as he washed her chest, then the rest of her torso. When his fingers moved to her slit, she couldn't crush the lust-filled moan that bubbled free. Her clit felt twice its normal size, and just a light graze had her bucking against his hand.

"Fuck. You're engorged. Turn. Now."

She gasped as he twisted her, trapping her back against the wall. His mouth came down hard on hers as he raised her arms, holding them in one of his hands—effectively pinning them to the tiled wall. He moved back, the heat in his eyes stealing her breath. He eased his grip, tapping his finger along her wrists.

"Keep them there. I swear if you move them, I'll tie them up with the damn shower head cord."

Just the thought had her squeezing her thighs together to stem the ache clenching her pussy. He snapped his gaze down her body, then shook his head.

"I see that's not a threat. Good to know." He went to his knees, using his thumbs to bare her to his gaze. "Fuck, so pretty." He leaned forward sucking her nub into his mouth.

"Shit. Oh God…"

He nipped at the hooded peak. "I want you to scream my name. I want the fucking shower to shake with your release."

He ground his face into her slit, licking and nipping

with the same abandonment he'd fucked her mouth. Her muscles clenched, cramps building along her abs and thighs when he sucked even harder, sending her crashing over. She shouted his name, her release coating her cleft when he stood, grabbing one thigh and locking it behind his back.

She didn't wait for him to touch her other thigh, lifting it and clamping it around his hip. His shaft nudged her channel, and she shouted again when he hilted himself inside her, balls slapping wetly against her flesh. The hard penetration sent a scattering of dots across her vision, and she wrapped her arms around his neck when her strength simply gave out.

He started up a rhythm, slamming her into the wall with every stroke. He didn't seem to care that she'd lowered her hands, though she felt certain he'd mention it later. Hell, maybe he'd spank her.

Just the thought had her climaxing again. She locked her mouth on his shoulder, using the pressure to stay conscious as he kept up the pace, nothing but his skin and the spray of the water making it past her lust-filled haze. He shifted slightly, then his finger found her ass, the length slowly sinking inside.

"Yes!" Her voice echoed around them, setting off a series of contractions in her pussy.

"Hell, yeah. I'm…"

Deke stiffened, cock bottomed out, the muscles beneath her fingers clenched tight before he was jerking his hips, emptying inside her. Hot, splashes sent more ripples cascading through her sex, and it was all she could do just to hang on—not slide down the wall onto her ass.

Deacon's harsh breathing sounded next to her ear,

each gasping pant slowly bringing her back down. The water had started to cool by the time he finally pulled back, meeting her gaze. He dipped down, coaxing her into a sensuous kiss.

He shook his head when they finally parted, resting his forehead on hers. "That...God."

She smiled, simply humming her reply.

He eased free, his rough sigh cooling the skin on her jaw. "I'm sorry."

She frowned at the look on his face. "For what? Making me scream until my voice gave out?"

"No. That pleases me more than you'll ever know. I'm sorry because in all the excitement, I didn't..."

Understanding dawned and brushed her fingers along his jaw. "I'm on the pill. For other reasons, but... You're the first man I've ever allowed to go bareback, so...if you're worried about catching—"

He cut her off with a hard kiss. "Fuck no. And I've never gone without, either, I just..." He released a weary breath, then smiled. "Does this mean we can play like this every time?"

"You might end up shortening your playtime that way, but it'd be nice not having anything between us but skin."

"That's a risk I'm willing to take." He shivered. "Shit, we're running out of hot water. Let's get you rinsed off, then maybe we can have some coffee before I pick another room to ravish you in."

"Or maybe I'll suck you dry, again. Only this time, I want you to come in my mouth."

"Christ..."

He turned, quickly cleaning himself off before soaping her again. He tsked when she moaned as he washed her pussy, shaking a finger at her then turning off the water. He opened the door, handing her a towel as he dabbed the other on his skin. "Rock, paper, scissors to see who makes the coffee?"

"I'll get it. If you promise to pick somewhere comfy for our next romp because I might just fall asleep before we're done."

"Oh, sweetheart. You'll be too busy coming to fall asleep. But I'll take that into account."

"Smartass."

She swatted his butt before detouring back into her room to grab a shirt, smiling to herself as she tugged his over her head. She inhaled, savoring the spicy scent of his cologne as it surrounded her, and she loved that she'd smell like him. Images danced in her head as she walked to the kitchen, dumping some coffee beans into the machine. Then she opened the fridge, scrounging around for something easy she could just toss on a plate. Knowing Deacon, he'd have her bent over a damn dresser before she could get more than a mouthful.

She chuckled at the thought, closing the door as she spun, colliding with a wall of muscles. A scream caught in her throat, and she pivoted, preparing to toss the guy over onto his ass, when she recognized the man's frame. The familiar aroma of soap and antibiotic disinfectant.

She grabbed her brother by the shirt then shoved him back, glaring at him. "Bloody hell, Riley. I damn near threw you on the floor. What the hell are you doing in my kitchen at seven o'clock in the morning?"

Riley didn't even flinch, crossing his arms over his massive chest. "Making sure you *were* still alive."

"What the hell are you talking about?"

"I've been trying to reach you for three days. Ever since Dave was killed. But you never picked up, never texted back."

Guilt gnawed at her consciousness, but she shoved it aside. "I needed some time."

"That's all you had to say, sis. But when there's a damn serial killer on the loose, a detective that works with your sister gets killed, and the woman in question goes silent..."

She sighed. She hated that he had a way of deflating her anger. Especially when he was annoyingly right. She leaned against the fridge. "I'm sorry. I should have let you know I was fine. Now if you don't mind..." She waved at the door. The last thing she needed was an awkward meeting between him and Deke.

Riley merely moved back to rest against the counter. "What's wrong? You trying to get rid of me?" He grinned at her scowl. "Does it have anything to do with that shirt you're wearing? Because I don't think it's yours. And I know it's not mine, not that I ever leave shit like that at your place, but..."

"Riley, don't start. Just—"

"Caitlyn? Everything okay? Thought I heard..." Deke tripped to a halt as he entered the kitchen, towel slung around his waist, drops of water still beading his chest. "Riley?"

Riley arched a brow, skirting his gaze back to her then over to Deke again. "Deacon. And now that we have all the names straight..." He focused on her. "I thought you said you needed time alone?"

# CHAPTER FOURTEEN

Deacon cursed inwardly. The last thing he needed was a smack-down with Caitlyn's big brother. Especially with everything so new. They needed time to get comfortable with being in a relationship. To quiet the voices he knew they both had rattling around in their heads. She wasn't the only one feeling off-kilter. Waking up with her nestled in his arms, her womanly fragrance surrounding him, had rocked him to the core. And he'd finally had to acknowledge the truth. Somewhere over the past several months, he'd fallen in love with her. Spending the past ten days at her side had only strengthened those feelings. Watching her work, knowing she had his back and trusting him enough to have hers—it'd dragged him all the way under with no hope of ever rising to the surface again.

Though, with her, he didn't need to. Didn't want to.

He glanced at Cait, noting the tight press of her mouth and the way she'd crossed her arms defensively over her chest. His girl wasn't pleased with the current situation, either.

*His girl.* Fuck, that shouldn't sound as good as it did.

Caitlyn didn't seem fazed by her brother's question. "I was alone. Deke showed up last night."

Riley smirked. "Then you both got naked, and he's still here this morning."

"Not how I would have phrased it, but yes. You have a problem with that?"

"Just stop, for a moment. Both of you." Deacon raked his hand through his hair, twisting to face Cait. "I'll be right back."

She snagged his elbow, worry creasing her brow. "Where are you going?"

He gave her a reassuring smile. "Something tells me this is the kind of conversation that requires pants. Not simply a towel."

Her lips quirked into a hint of a smile. He took a step, then changed his mind, spinning and closing the distance between them. Her eyes widened as he dipped down and gave her a quick kiss, ending with a brush of his thumb across her lips.

"I'll only be a moment, sweetheart."

He didn't bother looking at Riley. Deacon sensed the man's gaze following him down the hall, only vanishing when Deke slipped into Cait's room. He grabbed his jeans off the floor, quickly tugging them over his hips before heading back to the main area. He'd just reached the end of the hall when he heard Caitlyn curse at her brother. He turned the corner, cringing inwardly as Riley tossed Cait a bundle of clothing.

The man leaned against the couch, glaring at Deke

before focusing on his sister. "Seems yours didn't quite make it to your room."

Cait caught half the stuff, staring at it before dropping it at her feet. She hitched out her hip, looking devastatingly sexy in his shirt, one of her bare feet tapping restlessly on the floor. "Enough." She held up her hand, cutting Riley off. "No. You don't get to let yourself into *my* home, then proceed to act like an ass because you don't like what you found."

"I was worried about you."

"And I appreciate your concern. Yes, I should have called or texted. And I already said I'm sorry that I didn't. But as for the rest of it... I'm a grown-ass woman, Riley. I get to decide if I want a man to spend the night or not."

"Just because you can, doesn't mean you should."

"Screw that." She threw up her hands. "I don't get it. You're the one who's always telling me I should date more. Find a nice guy, let go of the past bullshit. But the moment I find someone I actually trust—who's interested in more than a few rounds in the sack—you get all protective."

"I realize you think he's got your back."

"He does."

"Still." Riley shifted his focus to Deke. "At the end of the day, he's a fed."

"So?" She groaned when her brother just stood there. "Seriously? You're going to crucify Deacon because of what happened to Joe?"

"If it weren't for those agents busting into the ER that night...demanding he treat that fucking psychopath..." He clenched his jaw, noticeably holding back his emotions.

Cait's expression softened instantly. She crossed over

to join her brother. "Riley. Sweetie. What happened that night was horrible. Unfair. But it wasn't anyone's fault but the guy who shot him." She placed a finger over his lips. "Trust me. I know firsthand that bad things just happen. There's no reason. No higher purpose. It's just shitty luck. But you have to stop holding others accountable simply because they share the same vocation. It was a fugitive that shot Joe. Not a fed. But even if it had been, it wasn't Deke. I trust him. You know how hard that is for me. How deep it runs."

Color rose high on Riley's cheeks. "Maybe you shouldn't put that much faith in him. He did nearly get you killed."

"He's the reason I wasn't."

"If those agents had done their damn job that night and protected Dad—"

"Two of those agents died trying to do just that."

"They never should have left that bastard alone with that rookie agent."

Cait sighed, and Deke closed the distance, palming the small of her back as a show of support.

She took a series of deep breaths, then held her head high, looking as if she'd come to some kind of decision. "Do you know why my parents were out driving the night they were killed?"

Riley's expression sobered. He glanced at Deke across Cait's shoulder, uncertainty flashing in the man's eyes. "You don't have to talk about that. I didn't mean—"

"It's long overdue. But I just couldn't bring myself to tell you. Or Joe. Being with the two of you was the first time since my parents died that I actually felt as if I belonged. That I didn't go to sleep wondering if I was safe.

And I didn't want to give you any reason to send me back."

"What?" Riley shook his head in genuine disbelief. "We never would have given you up. Shit, you were part of the family the second Dad walked into that exam room. He wouldn't have had it any other way."

"Still..." She sighed, glancing over her shoulder at Deke, as if assuring herself he hadn't moved. "I was sleeping over at a friend's place. I was supposed to stay the entire weekend. Had nagged my parents for weeks before they'd finally said yes. They thought I was far too young, but...I didn't listen. Then Cindy and I got in this stupid fight. Her mom got mad and told us we had to stay in Cindy's room for the rest of the evening. So I called my folks and told them I was sick. That I needed to come home. They tried to tell me that it was late, that they were tired, that I should just stick it out until morning, but..." A sob caught in her throat before she seemed to swallow it. "I begged them. Cried on the damn phone until they agreed. The next thing I knew the police were at Cindy's door, and my parents were dead."

Riley reached for her, pulling her into an embrace. Pain reflected in his eyes as he glanced at Deke, all the while holding Cait tight. "It wasn't your fault. It was a fucked up carjacking."

"I know. In my head, I know that it was just a brutal murder. But there's still a part of me that can't help but feel responsible. Because no matter what anyone says, they never would have been out there, never would have been possible targets, if I hadn't called."

Riley closed his eyes, rocking his sister in his arms. "That's what parents do. They sacrifice for their kids."

"Then you know why Joe had to be the one to treat that man. He never would have risked anyone else's life. That's just who he was." She eased back, cupping his jaw. "But that's not really who you blame, is it? You were supposed to be on call that night. Part of your last rotation before you took your exams. But you were sick. And now you blame yourself for not being the one to take the risk."

Her brother didn't answer. Just stood there, staring down at his sister as if he was frozen.

She wiped at her cheek, leaning against Deacon as he pressed his chest into her back. "You want to know the crazy thing? All this time you've been hating yourself for not being there...I've been thanking every god I can think of that I didn't lose you, too. Because I would have. I know it."

Riley looked away, kicking his toe against the wood floor. He released a weary breath as he faced them again, glancing at the way Cait had moved into Deacon's embrace, one arm wrapped around her upper shoulders, while the other palmed her waist, holding her tight to his chest.

The other man reached out and tousled her hair. "I never do win many arguments with you, brat."

"I try to throw you a bone every now and then."

He snorted. "So...you really like this guy?"

Deacon cleared his throat. "I'm standing right here."

Riley shrugged. "So? I want to hear it from her, because I'll know if she's lying." He focused on Cait. "Well? Is her worthy of my favorite sister?"

"I'm your only sister, and yes. He's worthy. And I care. More than I'd like to admit."

Riley shoved his hands in his pockets. "Fine. I'll give

the guy a chance. For you." He shifted his gaze to Deacon. "But if you hurt her, I'll make sure the autopsy says it was an accident."

Cait groaned. "And there he goes, threatening a federal officer."

"That's only a bad thing if I have to kill him." He stepped forward, dropping a kiss on her forehead, before nodding at Deke. "See that I don't."

"You really don't know when to just cut your losses, do you?"

"You're my sister. I'm supposed to be a pain in your ass."

"Then achievement unlocked...shit." She turned when music sounded in the background. She glanced at Deacon. "Yours or mine?"

Deacon frowned. "I'm pretty damn sure mine's in your room, so it's got to be yours. Though I'm not sure who'd be calling this early, seeing as your cockblock of a brother is already here." He grunted when she swatted him playfully in the chest.

She sighed. "That must mean it's work."

She headed for the kitchen, rifling through a pile of mail on one end of the counter before fishing out her phone. She stuck her tongue out at Riley when the man mumbled something about knowing why she'd been able to ignore his call, then swiped her finger across the surface. "Decker."

A small smile lifted her mouth. "Hey, Bridges. Early ass time to be calling. Don't tell me there's another body?" She nodded, inhaling sharply before glancing his way. "Text me the address. Are paramedics there, yet? Understood. Tell them I'm bringing my brother." She pulled the phone away, glancing at it before holding it against her ear again. "I'll be there in ten if I can manage it. Have the responding officers start getting statements. And I'll want all the video surveillance on any traffic cam, bank machine or business security for four blocks."

Deacon met her gaze, the inklings of uncertainty crawling "Everything okay?"

She pursed her lips, then looked at Riley. "I assume your bag's in your car? You'll need it. You can ride with us."

Riley didn't say a word, just made for the door, his footsteps quickly fading.

Deacon held his ground. "You're scaring me. What the hell's going on?"

She closed the distance, taking his hands in hers. "That was a friend of mine in dispatch. They received a call a few minutes ago. There was an attack outside that church just up the road from your sister's restaurant...I don't have all the details, but it's Trevor."

"Shit. Stacy?"

"Bridges didn't know."

She didn't resist when he pulled free, darting back to her room to grab his wallet and phone. He turned as his shirt hit him in the chest, Cait's bare skin rushing past him. She disappeared into her closet then popped out, jeans half on, a sweater twisted down to her ribs. She didn't slow, somehow managing to right her clothes as she grabbed her boots, hopping on one foot all the while continuing toward the door. He opened it, ushering her through then heading for her car. She shook her head when he motioned for the keys, reluctantly getting in the passenger side. Riley was already seated sitting in the back, black bag sitting resting on the seat next to him.

She started the engine, reversing out of her driveway then joining the light traffic. She hit some buttons, the shrill whine of her siren breaking the silence. Riley muttered to himself in the back as Cait wove through traffic, barely missing a car when she sped through a red light.

"You know, sis, if you kill us before we get there, I can't help your friend."

She barely acknowledged the man, focusing on the road. The scenery passed in a gray blur, not much registering until the siren cut out as she skidded to a halt amidst a volley of emergency vehicles, the flashing lights casting multicolored dots across the pavement.

Riley was out the door before the car fully stopped, running toward the medics crouched on the walkway across the street. Cait snagged Deke's hand when he reached for the door, holding firm until he met her gaze.

She gave his fingers a squeeze. "You worry about your family. I'll take care of the cop side of things, okay?"

He nodded, afraid any response would come out colored with anger and fear. She remained beside him as he made for the gathering of people, flashing her badge when anyone looked as if they were going to get in their way. Deke headed for where Riley knelt on the pavement when he heard someone shout his name. Deacon turned, conflicting emotions flooding his system as he spotted Stacy on the tailgate of one of the ambulances.

He bit back the fear still cresting his throat as he rushed over to her, catching her when she launched into his arms. Gut-wrenching sobs shook through her as he held her close, stroking her hair while whispering soothing words. It took a few moments before she finally drew a shuddering breath, easing out of his embrace.

He smiled down at her, tucking some of her hair behind her ear. "Better?"

She nodded, looking as if she might break down again, before visibly relaxing. She placed her head against his chest. "I'm so glad you're here."

"Nowhere else I'd be, sis." He frowned as he brushed his fingers over a piece of gauze on her forehead. "You're hurt."

She snorted, some anger bleeding through. "Please. I hit my head when that bastard pushed me out of the way. It's nothing. Trevor..." Her chin quivered, more tears spilling down her cheek.

"Easy, honey."

He brushed some of the moisture away, hating the fact more quickly took its place. He wanted to tell her it was going to be okay. But things were seldom all right unless taken by the nuts and forced into submission. Not to mention the fact, monsters were real. And the dark was something to be very afraid of. It didn't help that he had no idea how badly Trevor had been hurt, or if he was even still alive. Footsteps sounded behind him before Cait appeared off to his left.

She gave Stacy an encouraging smile. "Hey, don't go throwing the towel in yet. Didn't Deke tell you? I brought my brother along." She leaned in. "Don't tell him I said this but...the guy's a damn wizard. He's treating Trevor as we speak. Haven't heard Riley swear once, which means it can't be that bad."

Stacy furrowed her brow. "Your brother's a doctor?"

"I know. I'm the black sheep for sure. But I meant it. Riley's amazing." She shifted on her feet, glancing at Deke before focusing on Stacy. "I realize your mind must be going in ten different directions, but it'd really help us out if you could tell us what happened. While it's still fresh." She tipped down when Stacy tried to break eye contact. "I know you're worried about Trevor. But the best way to help him right now is to talk to us. Help us catch the bastard that hurt him."

Stacy glanced at him, eyes still panic-stricken.

Deke wrapped his arm around her. "Let's just sit down. You can fill us in on the main points. So we have a place to start." He shuffled her against his side as he sat on the edge of the ambulance with her. "I'll be beside you the whole time. Promise."

She nodded, leaning against him as she took a few deep breaths. More tears tracked down her cheeks, but she looked calmer. "We were delivering the leftovers to the church." She glanced up at Cait. "Trevor and I bring food here a couple of times a week. The Father runs a soup kitchen, and we like the idea of helping out. Being part of the solution and giving back. I had a few bags. Trevor was carrying the bulk of it. It usually takes a couple of trips. I'd just walked through the gate when…"

She broke into more tears, trembling against him.

He sighed, giving her another squeeze. "It's okay. It's over. You're safe."

"But…I don't know what to tell you. What I saw, it's…"

"Don't worry about what we'll think. Just tell us what happened."

"But it's crazy. You'll think I'm crazy."

He gave her a genuine smile. "Pretty damn sure I won't be one to judge. Cait, either. So spill. What did you see?"

Stacy pouted, glancing at where they were still working on Trevor before releasing a slow breath. "It all happened so fast. One minute I was swinging the rear gate open, the next, I get shoved to the ground, and some guy has Trevor by the neck." She turned to look directly at him. "He held Trev up with one hand, Deacon. One hand! Then Trevor starts screaming and there's blood on his shirt, like he's been scratched or something. That...guy put his other hand on Trev's head, and I swear Trevor's skin glowed. Like someone was shining a spotlight on it."

Deke looked at Cait, noting the tight press of her lips, the rigid line of her shoulders, and knew she'd already come to the same conclusion as he had. He nodded at his sister. "Then what happened?"

"I got up and sprayed that creep with my mace. Got him right in the eyes. He screamed and dropped Trevor. That's when I wrapped my arms around his chest and half dragged him toward the church. We'd just gotten through the gate, when that guy came at us again. Only..."

"Only what?"

She placed her elbows on her knees, palming her face. "It's crazy. *I'm* crazy."

Cait went to one knee in front of her, gently cupping Stacy's hands. "He couldn't follow you through the gate, could he?"

Stacy's head snapped up, her eyes widening. "How did you know?"

Cait just smiled. "Did he simply stop or did something else happen to him when he tried?"

Stacy's chin quivered, as she glanced at Deke. "He tried, but...it was like smoke came off his skin, and he screamed. He fell backwards then just...took off. I didn't even really see him move, he was just gone."

Cait nodded, not looking at all fazed by Stacy's account. "Just one more question. This guy. When he placed his hand on Trevor's head, when Trevor's skin glowed, did you notice anything odd about the attacker then?"

Stacy broke eye contact, staring at her hands intertwined on her lap. "I...I'm not sure what you're asking."

Cait gave his sister's leg a squeeze. "I think you do."

Stacy gazed up again, glancing at Deke, pursing her lips at his guarded nod. "I'm not sure, but...his skin. It might have looked sort of bluish, but wrinkly. More like leather with deep grooves in it. And he seemed bigger. Much bigger."

"Thank you." Cait rose. "Sorry, one last thing. Do you recall smelling anything when you were near the guy?"

"Smell? I'm not sure...wait! Rotten eggs. I remember wondering if maybe there was a gas leak just before I got shoved." Stacy shook her head. "None of this makes any sense. It must have been my imagination. Maybe it was how the food all mixed together when everything fell. Some weird effect from the rising sun that lit up his skin."

"You did great. I'm sure—"

"Cait!"

Riley's voice cut her off and she turned, mumbling a quick goodbye before darting over to her brother. Deke watched them interact, still holding Stacy—reassuring her when she stiffened beside him.

Cait nodded at Riley, then jogged back over to them, handing Deacon her keys. "Trevor needs a direct transfusion. I'm O negative, so... I'll meet you at hospital." She gave Stacy's hands a quick squeeze when his sister sobbed. "It's just to help keep Trevor stable until they can get him to the hospital. Honest. Riley says it looks promising. Have faith."

She raced back over, rattling off some instructions to a group of officers as she went. She followed Riley and the medics to the other ambulance, waving to Deke before getting in.

Deacon took a deep breath, nudging his sister. "Come on. We'll head over to the hospital. I'll get you some really bad coffee while we wait."

Stacy merely nodded, walking woodenly within his arms toward Cait's car. Deacon welcomed the silence, his mind tumbling over everything she'd said, knowing it wasn't a coincidence that the creature had attacked Trevor. The bastard had made it more than personal, and it was about time they took the fight back to him.

# CHAPTER FIFTEEN

"Jesus Christ, Decker. You look like shit."

Caitlyn glanced up as the captain's voice bellowed around her. Somehow the man had managed to walk up to her desk without her realizing it. Definitely a sign she needed more sleep.

She leaned back in her chair, cursing at the metallic squeak that grated on her already frayed nerves. "Thanks, Captain. I can always count on you to boost my fragile ego."

"If your ego was any bigger, you'd be captain." He braced his hip against her desk. "When's the last time you slept?"

*The other night in Deacon's arms.*

She bit back the response. While she didn't plan on hiding her burgeoning relationship with her temporary partner, there wasn't a chance in hell she'd broadcast it. Not while they were still working the case together. It was bad enough they didn't have any leads. She didn't need to give Rankin or Jamieson any additional reasons to end their joint venture.

She shrugged. "It's been a busy few days."

The man nodded, scanning the room before motioning to the empty chair beside her. "And you've been working the case the entire time, other than your visits to the hospital. Speaking of which...how's Agent McGraw?"

"He's doing well, all things considered. He's just driving Trevor home from the hospital. Riley called and said Trevor had improved enough he could be discharged."

"It's only been seventy-two hours. That's a good sign."

"Deke should be back any minute."

The man's lips quirked when she said Deacon's name. "I'm not keeping tabs on the man, Caitlyn. But I wouldn't be doing my job if I didn't check in. Make sure his head is still in the right place to watch my favorite detective's back."

"Favorite? Why does that thought scare me?"

He chuckled. "Because you're paranoid." His grin faded. "Seriously? You two okay? Do I need to give you more backup? Or tell the bureau they can shove this damn case up their collective asses?"

"After this creep killed Truman then attacked Trevor? No way." She forced a smile. "We're fine."

He nodded. "Any leads?"

"You'd think with the bastard providing us with two more bodies yesterday, we'd have more to go on. But it's just *more* of the same—nothing." She raked her hand through her hair. "I just got the rest of the video recordings from around the church and that parking lot where the two men were killed. I'm hoping I might be able to find a trace of our guy. Forensics should have some reports soon, as well. With any luck…"

"I have complete faith in you, Cait." He straightened, smirking when Deacon walked through the doors at the far end of the precinct. "Looks like your *partner's* here. The man is aware that if he hurts you, he'll have more than Riley to contend with, right?"

Cait's mouth gaped open as the captain winked at her then strode off, making some kind of hand sign as he walked past Deacon. Deke slowed, gazing back at the man until Rankin had returned to his office and closed the door.

Deke gave her a quizzical raise of his brow once he'd reached their desk, sinking into his chair. "Do I want to know why your captain just gave me that creepy 'I'm watching you' motion with his fingers?"

She palmed her face then scrubbed her hand down to her jaw. "Because he knows."

Deacon scrunched his nose. "Knows what?"

She glared at him.

"Oh." His eyes widened then he cleared his throat. "Oh. He *knows*." He motioned between them, his expression an open book. "About us."

"And now, everyone else does, too." She stared up at the ceiling, wishing she could be even a bit upset that Deke had visually outed them to anyone who'd been glancing their way, but she just couldn't muster the strength to give a damn. What she felt for Deacon far surpassed any ribbing she'd get from the other officers. Hell, she'd take it and more if it meant Deke was in her life to stay.

His chair scraped closer just before his hand landed on

her thigh. She dropped her gaze, focusing on his face. God, the man was stunning. Even with dark smudges under his eyes, his brow creased with exhaustion, he took her breath away.

His furrow deepened. "Cait..."

She shushed him with a squeeze of his hand. "Don't. Don't you dare apologize or something equally insulting. I don't care that he or anyone else knows we're involved. I'm not ashamed of what we have. I just hadn't planned on broadcasting the news until after we solved the case. Which seems like a damn impossible feat." She sighed. "You want to go through video footage with me?"

Deke held up one hand. "Just...wait a second. Can we go back to the part where your captain knows we're sleeping together and you don't care?"

She grinned. "Did you honestly think I'd want to keep our relationship a secret?"

His mouth opened and closed a few times before he sighed. "Not everyone in your precinct values my work the way you do. And they're bound to tease you."

"Guess that means I'm stuck working any interagency cases with you, then. And they're welcome to try. But I know for a fact I can kick most of their asses." She laughed. "Besides, I'd be proud to show you off anytime, anywhere."

His smile dropped her stomach. "So when I invite you to Assistant Director Jamieson's annual barbecue in a couple of months?"

"Just let me know how much skin I can show." She gave him a playful shove. "Can we get back to the case, now? We've got a few hours' worth of footage to go through, and that's narrowing the window down to twenty minutes or so each side of the attacks."

"My pleasure, sweetheart."

She smiled at the endearment, shifting around so they could both watch the monitor as they sorted through endless videos from the areas surrounding the crime scenes. Vehicles and people crossed the frames, nothing striking them as noteworthy.

Deke huffed when the video cut out, watching her as she keyed up another one. "God, it's like looking for a red hat in a black and white photo."

"I guess there's a reason this thing has been hunting as long as it has without getting caught." She tapped on some keys then glanced at her notepad. "A few people remembered a white truck in the area at both the church and that first alleyway."

"There haven't been any white trucks, yet. Hell, there hasn't been much of anything on these files."

"This next one is a traffic cam from a block away from the church. Out front of your sister's restaurant, actually. Maybe it got something."

He grinned at her. "I do love your optimism. Okay, roll it."

She started the footage. "I'll jump forward to just before your sister and Trevor left for the church."

She shuffled ahead to the correct time stamp, playing the video at regular speed. Deacon muttered something under his breath when Trevor's truck entered the frame, stopping at the light then speeding off. She reached for his hand, giving it a reassuring squeeze. He twisted his palm so he could return the gesture, but maintained his hold after she would have let go. He didn't say anything, focusing on the monitor again, a playful smile curling his lips.

She chuckled—the man was incorrigible. She studied the screen, watching as a number of vehicles crossed through the intersection before inhaling sharply. She paused the video, staring at a white truck centered in the frame. "I realize there are literally thousands of white trucks throughout Seattle, but...this is the first one we've captured on any of the tapes."

Deacon leaned in, looking as if he was trying to puzzle something out. "There's a sticker or logo or something in the left rear window. Just above the cab. Can you make out what that is?"

She tried zooming in, but the grainy texture only blurred the small image more. "Other than it's in the shape of a circle...not a clue."

"The bumper and hitch are blocking out too much of the plate to get anything useful." He tapped a finger against his chin. "Leave that there. Let's see if we can spot that same truck on any of the remaining footage from the other scene. I know this is a long shot, but..."

"But worth a look."

She keyed up another tape, going through three more before another white truck popped up on the screen. "There."

Deacon advanced it a few frames, pointing at the rear, flipping between the two paused images. "Plate's hidden again, but there's that same circular object in the rear window." He zoomed in. "Is it just me, or does that look like some kind of moon?"

"It's pretty grainy, but yeah. Not a regular image,

though. It's got swirls and lines inside it." She squinted. "Is that a letter in the middle?"

"Hard to tell. It could be... Fuck." He scraped back his chair. "Come on."

She frowned, grabbing her phone off her desk as she followed him toward the exit. "Where are we going?"

"That's an A in that moon drawing. A *tribal* moon drawing. Does that sound at all familiar?"

"An A? Tribal moon...no. Seriously?"

"Bet my ass it's not a coincidence that Beverly has a tribal moon as the logo for her *apothecary* shop."

Cait jogged to keep up with his long strides once they hit the pavement outside. "I agree, but..." She snagged his arm, stopping him. "It's not that much to go on. So let's be civil to start."

He gave her a stomach-flipping smile. "I'll be so damn charming she won't know what hit her."

"Deke."

He sighed, taking a deep breath. "I'm fine. I'll be professional. Promise."

She nodded, sighing when he moved to the driver's side, motioning for her to give him the keys. She tossed them at him, slipping into the passenger side. He started the engine then pulled into traffic.

Cait turned down the volume on the radio, twisting to face Deacon as he wove through traffic, the setting sun burning the clouds into pinks and purples. The light hit his profile, accentuating the golden streaks in his hair— the kind most women would pay a salon to put in. Christ, he was attractive. Though Cait realized it wasn't just the rugged good looks, or roguish charm. It was his sense of honor, his courage. The way he'd stood up to her brother, not allowing the man to intimidate him or scare him away. Hell, the fact Deke hadn't ditched her yet was a new level of commitment she hadn't experienced before.

Nervous excitement fluttered her stomach, and she couldn't help but wonder if she'd get tired of him. Of feeling damn well giddy just sitting next to him, regardless of what they were doing. Of finally feeling safe just being herself, knowing he'd have her back.

Deke chuckled, cupping her thigh before giving it a squeeze. "You okay?"

She gave herself a mental shake. "Of course. Why?"

"You turned to face me then just sat there. Staring. Looking pretty damn deep in thought."

Heat burned up her cheeks, but it was too late to break eye contact. Contradicting answers tumbling through her mind, but her heart answered first. "Just enjoying the view. You're easy on the eyes, sweetie."

His smile turned wicked at her endearment. "That's only because you're not sitting here, looking at you. You're spectacular, sweetheart. And not just on the outside." He cleared his throat. "I don't think I ever got a chance to thank you."

"For what?"

"Seriously? You drove me to that church, talked Stacy down off the wall, all the while gathering information. You completely took charge of that crime scene then proceeded to give up a few pints of your blood to keep Trevor alive. All without breaking a sweat. And I haven't even touched on how you got your brother to tag along, probably saving Trevor's life, or how you've kept me sane these past couple of days."

"First, you don't have to thank me for any of that.

Second, Riley's like that by nature. I know he doesn't come across that way, but he'd have gone regardless of who'd been hurt. And third, we've done nothing but work for forty-eight hours straight. Shit, I haven't even had a chance to kiss you."

"A wrong I intend to right. But that's not what I meant. I don't need to be naked with you to have you keep me sane. Just sitting here, knowing you'll have my back, regardless of what we walk into next..." He sighed. "Never had a partner like that. At work. At home. In my life, really." He winked at her. "Or in my bed. You are definitely one of a kind."

His words eased the prickly feeling she hadn't realized had been scratching at her sanity. While she knew the temporary hold on their relationship had been merely a by-product of work and stress—hospital visits and double homicides—she couldn't lie and say that a part of hadn't worried he'd been having second thoughts. Coming to the same conclusion most people in her life had—she just wasn't worth the effort. Hearing him talk like that...

She pushed the annoying thoughts away. Her childhood had sucked, but she'd made it through. Had somehow managed to gain a brother in the process. It was high time she let the other parts go.

Another chuckle grabbed her attention, and she realized she'd done it again. Drifted into her thoughts while just staring at him.

She swatted at his shoulder. "It's not funny."

"Oh, but it is. Am I scaring you?"

"Do I look scared?" She groaned when he chuckled again. "Trust me. If you could hear what I was thinking, you'd be the one running as fast as you could in the opposite direction."

"We're hunting a soul sucking creature. Pretty sure that means I don't scare easily. Especially, if any of those thoughts involve you being naked. My head wedged between your thighs."

"Christ. You really can't talk to me that way when there's no relief from *that* in sight. I'm already desperate."

"So when I ask you to spend the night with me at my place..."

"Guess sleep isn't in our future." She glanced out the window as he pulled to a stop beside the curb. "There's the truck. Sticker and everything. Funny how we never noticed it before."

"Maybe she keeps it in the garage. Or she usually parks it somewhere else. Even just down the street." He stepped out, looking at her over the top of the car. "Does something feel off to you?"

"Hate to break it to you, but this case has been off from the start. I'm not sure I could sense anything strange if it bit me in the ass."

He gaze dipped to her butt as she rounded the vehicle. "How about I just kiss your butt, instead. Ouch!" He rubbed his arm where she'd playfully swatted him. "I never realized you were so violent."

"Only when you're being an ass. Shall we?"

He grinned, crossing the street then checking out the truck. "Nothing obvious. No blood that I can see, or weapons. But there's something..." He inhaled, then gasped, drawing his weapon. "Sulfur."

Cait didn't need any further explanation. She drew her gun, following him up to the porch. The door stood slightly ajar, the space beyond cloaked in shadows. He made a series of signals with his hand, mouthing a countdown. He barged forward when he reached three, sweeping the area then moving off to his left. Cait went right, covering Deacon as he slowly made his way toward the rear of the house. He glanced in the first room, shaking his head as he motioned to the next. A soft groan sounded from the darkness, followed by a hushed scuffing sound.

Cait darted forward, pressing her back against one side of the doorway as Deacon took the other. He indicated he'd go first, giving her a hard look when she shook her head. She relented, covering him when he popped out, once again sweeping the area. A body sprawled across the floor in front of the shelves, the woman's hair bright against the dark wood. A bloodied knife rested a few feet away, as if it'd fallen from her grasp.

Deke headed for her, kneeling beside her. He reached for her neck, pressing his fingers against her skin. "She's alive. Multiple puncture wounds, maybe some head trauma."

Cait nodded, dialing nine-one-one as she kept watch at the doorway. She rattled off the address and known condition, cursing when an engine revved outside. She shouted to Deke, racing for the front door. She'd only just crested the porch when the white truck spun around on the street, screeching off in a cloud of burnt rubber. She got a flash of the driver's face, before the vehicle turned the corner, disappearing down the road.

"Shit!"

She ran back to the house, quickly clearing the rest of the rooms before turning on the lights as she returned to

Deke's side. Beverly's eyes were open as he attempted to keep pressure on her wounds.

Cait crouched beside the woman, gently cupping her shoulder. "Beverly? Can you hear me?"

Her gaze focused on Cait, a small nod her only reply.

Cait bent closer. "Can you tell us who attacked you?"

Beverly's eyes teared up, rolling back slightly as she groaned. She took a few panting breaths then pointed to the shelf. Cait twisted, scanning the rows until she spotted a picture. The same one she'd noticed the first time they'd visited.

She grabbed it, holding it out to Beverly. "Is this who hurt you?" At the woman's nod, Cait continued, looking up at Deacon. "He was in the vehicle that just sped off. I only saw him for a second, but I'm sure it was him." She glanced at Beverly, again. "Is he your son?"

Beverly shook her head, wincing as she tried to sit up.

Deke held her down. "Don't try to move. Help will be here soon."

Beverly snorted, pursing her lips before sighing. "Grandfather."

Cait coughed, glancing from the photo back to the other woman. "This man is at least thirty years younger than you in this picture. But he's your grandfather?"

She motioned weakly to her desk. "Book."

Cait rose, quickly crossing over to the desk. A large, leather-bound tome sat off to one side, a light layer of dust on the top. She picked it up, returning to Beverly's side then holding it out to her. "This one?"

Beverly grimaced in seeming pain. "One...forty-two."

Cait opened the cover, careful not to rip the brittle pages as she flipped to the correct number, staring at a drawing of a creature that looked eerily similar to the glimpses they'd gotten of the one that had attacked them. "Rinikarhu?"

"Yes. Yes." The last word hissed into a whimper, Beverly's eyes rolling back.

Deacon shushed her. "Don't try to talk anymore. Ambulance should be here any second."

She shook her head. "Read."

Cait met his gaze, then stared at the page, hoping she could decipher the handwritten note. "A violent demon spirit that possesses human males during their prime, granting the host immortality. But in order to retain its youthful appearance, rinikarhus consume the souls of other, healthy men of similar age every few decades. The number of souls needed, and duration of time between each feeding spree, depends on the energy within the souls and whether the last one is consumed during a full moon, which significantly increases the amount of energy the rinikarhu can absorb." She paused, trying to take it all in. "It says the only known weaknesses are silver and anything holy. They're extremely hard to kill as they have increased speed and strength but can be tracked by the sulfuric odor they emit during the weeks when they're consuming human souls. They're most vulnerable when they transform into their true form just before they latch on to their victim and suck out their soul through tiny barbs on their fingers." She looked up. "Christ, is this for real?"

Deacon sighed. "We've seen it."

"I know, it's just... Damn." She glanced at Beverly. "You were trying to kill it, weren't you? Finally put an end to the killings." She sighed at the woman's painful nod, focusing on Deke again. "That's why it didn't come after me, or Stacy. It only attacks men."

Deke glanced toward the door as a siren sounded in the distance. "If this thing possesses the person, can't we exorcise it or something?"

She skimmed through a few more notes. "It says that after the first set of feedings, the two entities become infused. The only way to get rid of the demon once they're joined is to kill both it and the host. Shit."

The whine of the siren increased.

Cait closed the book then bent lower, pointing to the knife. "Will that knife kill it if we get close enough?"

The woman nodded, reaching for Cait's hand. "Take it." She grunted through a few breaths. "He's injured. Won't risk attacking again until the full moon. That's when you have to kill him." Her teary gaze landed on Deacon. "So sorry. I was too afraid back then…"

Deke sighed. "It's okay. Save your strength. I hear the ambulance pulling up outside."

She shook her head, eyes bulging wide. "Should have told…" She groaned, breath wheezing out. "Nothing left of the man. Just…evil."

Her voice trailed off as paramedics entered the room, rushing over to her. Deke backed away, motioning to the knife. Cait picked it up, moving off in order to give the medics room. They answered what questions they could, following the EMTs outside as they shoved Beverly into the ambulance, siren blaring, lights flashing. It sped off, the sudden lack of noise strangely unnerving. They headed back into the house, returning to the room.

Deke scanned the area, shaking his head. "Guess we'll have to call it in. Not sure how we're going to explain our guy did this. He's never attacked a woman before."

Cait squeezed his arm. "He's masquerading as her son this go 'round. Not a stretch to say we're assuming she confronted him, and he attacked her. Fled when we arrived. We don't actually know how it all went down, so...we wouldn't be lying."

"You know if we go that route, it'll blow our same killer theory right out of the water."

"The man looks like he's in his twenties. There's no way anyone else will believe he's her grandfather, instead of her son." She moved in front of him when he looked as if he was going to leave. "I know you want to prove your father right, especially since he was, but... Did you really think we'd be able to put soul-sucking creature, or rinikarhu, in the report? That your boss or mine would accept that a...a...demon killed all these people in order to maintain its immortality? I *know* it's true, and it sounds crazier than shit to me." She smoothed her hands up his chest. "We'll work the family pact idea. Say that the previous father made his son kill with him or something. That's how all the murders were identical. Gave the perfect illusion of a single killer. No one will fault your dad for jumping to the conclusions he did."

He snorted, moving out of her hold. "So we're just going to throw my dad, and everything he died for, under the bus? Lie because it's easy? Believable? That's not why I became a federal officer."

She spun as he walked past her. "No, we're going to do what we have to do in order to see justice served. *That's* why you joined the bureau. And we'll do that. We'll nail this son of a bitch."

"Let's say we do. Everyone will still think my dad was nuts. That I'm nuts for ever believing him."

"What they'll think is that you just solved a serial killer case that's spanned eighty years and resulted in over a dozen deaths. Don't diminish what you've pulled off, here. What you and your father made possible in the first place. Trust me, everything else will fade away."

"Call me crazy, but I'd rather clear my dad's name than get a pat on the back for a job well done."

"Deacon…"

He pulled out his phone. "I'll call it in. Wait for CSI outside. You'd best put that book and knife in your car before they get here, or we'll lose what little advantage we might have."

Cait closed her eyes, his fading footsteps mimicking the empty thud of her heart. This was quickly turning ugly, and it wasn't just the case.

# CHAPTER SIXTEEN

Deacon sat on his couch, nursing his third beer as he stared at some old family movies playing on the television. He'd spent a couple of hours at Beverly's shop, going through books and other items as the CSI guys swabbed and photographed everything. He'd found a few more photos of Byron Howard—Beverly's grandfather turned son. There was no mistaking the older images were of the same man—clothes, hairstyle and color altered to suit the times. But the eyes, the shape of his jaw—the bastard hadn't aged more than a few years over the past eighty he'd been possessed by the rinikarhu. Not that a single soul would believe Deke if he told them. Fuck, showed them. They'd chalk it up to family resemblance. And it's not as if he had any DNA from the previous crimes as proof, even if they caught the bastard.

He tilted his head back against the cushions, listening to his child self giggle on the screen as his dad chased him around the yard. Thomas McGraw had been the kind of man who'd filmed everything. Had wanted visual records of birthdays and gatherings. Hell, of any first he could think of. Deke hadn't really appreciated it, back then, but now...now it gave him a chance to see his dad. Hear the man's voice. Deke didn't pull them out very often. But when he realized he couldn't quite remember the funny snort his dad made when he chuckled, Deke would sit down—watch for a few hours. Pretend he wasn't gutted by the fact his father would never get the recognition he deserved for sacrificing his life in an attempt to stop a monster.

Deke had meant what he'd told Caitlyn. He didn't care about a damn commendation for his work. He didn't give a shit about anything other than stopping the creature and proving that his dad hadn't been having some kind of breakdown. That he'd seen the truth when everyone else had put on blinders. Too afraid to believe there might be something far more dangerous in the world than people. That monsters were real.

His stomach roiled. That wasn't true. He cared about Caitlyn, too. More than he should. Which was the real reason he was about to reach for his fourth beer. Ever since she'd had the courage to voice their logical course of action, he'd distanced himself. Put up barriers to keep her from seeing how much the reality of their circumstances hurt him. While a part of him had always known he'd never be able to reveal the true aspects of the case, damn if he didn't want to. Didn't want to march into Jamieson's office, toss the book and bloody knife on the man's desk, and force him to see it for what it was.

But she'd been right. The world needed a tangible story. One that wouldn't end up with them in the psychiatric ward, their careers a distant memory. She'd done nothing but stand by his side since the start. But hearing her say the words out loud... It'd hit him hard, and he'd gone out of his way to avoid being alone with her since. Hell, when Stacy had called and asked if he'd stop by the restaurant on his way home, he'd practically ran out the door—nothing more than a mumbled, "got to go" as an explanation. And he'd been sitting on the damn couch, brooding, ever since.

He glanced at the television, noting the time. Nearly midnight. If he hadn't been such a colossal ass, he could be holding Cait right now. Snuggling with her in his bed, the afterglow of their lovemaking still coloring her skin. Instead, he was slowly getting drunk, letting the best thing that had ever happen to him slip away.

He scrubbed a hand down his face, wondering if he should call her, when a throat cleared behind him. He stood, reaching for his gun as he spun, aiming it at the hallway behind him. Green eyes crinkled with humor as she leaned against the doorframe, a case of coolers in one hand, a bag in the other.

She arched one brow, seemingly unfazed by his reaction. "Do you always leave your door unlocked?"

He released a harsh breath, holstering his weapon then placing it on the table before crossing his arms over his chest. "Do you always just walk into someone's house unannounced?"

"Someone's?" She snorted. "Here I thought I was walking into my *boyfriend's* house after getting an invitation earlier in the day, but...perhaps I was mistaken." The cockiness faded from her expression. "Besides, I was pretty damn sure you wouldn't answer the door if you knew it was me, so..."

"You make it sound as if I'm avoiding you."

"Maybe because you are." She tsked at his frown. "At least have the decency not to lie to my face, Deke. You owe me that much."

"Did you ever stop to consider that maybe I just need a bit of time? Alone?"

"Actually, you made that quite obvious."

"Yet, you're standing in my living room."

"Because if you're backing out of whatever we were trying to get going, then you're going to have to tell me to fuck off to my face."

He sighed as she tossed his words from that first day as partners back at him. "Still direct, I see." He motioned to the carton in her hand. "You brought your own?"

"You didn't seem like the hard lemonade type."

He waved at the couch, sinking into the cushions again before crossing his feet at his ankles as he rested them on the edge of the coffee table. She padded across the floor—hushed footsteps that made his stomach clench in anticipation—then claimed the cushion next to him. Close, but not touching. She twisted off a cap, taking a long pull. He tried to ignore the way the bottle looked caressed by her lips, knowing he'd get lost in the tones of her skin, or the way her hair hung in a deep auburn curtain around her shoulders. The contented little hum she made after she swallowed. She'd made that same sound when she'd gone down on him in the shower, and now wasn't the time to let his dick do the talking for him.

A small smile lifted one corner of her mouth as she watched the images play across the screen. "You really do look like him. Sound like him, too." She laughed along when his father erupted into a fit of laughter on the movie. "God, you even do that cute little snorting thing. It's uncanny."

He scoffed. "I do not."

She glanced sideways at him, not fully taking her gaze off of the television. "Yeah. You do."

"You're delusional."

"I didn't say it was a bad thing. I think it's nice. That you're so much like him. That you get to remember what he sounded like. Looked like. How much he loved you." She took another swig. "Trust me, I'd give anything to have something of my parents. A reminder that those ten years in foster care hadn't been what they'd wanted, either."

"You don't have anything? Not even a photo?"

He cursed inwardly as the question just popped free, hanging between them. He knew instantly by the purse of her lips, the way her entire body stiffened, that he'd stepped into uncharted waters. Ones that were most likely littered with mines. He waited, trying to decide what he'd do when she made a move to leave, only to stare in disbelief when she shrugged, relaxing into the cushion. The usual tough facade she wore like armor slipped away, leaving a very different side of Cait sitting there. Open. Vulnerable.

She glanced at the bottle in her hands, looking at it as if it might fall from her grasp. "I had a shoebox with some old photos. My dad's watch. A necklace my mom used to wear all the time, but...I had to leave it behind at that last place." She snorted. "Actually, left isn't the correct word. The family destroyed it before Joe could get over there to retrieve it for me. Payback, I suppose."

"Payback? For what?"

"Getting the father arrested for sexual assault of a minor." A grim line shaped her lips. "And there was that pesky attempted murder charge... That didn't go over well with his wife and son."

A loud roar sounded inside his head as he turned to face her, one arm stretched across the back of the couch, the other thumbing the lip of his beer. Christ, had he heard her correctly? The desolate expression on her face more than confirmed it.

He closed his eyes, tamping down the resulting anger before gazing at her. She hadn't moved, her focus still fixed on the television, her lips twitching with what he suspected was an effort to remain in control. Not allow him to see any form of weakness.

He lightly touched her shoulder, hating the fact she tensed. "Cait."

Her eyes closed for a moment, the muscle in her jaw jumping as she clenched it. Unshed tears glistened in the green depths when she finally opened them again, still not looking directly at him. "We all have demons we'd like to vanquish, Deke. Sometimes, it's just not possible."

"Is that how you met Joe? He treated you after..."

She glanced at him, holding his gaze when he thought for sure she'd look away. "After my foster father tried to rape me, then cut me up because I was initially able to kick his ass off of me? Yeah, Joe was the emergency physician. He walked into that exam room, took one look at me and called the police. Of course, it was my word against theirs. They all lied. Said I'd come home from a party that way. Drunk. High. That I'd attacked them. They even went so far as to say they felt sorry for me. Would welcome me back."

There was no mistaking the hatred dripping from her words, or the pain creasing her brow and deepening the lines around her mouth. And he couldn't help but wonder if she'd ever told anyone this story. Or if she'd locked it inside herself for over a decade. Hiding it away with the parts of herself she saw as weak. That had allowed her to put herself in that position to begin with.

She looked toward the television again. "Joe stood up for me. Started rattling off stuff to the cops about how my wounds didn't match what they'd claimed. That they were too fresh. The wrong direction. I don't remember much. I *do* remember that I wouldn't let Joe touch me for like two hours. I just sat in the corner, holding my knees, keeping that damn gown they give you wrapped around me as I rocked back and forth. Praying that my mother's ghost would show up and just take me with her. It wasn't until I'd lost so much blood I was starting to see dots that he convinced me he wouldn't hurt me. Wouldn't touch me other than to treat the wounds."

She smiled. "The man was a saint. Crazy to take me in, but a saint, nonetheless. Child services came along and wanted to cart me off to some juvenile detention center to heal. Said it was the only place they had any kind of medical facilities. Joe refused. Wouldn't release me until they'd agreed to allow him to be my temporary guardian. I'd planned on running away the moment I felt strong enough, but..."

She turned to face him again, a few of the tears slipping free. "I guess he and Riley got under my defenses. Gave me a reason to trust, again. Not that I do that very easily. Trust people. I just can't help but assume the worst until they prove otherwise. Except you. You got under there, too. From day one."

A shiver worked through her before she suddenly rose to her feet, clanking the bottle down on the table. She snagged her bottom lip, worrying it between her teeth as she took a couple of quick steps back. "And I shouldn't have told you that. Any of it. I'll see myself out."

She bolted for the door, getting halfway there before he caught up to her. She didn't resist when he hooked her elbow, spinning her around. He tried to go gently, not wanting to scare or provoke her, but just one look at her face—at the tears dotting her cheeks, the fear reflected in her eyes—had him backing her against the wall. One hand cupping her head as the other landed beside her hip, effectively shielding her.

He didn't talk, just rested his forehead on hers, savoring the feathery caress of her breath across his neck. It grounded him. Proof he hadn't yet screwed up everything to the point he'd lost her for good. Her hands landed on his chest, each tiny finger anchoring him to her. She didn't move, simply stood there, trembling through each breath.

He nuzzled her nose, dropping a chaste kiss on the tip when he finally eased back. "Did you honestly think I'd just let you leave? After telling me all that?"

She swallowed thickly, a few more tears washing down her face. She cringed, and he knew she was fighting the urge to wipe them away. "I never should have told you that. God, what was I thinking?"

"That maybe you understood better than anyone how it feels to think you failed. To worry that you don't measure up. Fuck..." He pushed out a slow breath, hoping the simple act would keep him calm. "I had no idea you'd had to suffer through shit like that. That you'd lost everything."

"I have Riley. That's more than I ever thought I'd have. I'm lucky. I know that. And I'd go through it all again if it meant I'd still end up with him and Joe. That I'd get so much more than I deserved."

"You deserved to be loved. To be safe. How can you think any less?"

"Old habits. You get told often enough that you're worthless. That the only thing you'll ever be good for is a quick, cheap fuck...you start to believe it. I work hard at blocking those voices, but they're still there. They'll always be there."

"You know none of that's true." He wanted to add that Riley wasn't the only one she had, but damn, he'd done little today to prove that. And after learning the truth, he realized actions meant far more to her than words. Actions didn't lie. Didn't leave her wondering if he was just another player. If her trust had been misplaced.

She huffed, finally pushing against him. "I don't need your pity."

"I'm not giving you my pity. Christ..." He wanted to say, he was giving her his love, but it just wouldn't form on his tongue. Make it past the erratic beating of his heart.

"Now you know why I never tell anyone about my past." She shoved at him again. "I shouldn't have come over. I'll leave."

"I don't want you to leave." He sighed, kicking at the floor as he backed up a bit, giving her some space. "I know I acted like an ass today. That I distanced myself when all you did was have the guts to tell me the truth. How I knew it had to play out but didn't want to admit. So, stay." He held up his hands. "We don't have to have make out, get naked. Hell, we don't have to do anything other than sit on the couch, drink far too much alcohol, then fall asleep with the damn television still playing those stupid home movies. I won't ask for more than you're willing to give, I just… I want you to stay."

"I should read more of that book. Prepare."

"Beverly said he won't attack until the next full moon."

"That's less than a week away."

"Which mean we can spare one evening without the entire world falling apart. We've got an APB out on Byron and his truck. A police detail guarding Beverly in case he decides he needs to finish the job. We'll know if the bastard pops his head out. There's nothing more we can do tonight. Besides, we're both exhausted. We won't be much good to anyone if we can't stay awake." He gave her his best smile. "Just one night. We'll pick everything up tomorrow."

She glanced at the doorway, indecision clouding her eyes. She seemed to weigh the options over in her mind, finally meeting his gaze. "I did bring a carton of coolers. And *Constantine* is available on Netflix."

He cracked a smile. "Angels. Demons. Sounds like our kind of movie. Popcorn?"

"Sure."

"You fire it up. I'll pop the corn."

She nodded, heading back toward the couch. But he didn't miss the slight hesitation in her step. The way she rubbed her arms as she sat down, looking as if she wasn't sure how close to get to his spot. She was wary. And it was his fault.

He cursed inwardly, shuffling into the kitchen. He got their snack, handing her the bowl once he'd made his way back. She took it, offering her thanks as he sat beside her. He wanted to move in closer, take her in his arms, but he wasn't sure she'd welcome him just yet. She still seemed raw. Unnerved by her confession. Instead, he cracked open a new beer, passing over her cooler before relaxing against the couch.

The movie started, breaking the uneasy silence. She placed the popcorn between them, some of the tension in her muscles easing as she finished her cooler, then opened another, humming as she took a deep pull. He tried not to stare at her. Catalogue the way her expression changed with each scene of the movie. Or the way she licked the rim of the bottle, wishing she'd use her tongue on him. Let him taste the sweet essence that was all her. But he managed to hold off, chuckling when her eyelids started to droop. She burrowed into the cushions, finally resting her head against the back.

Deke watched her drift, fighting to stay awake but obviously just too tired to win the battle. When her head lolled toward her chest, he stood, gently taking the bottle from her hand. Then he moved in front of her, scooping her into his arms. Her eyelids fluttered, giving him glimpses of green as she rested her head against his chest.

He dropped a kiss on her forehead. "Sleep. We can talk in the morning."

She mumbled something incoherent, not truly opening her eyes. He made his way to his bedroom, placing her on the bed. Then he tugged off her pants and socks, rolling her enough to draw down the covers. She grunted when he moved her back, scowling as she blinked at him a few times.

He smiled. "Just getting you more comfortable. Go back to sleep."

Her brow furrowed, then eased. "Come to bed."

His heart tripped, skipping into a shaky rhythm. God, just hearing her ask him to join her, even if it was more of an automatic response, made his chest tighten as his dick spiked against his pants. He brushed back her hair, giving her another kiss. Then he readied himself for bed before stripping down to his boxers. Warm, soft skin brushed against him as he snuggled into her, drawing her close with a hand between her breasts. She wiggled into position, rubbing his cock until he thought he'd come all over her ass, then sighed, drifting off again.

Deacon closed his eyes. He'd more than screwed up, but he'd find a way to make it right. Because lying there, Caitlyn cuddled against him, her breath feathering across his arm, felt more than good. It felt right. Loosened the knot in his gut. Filled the hole he'd had since his dad had been killed. And he knew he'd do whatever it took to be the man she needed. The one she'd trusted without hesitation. The one who would rather die than let her down again.

# CHAPTER SEVENTEEN

Caitlyn hummed, burrowing into the warm, muscular frame behind her. A steady thrum vibrated against her back, a slow breath tickling her neck. She blinked, allowing her eyes to adjust to the grayed surroundings. Objects ghosted into view amidst the shadows, her memories shuffling in her head.

She stiffened. The last thing she remembered, she'd been watching the movie on Deke's couch, wondering whether she should have simply left when she'd had the chance. Though a part of her had wanted to stay, sitting there, so close yet feeling miles apart, had taken a toll. Made her question why she'd ever thought she could have a normal relationship. She was damaged goods. Scarred in a way she doubted time would ever truly fade. Her best option was to keep things on the fringes. Occasional romps with guys that attracted her but would never possess her heart sounded far safer, smarter, than thinking she could hold on to a guy like Deacon. And she feared it was only a matter of time before he realized he'd made a mistake and left, taking what she'd managed to save of her heart with him.

The thought more than sobered her. She'd already fallen way too hard for him. Any further, and she'd never find her way back. Never be able to rebuild herself without having Deacon fill in some of the spaces.

His arms tightened around her, his lips dancing along her nape. "Call me crazy, sweetheart, but my gut's telling me you're about ready to run screaming out of here."

Her stomach quivered at his words, she just didn't know if it was because he'd said her thoughts out loud or because he'd spoken the truth. She glanced back at him. "If I screamed, it would have defeated the running part. I would have woken you up."

He smirked. "So, you were hoping to sneak out."

She sighed, wishing she had the strength to lie. "I'll be honest. The thought had crossed my mind."

He pushed onto his elbow, rolling her unto her back. Those brilliant blue eyes of his stared down at her, an unreadable expression on his face. "Why?"

"I think you already know the answer."

The muscle in his jaw flexed. "I behaved poorly yesterday. Shutting you out. Using Stacy as an excuse to ditch you. I'll own that. I'm not proud of how I reacted, but it doesn't mean anything more than I had a bad day." He reached down, brushing some of her hair back from her face. "Trust me. If you hadn't shown up, I would have ended up at your place, again. Banging on your damn door until you either opened it or your neighbors called the cops."

Her skin tingled beneath his gentle caress, his voice sending shivers across her skin. God, she was too affected by him. Too invested in his happiness. Her breathing sped up, the room suddenly hot.

Deke smiled in that way that dropped her stomach. "This is new for me, too. And knowing I hurt you yesterday… It guts me. I know how much it cost you to come over. Make the first move. Tell me about Joe and Riley. I'm hoping that means you're not ready to throw it all away because I couldn't think past my own demons." He dipped down, brushing his mouth over hers but not kissing her. "If you'll give me another chance, I promise I won't let you down, again."

The honesty in his voice pooled tears in her eyes. "You didn't let me down."

"I did." He silenced her with a finger across her lips. "Last night, when you said you hadn't lost everything because you had Riley. God, I wanted you to say you had me, too. That's when I realized just how scared you really were. That I'd acted like all those men who'd merely taken what they'd wanted then pushed you aside. That's not who I am. I know I didn't act that way, but…"

Her stomach rose to her throat, and her heart thrashed against her ribs so hard it hurt. She reached for his face, palming his cheek as she brushed her thumb across the corner of his mouth. "I think the fact I spent the night in your bed, and all you did was hold me, shows me the kind of man you are."

"Believe me. I wanted to do so much more than just hold you. Still do."

She let a smile lift her lips. "I'm not sleeping, anymore."

"So, I'm forgiven?"

"I guess that depends."

"On what?"

"On how mind blowing the make-up sex is."

Deke's pupils dilated as his breathing roughened. "Challenge accepted." He bent forward, nipping at her bottom lip. "I hope you're well-rested, because you'll be spending the next couple of hours screaming my name."

She snagged his lip when he dipped down again, tugging on it before letting it slip free. She laved the flesh, smiling at his hushed moan. "Not if I make you scream first."

He climbed on top of her, straddling her hips, his weight braced on his elbows. "Oh, sweetheart. You're welcome to try…"

His voice keened into a startled gasp as she bridged upwards, dipping her left side and effectively tossing him off. His back hit a moment before she scrambled on top of him, cinching her hands around his wrists and pinning him to the bed. She shifted her weight, preventing him from simply mimicking her tactic, fully aware he could overpower her if he wanted. There was no denying he was far stronger than her, with more than enough moves to seize control. The fact his face lit into a smile, and he seemed content to lie there, trapped, warmed her heart.

He let his gaze travel the length of her. "I'll assume you have something specific in mind?"

"I had thought about handcuffing you to the headboard, but that would require me leaving the bed. And I'm not quite prepared to do that just yet. Don't suppose you'd behave and lie still while I have my way with you?"

"And by 'having your way' you mean…"

"A blowjob worthy of your submission."

"Like in the shower?"

"That's the benchmark. Let's see if I can improve on that."

His muscles twitched beneath her, a rough exhalation marking his acceptance. She smiled, dipping down for a long, slow kiss before releasing his wrists. She smoothed her hands along his arms, admiring the way his biceps flexed at the gentle contact, accentuating his strength. He was all angles and planes.

Cait kissed and licked her way to his chest, circling his flat nipple before doing her best to suck it into her mouth. He grunted in response, a throaty moan quickly following. She nipped at it, then moved to the other side, repeating the same actions, loving the way his cock hardened against her abs as she moved down his body, tracing each rib with her fingers and tongue.

She stopped when she reached the waistband of his boxers, tugging at it with her teeth a few times before shifting her weight so she could slip her fingers beneath the band and yank them down. He lifted his hips, allowing her to peel the garment off as she shuffled to the end of the bed. The underwear hit the floor with a hushed whoosh, the soft sound making her stomach flutter with anticipation. God, no guy had ever gotten her this excited. Just the thought of wrapping her lips around his shaft, watching him lose control—it creamed arousal along her slit.

Deacon chuckled. "Oh, sweetheart. Are you sure you're going to hold off long enough to make me shout? Because if your nipples get any harder..."

She crawled over him again, brushing her knuckles

back and forth along his length as she smiled at him. "I'll manage."

"Why suffer when you don't have to? Turn around, and we can both play."

"God." Shit, she wouldn't last long if he put his tongue on her clit.

"What's wrong? Afraid I'll win?"

"I don't see how making me come is losing but…"

"Then get that pretty pussy up here. Grind yourself on my face while you suck me to your heart's content." He fucking winked at her. "If you're a good girl, I'll make sure you don't come until I do."

"Fuck being a good girl. And you're on."

She spun, straddling his waist. His fingers landed on her hips, the pads digging in slightly as he snagged her panties and dragged them over her hips. She lifted each leg, helping him dispose of the thin fabric, before settling with her knees on either side of his chest.

He tsked her, palming her thighs and pulling her toward him. "I can't play if I can't reach you. I want you straddling my head, your clit pressed hard against my tongue."

More juice creamed her folds at his words, as butterflies bounced around in her stomach. She bit her lip, inching back, gasping when he blew a heated breath across her slit.

"Much better." His tongue dipped inside. "Shit, you're dripping."

She gave herself a mental shake. Damn cold day in hell she'd lose a challenge, which meant making the man shoot down her throat in record time. She took a calming breath, once again focusing on his shaft. The head was swollen, flushed, leaking drops of fluid from the thin slit. She leaned forward, licking away the slick essence, humming at the spicy flavor of him.

Deke moaned behind her, his hips tilting up to meet her next pass. She licked the entire head this time, flicking her tongue across the opening before slowly taking him deep. The raspy version of her name that followed her descent made her clit flutter and her pussy clench emptily. Christ, she could climax from the man's voice alone.

A finger moved the length of her cleft, thrusting inside her. "I love that touching me excites you as much as when I touch you. God, you're incredible."

His tongue repeated the path, dipping inside her sex before swirling her arousal around her clit. Pleasure whipped through her core, and she barely managed to crush the shout that swelled in her chest. Instead, she focused on Deacon. On licking his cock, increasing the pressure as she drew back then plunged forward, taking him to the back of her throat. On the sounds he made as she rose and fell along his length, never allowing the head to fully slip free of her mouth.

Deke seemed to falter for a while, losing rhythm with his fingers and tongue. The muscles in his stomach and thighs tensed, and she knew he was close. She increased her efforts, loving the feel of his hard length filling her mouth, so damn big her eyes began to water from the strain. She was full of him, and she'd never felt more powerful. She moved one hand to his balls, massaging the taut sac with every intention of finger fucking his ass, when he hissed out a breath. The sudden swirl of air across her heated flesh made her pussy contract around his fingers.

Deacon smiled against her skin. "Damn. You are masterful. And I think you've got me close enough I can pick up my pace now. But mark my words, you'll explode before I do."

He latched onto her nub, sucking on it as he started thrusting his fingers into her again. The motion rocked the mattress, banging the bed against the wall. Searing pleasure tore through her groin, threatening to unhinge her with every stroke. She tried to breath around his cock, still working it in and out of her mouth, as her release gathered strength, beading her skin with sweat. She held on, not sure how long she'd last when his finger sank into her ass.

Her stomach clenched, her impending orgasm burning along her spine. Dots flickered across her vision, and she knew she was only moments away from screaming Deke's name. His smug chuckle against her pussy had her moving. She slicked up her finger, then circled his ass, copying the same, mind-numbing penetration he was giving her—sinking her finger inside until she hit his prostrate. Deacon stiffened beneath her, his hips canting upwards.

She grinned inwardly, thrusting her finger back and forth, while moving her mouth along his length. He might claim victory, but she'd push him as far as she could. Deacon's movements became erratic until the finger in her ass stopped moving as his breath caressed her wet flesh.

"Shit, sweetheart. I'm going come. Decide where you want it."

She didn't answer him, knowing he'd recover slightly if she stopped, even for a moment. Instead, she kept bobbing along his cock, grazing his gland, waiting for that moment when he'd surrender to her. It only took a few more strokes before the crown flared, a warning of his impending release.

She kept moving, knowing the instant she had him. He moaned her name against her flesh, as his head fell back to the mattress, the soft thud marking her victory. She managed three more passes before he thrust into her descent, his cock emptying inside her mouth. Her name sounded around them as she pumped him through his release, not stopping until his muscles eased, his shaft softening.

Cait drew down his length one more time before allowing him to pop free. She dropped a kiss on his hip, using the headboard to lever herself up until she could move off of him. Pleasure colored his cheeks, his eyes squeezed shut.

She settled on his chest, elbows on either side, a smug grin tilting her lips. "Something tells me you were a bit too...cocky for your own good. It appears I won."

He chuckled, finally opening his eyes. A sea of stunning blue gazed up at her, his easy smile warming her chest. "I'll hand it to you, sweetheart. I didn't think you'd be able to hold out that long." He winked at her. "You've usually got a hair trigger."

"Then why is your release coating my tongue instead of mine on yours?"

The blue in his eyes darkened. "A minor oversight on my part. Not that it matters, now. That kind of sass can't go unpunished."

He moved, tossing her over then pouncing on top. His weight pinned her to the bed, his mouth possessing hers with a fierce determination she hadn't felt before. She fought for control, tangling her tongue with his, squirming against his hold until her strength gave out, and she conceded. Deacon didn't ease up, still plundering her mouth as he lifted her arms, transferring both of her wrists into one of his hands. His grip held them in place as his other hand smoothed down her torso, moving between her legs.

He finally broke the kiss, nipping at her shoulder as his forefinger grazed her clit. "You're going to come for me. Hard. Fast. Then I'm going to pound into you so damn deep you won't question my intentions, again."

He dipped down, latching onto one nipple as his fingers tortured her clit, moving back and forth so damn quick she didn't have time to do more than hold her breath as her climax shot forward, keeping her on the edge as the scenery started to darken. Time faded into the hot press of his mouth and the never-ending precipice she couldn't quite crest. Emotions clawed to the surface, those voices in her head breaking through her barriers. How long would he wait for her to come before deciding she wasn't worth his effort? His love? That their relationship was a waste of his time?

Deke moved along her body, finally nipping at her ear. "Breathe, sweetheart. Not going to stop until you go over. But you need to breathe."

She tried to suck in a shallow breath, shouting it out as her muscles clenched, so damn close but not quite enough.

"Cait. Look at me."

She thrashed her head across the pillow, tears leaking from her eyes.

"Caitlyn."

She managed to pry her eyelids open, staring into Deacon's face. The hand between her legs gentled, allowing her orgasm to ebb. "No."

"Easy. As much as I would love to say I made you pass out...watch me. Focus on me. This isn't a competition, sweetheart. I've got nothing but time. And there's nothing I'd rather do than touch you. Love you every way I can. So, get out of your head. Stop trying to make it happen and just feel how your body warms to mine. How well we fit together. How hard you're going to come because you will."

He kissed her. Softly. His lips barely touching hers as he circled her clit, slowly building her back up. He didn't waiver, his gaze fixed on hers, his body poised above her, the sheer size of him trapping her against the mattress. He didn't rush, didn't falter, rolling waves of heat through her core until her stomach began to tighten. Fire shot through her groin, culminating in her pussy as her body heaved, once again suspended on the edge.

Deacon smiled. "Damn, you're beautiful. Strung tight. Writhing beneath me. It's time, sweetheart. Come for me."

He claimed her mouth in a kiss that set her off. She arched, clawing at his back as she broke, feeling as if every part of her was flying out in a different direction. He kept moving, kept kissing her until she collapsed beneath him, body shaking. Deke eased away, staying dangerously close as he watched her come back down.

Billows of release still tingled through her, but it was Deacon's gaze that held her captive. It was as if he could see through her. Sense the love she'd been trying hard to hide, especially after the way he'd distanced himself yesterday.

He leaned closer, daring her to look away. "That was incredible. Watching you give yourself over to your release, to me...I could spend a lifetime like this."

More tears slipped down her cheeks, but he didn't pull away. Instead, he gathered her close, brushing some of the moisture away with his thumb.

"Do you need more time to recover? Or can I love you?"

Her chin quivered, her love reflected in his eyes. "I'm yours."

# CHAPTER EIGHTEEN

*I'm yours.*

Deacon stared at Caitlyn, her words resonating in his head. She was pinned beneath him, her emotions exposed as the remnants of her orgasm washed through her. Tears gathered in her eyes, a deep flush staining her skin as tremors shook through her. She'd never looked more beautiful. And she was his. Not just for tonight. Watching her trust him to take her over, to put her pleasure above everything else, had humbled him. Had made it painfully clear that he was in this for the long haul. He knew he'd never find another woman who understood and accepted him the way she did. Hell, she'd agree to hunt a soul-sucking monster with nothing more than his assurances the damn thing was real.

He nuzzled her nose, tasting her mouth with a slow, deep kiss. She squeezed his back, her nails no longer biting into his skin, but her touch just as desperate. He settled between her thighs, smiling when she wrapped her legs around him, locking her heels against the small of his back. While he'd planned on flipping her over—pounding into her from behind, her ass cushioning every thrust—he knew that wasn't what she needed. What she deserved.

Every swirl of her fingers, every twitch of her lips told him she needed to be loved. Cherished. And damn if he didn't want to give that to her. Know he'd been the reason for the loving gleam in her eyes and the contented smile on her face. That he'd shown her she hadn't been wrong in trusting him.

He tilted his hips, nudging her sex, moaning when she met the gentle intrusion, taking the first few inches inside her. Warm, wet heat engulfed his cock, the simple feel of skin on skin drawing him under. He still couldn't believe he got to love her this way. Nothing between them but heat.

Caitlyn scratched her fingers up to his neck, spearing one hand through his hair as the other cupped his shoulder, anchoring him to her. He lowered slightly, grazing his chest against hers with every frenzied inhalation. Their breath mixed, her focus narrowed on him. He thrust forward, hilting himself inside her sheath. Her eyelids fluttered then closed as her mouth pursed into an O.

He kissed her nose, waiting until she opened her eyes. "Don't look away, sweetheart. Eyes on me."

He transferred more of his weight onto his elbows then moved his hands to her shoulders, palming her skin and holding her in place. He grazed his fingers against her neck, feeling her muscles cord before settling them on her collarbones. He wanted to possess more of her. Surround her until she couldn't move, couldn't breathe without including him.

Her eyes widened, and he waited to see if she'd ask him to back off. Lessen the intensity, the intimacy, of their coupling. She stared up at him, chest heaving against his, every damn inch of them touching before allowing her head to loll into the pillow.

He smiled at her visible surrender, claiming her mouth as he started up a slow rhythm. He didn't want to rush it. Didn't want the moment to end. Have the rest of the world intrude again. He wanted to stay there. Caitlyn's body pressing against his the only tangible thought. Watch her react to his every move. How her eyes dilated, the black eclipsing the green. Or how the flush on her skin deepened, matching the dusky color of her nipples.

Caitlyn arched into each gentle thrust, her gaze fixed on his. She seemed just as invested. Just as encompassed by the moment. He kept pumping, the steady motion slowly clawing at his control. The wet echo of his cock through her channel surrounded them, a steady backdrop to the breathy little moans that rumbled from her chest.

He inhaled, rewarded with the heady scent of their combined arousal. A spicy aroma with a hint of sweetness. He licked at her lips, giving her his mouth when she ate at him, seemingly desperate for more. Fire burned beneath his flesh, pulling his balls tight as his release coiled around the base of his spine. He tried to block out the sensations. Focus on something other than the way her pussy rippled, or how she'd released his mouth and locked hers onto his shoulder. How every thrust bound him more to her until he knew he'd never be able to separate himself from her. See a future without her by his side. But it was useless.

Every breath, every move became a joint effort. She

rolled her hips as he levered into her, countering his strokes, pushing them closer to the edge. He didn't think about finishing, focusing on the way she gasped as he entered her. The slight huff of disappointment when he withdrew. How her pussy creamed when he whispered her name, or the steady thrashing of her heart against his palm.

Deke lost track of time, nothing registering but the smooth glide of his body inside hers. The building heat as his release surged forward, fraying what was left of his resolve. He closed his eyes for a moment, dragging in several ragged breaths, when her breath caught.

He opened his eyes just as hers rolled back, her body arching into him. His name sounded above the pounding of his pulse in his ears as her pussy contracted around him, the rhythmic pulses triggering his own climax. Liquid fire coiled in his sac, suspending him on the edge for three agonizing heartbeats before shooting forward, taking him with it. He stiffened, suspended above her, paralyzed with his impending release before his cock exploded, jerking his hips against her.

She moaned his name, the low sound drawing out his climax. He didn't know how many times he pulsed inside her, the sticky fluid dripping out to coat his skin, before his strength gave out. He collapsed on top of her, barely bracing any of his weight, his limbs feeling like rubber.

Cait shifted her hands to his back, holding him tight as she trembled beneath him. He knew by her shuddering gasps, by the way her fingers flexed against his skin, that she hadn't fully descended from her orgasm, yet. He grinned at the thought, finally finding the strength to lever up enough to look at her. Her bottom lip was snagged between her teeth, her eyes squeezed shut. Her cheeks were hued a deep pink, her forehead dotted with sweat.

He kissed her nose, smiling at the flutter of eyelashes before she managed to look up at him. "God, you're stunning."

An easy smile lit up her face as tears collected behind her eyes. "Says the man who made me see stars. Again."

"Seems only fair after you won our little challenge."

He moved to roll off her when she tightened her hold.

She shook her head. "Don't go, yet."

"Wouldn't you be more comfortable being able to breathe?"

"I can breathe just fine. I like having you pressed against me. It makes me feel...safe. And it's been a long time since I've truly felt that way."

His throat constricted around a lump of emotion. "Whatever you need, if I can give it to you, it's yours."

Her eyes crinkled as she laughed. "How about a kiss?"

He leaned in, sealing his mouth to hers. She responded in kind, not rushing or seeming to care that he could barely see straight by the time she eased back. She licked her lips once they'd parted, and he couldn't resist from kissing her again. Harder. Deeper. Until her chest heaved against his, this time.

He pushed onto his knees, offering her his hand. "Join me in the shower."

She accepted, swatting him when he picked her up. "You need to stop carrying me to the shower every time you offer one."

"Sorry, no can do. I like having you in my arms too much." He dropped a peck on her forehead. "And it's the only way I know you won't run off on me."

"After your performance in the bedroom, there's no way I'm going anywhere."

"So, I'm officially forgiven for being a jackass, as you put it?"

"Completely."

He grinned, setting her on her feet before readying the shower and grabbing them some towels. Caitlyn watched him dart around the bathroom, a devilish smile on her face.

He cocked an eyebrow at her once he was finished. "What?"

She shrugged. "Nothing. You're just…incredible."

"Because I can turn on a shower and grab a couple of towels?"

Her expression sobered. "No. Because regardless of what you're doing, you always make me feel as if I belong. That I'm not an obligation that results from having sex with someone." She quirked one side of her lips. "That I'm special."

His heart skipped, robbing his breath as he stared at her. Stunned. He closed the scant distance, cupping her jaw. "You do belong. Here…with me. And you have no idea just how special you are." He tapped her ass. "Now get into the shower before I bend you over the counter, clean or not."

She twisted her head slightly, kissing his palm. "Why bend me over the counter, when you can accomplish both and take me in the shower?"

Deke reacted, snaking his arm around her waist as he tugged her against him. He crushed his mouth to hers, thrusting his tongue inside the moment her lips parted. Caitlyn grabbed his shoulders, anchoring herself to him as he lifted her slightly, then spun, taking them both into the shower stall. She gasped as her back hit the tiles, her chest heaving against his when he finally released her.

He didn't speak, just grabbed the soap and made quick work of washing them both off. He didn't worry about being thorough. They were just going to get messy again.

Caitlyn's eyes dilated further with every swirl of his hands over her body until the green ring surrounding her pupils was nothing more than a thin band. Her nipples peaked against her breasts, the tips flushed a dark pink. He captured one in his mouth, sucking on it as he shoved the soap back on the shelf, smoothing his other hand along the curve of her ass. She arched against him, claiming his mouth once he'd released her nipple.

He stepped back after she'd broken the kiss, giving her just enough space to turn. "Face the wall. Hands by your shoulders."

She spun, inhaling when her chest touched the tiles. He knew it probably felt cold, but he'd warm her up. He tapped one ankle, getting her to spread her feet apart as he skimmed his hand up her back and into her hair.

He fisted the wet strands, tipping her head back. "Stick that beautiful ass out for me."

She moaned, the sound morphing into a hiss as he tugged on her hair, keeping her head where he wanted it. She moved her hands down the wall, ensuring they were poised beside her shoulders as she bent over slightly, grinding her ass against his groin. He rubbed his free hand over her flesh, giving it a light slap. Her muscles tensed, drawing a mumbled cry from her.

Deke slipped his fingers down her crease, dipping into her sex. "Fuck, still wet."

"Don't tease me."

"Oh, sweetheart. You know that kind of confession just makes me want to have you squirming again. At my mercy for the next hour. Getting you close over and over until you can't see straight."

"If you want me desperate, then you've already succeeded."

"Fine. Seeing as you shattered so wonderfully for me last time, I won't make you wait. But next time…"

He smiled when she shivered, knowing she was already picturing their next encounter. That she was counting on there being one. Shit, there'd be endless next encounters if he had anything to say about it.

Cait moaned as he sank his finger inside her, gathering some of her slick fluid before spreading it around her clit. She bucked her hips forward, grunting when he gave her ass another slap. This one a bit harder than the last.

"Don't tilt away from me. I want your ass presented to me like a fucking present."

"I can't help it. When you touch me… Oh God."

She gasped when he spanked her again as her hips punched forward a second time, his finger working her clit. She shuddered in response, then let her head bow forward as she pushed her butt toward him, seemingly determined not to move it during the next pass.

He slipped his finger inside her again, rubbing more of her arousal along her folds. Tremors rocked through her arms and legs, but she kept her hips still, finally arching back into his touch. He hummed his approval, watching the water spray across her skin as he alternated between claiming her pussy and fingering her clit.

He leaned over her, licking the shell of her ear.

"Something tells me you enjoyed having my hand connect with your ass, even just a couple of times."

She glanced at him. "If I say yes, will you put me over your lap next time? Maybe use the handcuffs?"

"Fucking right."

Her lips twitched into a smile. "Then yes."

"Shit." He grunted. "I'm going to bend behind you, and you're going to come all over my tongue. Then I'm going to pound you against this wall. And nothing's going to sway me this time."

"God…"

The word became a raspy plea as he knelt behind her, tilting her hips even more as he swiped his tongue through her slit. Warm, sweet fluid filled his senses, her flavor slightly diluted by the spray from the shower. He moved both hands to her inner thighs, using his thumbs to hold her pussy open—give him complete access. She shouted his name as he buried his face in her cleft, eating at her flesh, licking every drop of arousal from her smooth skin. Her thighs trembled, her clit fluttering against his tongue.

He kept sucking, humming at the taste of her, loving how the tiny vibrations drew a strangled cry from somewhere deep inside. Her feet slid farther apart, pressing her clit harder against his mouth.

"Now. Don't stop. Yes."

She drew out the last word as her pussy contracted, pulsing as her orgasm washed over her. He kept licking, tasting her release until she sobbed, begging him to fuck her. He rose, grasping her hips and slamming home. Another set of contractions rippled around his cock, the sensation snapping his control.

Deke slid one hand up to her shoulder, holding it tightly as he pounded into her, making her ass shimmy with every hard thrust. She met each stroke, angling her groin to take him even deeper—graze her G-spot with every pass. His name became an unending chant before her head dropped to her chest, and she broke.

The rush of warm fluid pushed him over. He dug his fingers into her hips, thrusting through the firm contractions squeezing his shaft, until the fire blazing in his sac shot forward, emptying his release inside her.

Deacon moaned through his climax, finally draping over her back as he fought just to breathe. Darkness edged his vision, his pulse an erratic tempo in his head. He wrapped his arms around her ribs, holding her tight. Her heart thrashed against his palms, her breathing as frantic as his.

He smiled against her skin, waiting until he wasn't gasping for air before lifting one hand and tucking her wet strands behind her ear. "I swear, if this gets any better, you're going to kill me."

She snorted, her limbs still shaking. "Then we'll die together, because...damn."

"I could think of worse ways to go." He forced himself to straighten—remove his weakening erection. "Come on. I'll clean you up again." He tsked when she glanced back at him, arching her brow. "No. No more sex for you until I can see straight. I'm spent."

She sighed as he gathered her in his arms, turning her into the spray. "Fine. But you'd better recover fast. You promised me a spanking. And I have a feeling I've been a very bad girl."

"Christ." He chuckled. "That you have. In the best

possible way." He grabbed the soap again. "A quick rinse, then I'll get us some coffee. Food. We can go over that book. That is what's in that bag you brought over, right?"

"Thought there might be more information. Something to give us an edge."

"Let's hope so, because if Beverly's right...he'll be hunting for his next victim with every intention of killing his prey when the full moon rises."

# CHAPTER NINETEEN

Caitlyn squeezed the bridge of her nose, hoping the pressure would clear her vision once she dared to open her eyes. They'd spent the past four days scouring every resource available for more information on a rinikarhu, but hadn't discovered anything that would guarantee them certain victory. In fact, the more they learned about the lore surrounding the creature, the more killing it seemed an impossible feat. And there was nothing in the evidence from the murders to shed any additional light on where the bastard might strike next. All his previous rituals had gone for shit once he'd started targeting them. Making it personal. No more notes. Just blood. Death.

"Shit." Deacon pounded his hand on the table, slamming his laptop closed. "Everything I unearth says the same damn thing. Silver blade to the heart just before they feed. Which means we have to let this thing take a victim or volunteer to become one in order to kill it." He sighed, raking his hand through his hair. "Neither sounds like a good option."

"The book only says it's the easier way to kill them. Not the only."

"After our dismal failures, thus far, I'm thinking even easy isn't going to remotely easy."

"Maybe we just need to douse the bastard in holy water then stab him repeatedly in the heart?"

"Not bad, except where we have to get close enough to do both. I'd rather kill the bastard from several feet away, but I suppose that's not going to be possible."

Cait sighed, reaching across the table and taking Deke's hand in hers. They'd needed a change of scenery and had ventured to Stacy's once again, hiding away at the same isolated table she'd given them that first night, even though the place wouldn't be open for another hour or so.

Cait gave his hand a squeeze. "If it bleeds, we can kill it."

"We never actually confirmed that blood belonged to Byron." He blew out an exasperated breath. "This wouldn't feel so damn hopeless if we could simply talk to Beverly."

"The woman's still in the ICU. She's been in a coma since they operated on her. We'll be lucky if she doesn't die."

He scowled. "I know. Believe me, I know."

She rose then moved in behind his chair, palming his shoulders as she dug her fingers into his muscles in a firm circular motion. He moaned, allowing his head to loll forward.

She tsked him. "Damn, you're tense."

"We're trying to find a weakness for a man possessed by a demon who just happens to eat souls. Some stress is justified." He moaned again. "God, sweetheart. Don't stop."

"I don't need an excuse to touch you. I could do this for hours."

"I wouldn't stop you. Can't remember the last time I got a massage. Not really a spa kind of guy."

"Surely one of our previous conquests gave you a massage?"

He glanced back at her. "Nope. Never."

"Never?"

He sighed, placing his hands over hers before tugging her around the chair and into his lap. He gave her a quick kiss. "Why is that so hard to believe?"

"Maybe because it's something girlfriends do, especially when their boyfriend has the kind of body that begs to be touched."

"No one really lasted long enough to be labeled that. They were all one-night stands or a convenient weekend fling. It was just sex."

Heat blossomed in her stomach, making it suddenly hard to breathe. "So...no massages?"

His mouth lifted into a wicked grin. "No massages. No watching movies. No sleeping over for the sake of sleeping." He paused as if deciding how much to reveal. "No making love. None of the things we've shared."

His words hit home, and she couldn't do anything other than stare at him, mouth slightly open, her breath a raspy whisper of air between them.

He reached up, running his hand along her jaw as he thumbed the corner of her mouth. "Are you starting to see just how special you are to me? I'm falling for you. Have been since the day we met. I just didn't realize how hard until you stood in your captain's office and put your reputation, your career...your life, on the line for me. Since then..." He whistled. "It's been a slow descent into madness. One I don't want to recover from."

Her heart pounded against her ribs, and she swore he could see the damn thing thrashing beneath her shirt. "Deacon..."

He silenced her with a slow brush of his lips on hers before shaking his head. "That wasn't a plug so you'd confess your undying love for me. After everything you've told me... Christ, sweetheart. I consider it a miracle you ever let me in. Even after royally fucking up, and pushing you away, you showed up on my doorstep. That tells me everything I need to know." He winked at her. "But I won't stop you the next time you try."

She shook her head, leaning forward and taking his mouth with hers. Emotions she didn't know how to convey roiled through her, and she wished they could stay in that moment—hearts beating in sync, nothing between them but endless possibilities. The promise of a future she'd never considered until Deacon had walked into her life and stolen her heart.

She rested her forehead against his once he'd finally broken the kiss, drinking in the spicy scent of him. The way his fingers drew lazy circles down her back. And she knew he wasn't the only one who'd fallen.

She laid her arms along his shoulders, meeting his hungry gaze. "You're not alone in this. I just..."

He nodded. "I know. I'm scared, too. But like I said before. You're worth getting burned over. Now back to the demon—"

A blare of music drowned him out. Cait glanced at the

table, sighing when her phone vibrated across the surface, Riley's name flashing on the screen.

Deke scoffed. "It's like he knows I'm about to seduce you again."

"We're in your sister's restaurant. And you were about to talk about the case."

"But I was undressing you in my mind. That counts."

Her cheeks heated at the thought as she reached over and swiped her finger across the surface before putting the call on speaker. "Are you determined to be a cockblock, big brother? Because I might have to start screening my calls."

Riley huffed into the phone. "Must you give me a visual every damn time? I already want to gouge my eyes out after walking in on the two of you the other day. In the goddamn kitchen."

She smiled at the memory, knowing she'd never be able to look at her countertop without remembering what Deacon had done to her on it. "You'd been warned."

"It was lunchtime. I figured I'd be safe. Besides, you usually don't stop to breathe once you're knee deep in a case."

"We still need to eat occasionally, Riley."

"That wasn't eating. Or if it was, I'm thankful I didn't see *that*." Riley sighed. "He still treating you well? Because I meant what I said. They'll never find his body."

She scrubbed her hand down her face. "You're on speaker. Surely you knew that?"

"Duh. But this way I don't have to repeat myself the next time I see him. Now answer me. And I'll know by the sound of your voice if you're lying."

"You're such a jerk."

"It's part of my charm. So, is he?"

"Fine. You want the truth? I told him."

"Told him? About what?" He inhaled, the raspy sound filling the room. "How you came to live with us? But you've never..."

She released a shaky breath. "I know."

"Fuck. Guess that answers my question. All of them."

"So, is that the only reason you called? To check up on Deacon's behavior?"

"That was just for my peace of mind. You might be a brat, but you're the only one I have. I called regarding Beverly Howard. She's awake."

"Thank God." Cait straightened. "I didn't realize she was your patient."

"She isn't, but since everyone knows you're my kid sister, and there was a note saying to contact you or Special Agent McGraw if she woke up...they asked me to call."

"Is she okay?"

"Physically, she's healing. I took a look at her chart. Couldn't help but notice she had similar wounds to those I treated you and Deacon for. That other guy, Trevor, too. Care to elaborate?"

"Ongoing investigation—"

"Don't. Don't even start with that."

"Fine. She was most likely attacked by our guy. What's wrong?"

"It's her mental wellness." He huffed again, and she could picture him spearing his fingers through his hair, spiking it out in every direction. "I'm...concerned about it."

"Why?"

"Ever since she regained consciousness, she's been saying some pretty weird shit, sis. Stuff about demons and immortality. Normally, I wouldn't even give any of it a second thought, except..."

A shiver crawled down Cait's spine. Fuck, her brother knew. "Except, what?"

"She mentioned a name. A rinikarhu. It's some kind of soul-sucking demon. Which, again, I wouldn't put much stock in, but I looked it up. Curious how the few things I was able to dig up about it says it has barbs on its fingers that leave fingerprint-like markings behind. Just like in all those files you had me look at. The kind of thing I yanked out of Deacon and his brother-in-law. And there's that disturbing detail where all the victims died instantaneously. As if—"

"Their souls were sucked out."

"Shit!" Riley's voice rose in pitch. "You knew? All along you've been after some kind of creature and you didn't tell me?"

"Seriously? Would you have believed me if I had?"

"That's beside the point."

"No, that's exactly the point. The whole point behind this crazy-ass investigation. Why we didn't want to go to the hospital. Why we haven't said much at all. Everyone will think we're mentally unwell, as you put it."

"So, you're saying this...rinikarhu. It's real?"

"You saw the barb yourself. The claw marks on my side." She sighed at the sudden silence on the other end of the phone. "Look, I know this sounds crazy, but...it's real."

"So this thing attacked you and Deacon, then what...

went after Trevor because he was in the wrong place at the wrong time?"

"We think it might be more than that. That it's targeting Deacon or those directly linked to him. It all stems back to Deke's father, but that's a whole other story. It's also what killed Truman." She snorted. "Wait... you believe me?"

"Honestly, sis? I don't know. But I'm willing to give you the benefit of the doubt, for now." He paused, then sighed. "I wasn't going to say anything because I'd assumed Beverly was nuts, but... When she's actually coherent, she's been going on about having to warn you. That she's got some kind of message for you."

"What message?"

"I have no idea. She doesn't stay lucid long enough to get it out. She's still weak. I'm afraid you'll have to ask her once she's stronger."

"How long before she's strong enough?"

"Awhile. She went a bit ballistic when one of the nurses tried to draw some blood. She's been sedated. She's just too weak to pull out stitches or re-injure herself thrashing around. Why don't you and Deacon drop by just before I go off shift? Close to seven. The sedative should have worn off by then, and I'll make sure she isn't given any more until after you leave."

"Damn, that's only a few hours before the moon rises. That won't give us much time if she has any kind of lead for us."

"The moon rises?"

"Forget it. Fine, we'll drop by then. I might even bring you some coffee."

"Promises, promises. Oh, and Deacon, I know you're listening. Watch her back."

Cait groaned as the line went dead. The man was infuriating at times.

Deacon chuckled. "Dare I say he's warming up to me?"

She smiled, dropping a quick kiss on his mouth. "Oh, sweetie, this is how he is when he likes someone."

"Lucky me. Shitty timing about Beverly. We could use a break."

"At least, we'll get a chance before it's too late. The question is...where the hell do we go now? The warehouse again?"

"We've searched there every day. If Byron was using that place as some sort of lair, he's gone now. Let's go over to Beverly's. I keep getting the feeling we're missing something."

"Sounds as good a place as any." She tried to stand only to have him hold her in place on his lap. "What?"

His eyes narrowed a he stared at her. "Have you really never told anyone that story before?"

Her stomach quivered at the genuine concern in his voice. She leaned in, getting close without actually touching her mouth to his. "Not once."

"So why did you tell me? You could have told me to bugger off, instead. I wouldn't have pushed."

"You're the first person I care enough about that I wanted to know the truth. Because as painful as those memories are, as much as they still haunt me, it'd hurt far more to lose you. You're not the only one who's fallen."

The muscle in his jaw jumped before his mouth lifted into a stunning smile. "Good answer."

He captured her lips with his, the kiss more intimate,

more telling, than anything else they'd shared. He didn't rush, lingering with his mouth against hers until a throat cleared beside them. Cait turned, cheeks heating as her gaze clashed with Stacy's.

The woman arched a brow. "I thought you two were working?"

Deke flashed the woman a wicked smile. "We are."

Stacy shook her head. "At what? Making babies?"

"At making *us* work."

Her expression softened. "You're too damn charming for your own good, big brother. I just wanted to let you know I'm heading out to run an errand, but I left a fresh pot of coffee for you if you'd like some."

Cait gasped as Deke stood with her still in his arms. He kissed her again then placed her on her feet.

He winked at her. "I'll grab us a couple of to-go mugs before sis changes her mind."

Cait rolled her eyes as he darted away. "Sometimes, it astounds me that he's actually a federal agent."

Stacy grinned. "Trevor's the same way. A two-hundred pound, heavily muscled kid." She cocked her head to the side. "So it appears you two have definitely moved beyond casual partners."

Cait pursed her lips, not quite sure what to say. "He's a hard man to resist."

"From what I've seen, he's chosen wisely." She stepped forward, giving Cait's hand a squeeze. "I'm not sure I thanked you…for what you did for Trevor."

"No need. I'm just glad he's all right. You, too. It would have gutted Deke to lose either of you."

"Thinking you're on that list, as well, now." She let go

as Deacon reappeared, carrying two large cups. "Please thank your brother again for me."

"I will."

Deke arched a brow as his sister tiptoed up, placing a kiss on his cheek before heading back to the kitchen. "What was that about?"

Cait grinned. "I think she likes me."

Deke chuckled. "Of course she likes you. You're amazing. You just aren't used to people expressing that in a normal fashion when you only have Riley for comparison."

"He's not that bad." She laughed at his expression. "Okay, he's protective. But his heart's in the right place."

"In that case, we'll drop by here again on our way to meet him later. Bring him some of Stacy's coffee. The man will adore me after that."

"Don't get your hopes up, but... I'm sure he'll appreciate it. You ready?"

"I just hope we find something useful at Beverly's. Knowing that bastard is hunting his next victim as we speak." He huffed. "I hate feeling so damn helpless."

"We'll scour the place. Again. And we'll catch this guy tonight. One way or another he's going to expose himself. We just have to believe."

"If he succeeds..."

Cait merely nodded, following Deke out. If the bastard succeeded, chances were he'd make due with whatever energy he'd gained then go into hiding. And they'd be cursed for another decade or two of knowing they'd failed.

# CHAPTER TWENTY

Deacon rested his hand on the small of Caitlyn's back as he followed her through the sliding doors into the hospital. They'd spent hours searching through Beverly's house—looking for anything that seemed remotely connected to Byron Howard. But other than a few more old photos, the entire trip had been a bust. Then they'd gotten a lead regarding a possible sighting, but after thirty minutes of traipsing through another deserted warehouse, they'd finally called it quits and headed for the hospital. Praying Beverly would somehow pull their asses out of the fire.

Cait cursed under her breath, weaving through the crowd of people waiting to be seen. "I really don't like hospitals."

Deke gave her hip a light squeeze. "Can't say I do, either."

"I don't know how Riley stands being in one day in, day out. Speaking of which, he's not going to be pleased we're late. His shift ended ten minutes ago. I'm actually surprised he wasn't waiting outside for us, brooding."

"You're a detective in the midst of a hellish case. I'm sure he'll understand that we got sidetracked in that warehouse. If it'd paid off..."

"Yeah, we'd either be celebrating or dead."

He chuckled. "You do have a unique way of seeing things. Of course, that's one of the traits I love most about you."

She stumbled at his choice of words, glancing over at him before stopping at the nurses' station. He grinned, enjoying the play of emotions across her face.

A woman in green scrubs looked up, nearly dismissing them before breaking into a huge grin. She stood, crossing her arms on the counter as she leaned toward them. "Why, Detective Caitlyn Decker. Haven't seen you in here in some time." She eyed Deacon, arching a brow. "And with a handsome man. Who's your new partner?"

Cait returned the woman's easy smile, motioning to Deke. "Doris, this is Special Agent Deacon McGraw. He's on loan from the bureau. Deke, this is Doris Poulson, hands down the best trauma nurse you'll ever meet." Cait glanced at him. "She also happens to be the kind woman who helped treat me way back when. She's got the patience of a saint."

Doris snorted. "I'd like to see that asshole try to take you on, now. Bastard would have gotten his damn ass kicked." Her expression softened as she tapped her watch. "Still late, I see. Your brother said you'd be in here looking for him about twenty minutes ago."

"You know how cases are, Doris."

"That's not the reason you're always late, and you know it."

"True. But today it is. Do you know where he is?"

Doris laughed. "That man just doesn't know when to call it quits, either. He went into exam room two about fifteen minutes ago. Took one last patient. A friend of his, I assume. Guy asked for him by name. And you know how Riley is when someone he knows is hurt."

"And he says I have a bleeding heart. Thanks. We'll go see if he's finished."

Deke moved in beside her as she headed for a hallway. "Doris is right. You'd kick that bastard's ass and then some."

Cait glanced at him, confidence shaping her features. "Funny. Over the past few days I've come to realize he wouldn't be worth my effort. Or another moment of my time."

"That's my girl."

She stumbled again at his words, a light blush staining her cheeks. He grinned. About bloody time she started accepting that he wasn't going anywhere. That spending the last four days together had made him realize how empty his life had been before she'd dared him to dream for something more. To break out of his comfort zone and take a risk that actually mattered, instead of going through the motions, all the while never lowering his defenses enough for anyone to get through. But then, she'd knocked down the damn walls with nothing more than her smile.

He stopped when they reached a door, waiting as Cait rapped her knuckles against the wood.

"Riley?" She frowned when nothing sounded beyond

the door. She knocked again. "Riley?" She cracked open the door, peering through the sliver of space before shoving the door aside, marching in then spinning to face Deke. "Where the hell is he? Doris said exam room two."

"Maybe he's already finished and went to grab his stuff out of his locker? Or the guy needed to get x-rays or something?"

She shook her head, bouncing her hair about her shoulders. "No. He wouldn't leave without telling Doris where he was going. Not when he was expecting us, knowing how important talking to Beverly is. In fact, why the hell didn't he just call me?"

She pulled out her cell, dialing his number, pacing across the room, obviously waiting for it to ring. She stopped as she neared the other side. "Wait. Do you smell that?"

Deke joined her. A hint of sulfur permeated the air, the familiar aroma making his skin bead. He turned toward her, just as a muffled echo of music sounded from a bin next to them.

Cait spun again, darting over to a hamper full of old scrubs. She rooted through, fishing out a phone wrapped in a blood-stained shirt, her name flashing across the screen. The color drained from her face as she stared at the offering, knuckles white, chin quivering. "Oh my God."

Deacon closed the space, taking the shirt and phone out of her hands as he pulled her close, secretly wondering if she might pass out. He wrapped one arm around her waist, keeping his head next to hers. "Breathe, sweetheart. Everything's going to be okay. This might not be anything. He's a doctor. I'm sure he ruins his share of shirts. Let's not panic until we know what we're dealing with."

"I know you smelled the sulfur. It's all over his damn shirt. Not his scrubs, his actual shirt. Besides, if he'd just cut himself, he'd be in here, swearing up a blue streak. Hating the fact another doctor had to stitch him up. And if it'd been an emergency, Doris would have known. She would have told us he was in surgery or something. This… I know when something's seriously wrong, Deke. And my spider sense is off the chart." She pulled out of his embrace, the detective in her back in control. "You still have those pictures of Byron Howard?"

"Most are back in your car. I've got one in my pocket I was looking at. There's something about it that feels familiar. I just can't place it. Why?"

"Let's go."

She turned, running back through the hallway to the main desk. Doris glanced up as she rounded the desk, moving deliberately toward her.

The other woman frowned. "Honey? Everything okay? You look like you've seen a ghost."

"Did Riley leave?"

Doris stared at Cait as if she'd lost her mind. "He's in exam room two, honey. I saw him go in there, myself. The man hasn't left, or I'd have noticed. He has to walk past here to get to his locker."

"He's gone." She pointed to the shirt in Deke's hand. "That's his shirt. Any reason it'd be covered in blood?"

"What?" Doris fingered the sleeve, doubt reflecting in her eyes. "Lots of people come in here bleeding. It's probably not his blood."

"Has he treated that kind of emergency in that exam room today? Since you saw him last?"

"Caitlyn, I...I'm sorry. I don't know. I'm pretty sure he was wearing that shirt when he went in for that last patient. I remember commenting how nice he looked in it, and that he should put a gown over it so he didn't ruin it. But I can't swear by that."

"Deke, show her the photo. Is this Riley's *friend*?"

Doris squinted as she took the picture Deke held out, tilting her head as if trying to remember. Then she nodded. "That's him. His hair was darker. Longer. But that's definitely the same guy."

"You said he asked for Riley by name?"

"Yes. Said he needed to see Riley Decker. He's around Riley's age, maybe a bit younger. I figured they played sports together or something."

A tremble shuddered through Cait as she merely nodded.

Deke put a comforting hand on her shoulder as he focused on Doris. "You're sure you didn't see them leave? Either of them?"

"No. Neither of them walked past this desk. I don't miss that kind of stuff when there's an endless line of patients. I'm always looking to see when a doctor is free. And Riley's one of our best."

"Okay. I'm going to go do a quick sweep of the garage—"

"I'm coming with you." Cait glared at him when he shook his head. "I'm coming. Facing that guy alone isn't an option, and we can't help Riley if either of us gets hurt."

Deke sighed. "Fine. Doris. I need you to page security

for me. Have them roll back all the footage on every damn camera throughout the hospital until just before the time when Riley entered that room. I want them to go frame by frame. See if they caught Riley or that patient leaving on any of the videos. We'll be right back." He scribbled his number across a piece of paper. "Call me if anything comes up. But if you see them, don't confront them. Just call me, okay?"

She nodded, already reaching for the phone. Deke grabbed Cait's hand, heading for the elevator. He didn't speak, just stepped inside and pushed the button for the lower level. The machine shook, dropping a couple of floors before opening. He motioned to his right, drawing his gun as he made his way into the parking garage. Lights hummed overhead, the florescent glare casting harsh shadows across the cement.

He skirted to the outside of the first row, nodding as Caitlyn copied his tactics on the opposite side of the row of cars. He moved methodically, checking between and under vehicles before moving to the next row.

"Deacon! Over here."

He darted over to her, stopping beside her as she knelt on the pavement. "What did you find?"

She reached into her pocket, removing a spare glove then grabbed an object off the ground, holding it up to the light. "Joe's dog tags. Riley's worn them ever since Joe died. He'd never take them off."

Deke carefully cupped the glove, transferring the necklace to his hand. He took a closer look, noting charred bits along the links and around the pendants. "I'm betting the chain and the brackets around the tags are made of silver. Looks like it burned something."

"Yeah. Byron Howard. This whole area reeks of him."

Deacon clenched his jaw as Cait surged to her feet. "No way he carried your brother out of here without anyone seeing something. Or getting caught on camera. Where's Riley's car?"

She pointed at the empty space. "Missing. I'll put out an APB on it. But they've got fifteen, maybe twenty minutes on us."

"We'll find him. Let's head back inside. We'll see if security found anything on the tapes." Deke palmed his phone, motioning her to follow him. "It's Agent McGraw. Get me Assistant Director Jamieson. Now. It's an emergency." He covered the speaker with his hand. "I'll have roadblocks set up. Mobilize every damn agent if I have to. He's not getting through."

Caitlyn nodded woodenly, trailing after him as he explained the situation to his boss. Deke heard her call in Riley's vehicle information, but he could tell by the monotone pitch of her voice, she'd put herself on automatic. Going through the motions without allowing herself to think. Feel.

Deke closed his eyes as they rode up the elevator, praying she wouldn't have to face the cold reality that Riley wouldn't make it through this alive. That by the time they found him, he'd be just another number for the file.

Doris rushed over when they walked into the ER. "Security says your brother's car drove out of here about ten minutes ago. But they can't tell which way it was headed."

Deke nodded. "I'll call it in. See if I can get dispatch to go over some of the live traffic footage. Catch a glimpse.

Call security back for me. See if they can backtrack further and see when and where this guy entered the hospital."

She nodded, rushing off, again.

Deke grabbed Cait's hands, waiting until she looked at him. "He's still alive. You heard what Beverly said before. He won't do anything until the moon's up."

"You mean in like three hours?"

He cringed at the hollow tone, the tears gathering in her eyes. "We still have time. I'll call dispatch. Get them on those traffic cams. But we need to go and talk to Beverly. She's our best hope at uncovering where that bastard took your brother."

"What makes you think she even knows?"

"Riley said she wanted to warn us. She's got to know something."

"We should be out there. Searching for him."

"Driving around in circles won't save Riley's life. You know that." He palmed her jaw, brushing his thumb along her cheek, hating the dampness that greeted his caress. "I know how hard this is for you. How crippling it feels. And I'm going to do everything I can to get him back. But you have to trust me."

She coughed as if holding back a sob, nodding.

He tucked some of her hair behind her ear. "Good girl. Now, let's go have a chat with Beverly. And we won't leave until she's told us everything."

A few tears slipped down Cait's cheek before she swiped them away, marching toward the elevators again. He followed, not pressuring her to talk as they rode in silence. But he sensed the mixture of fear and pain radiating off her. The labored breaths that filled the small space, the increased white in her eyes. The way she forced herself to swallow as she fisted her hands at her sides. He'd felt all of that and more when she'd driven him to the church. But at least he'd had Riley on his side. Knew the man would do everything possible to save Trevor. But all Riley had was them.

He pushed back his shoulders as he exited the machine. Not a chance in hell he was going to let Caitlyn down. Be responsible for her losing her brother. They'd get the man back. Period.

He headed for the nurses' station, asking which room Beverly had been moved to since regaining consciousness, then strode off. He flashed his badge to the officer still guarding the door before continuing in. Beverly was sitting in the bed, staring out the window as if she'd never seen the sun setting before. The woman jumped when he circled to the far side of the bed, bracing both palms on the rail.

She glanced at Caitlyn, a slight grimace shaping her lips. "I've been asking for you."

Deacon leaned in. "And here we are."

"I know the full moon is tonight. You have to stop him before he finds his next victim. Once that happens, you'll lose him for another twenty or more years."

"Nothing we want to do more, but we need to know where Byron would take that victim."

She paled. "He already has one? Then it's too late."

Deke shook his head. "We still have time to stop him. We just need to know where he'd go."

"I don't know."

"You have to know something. You've been living with him all your life. What aren't you telling us?"

"Nothing I—"

"He took my brother." Caitlyn moved in beside Deke. "I won't lose him to that monster. Not when you can help us stop him."

Beverly shook her head, her heart rate increasing across the monitor, the metallic ping echoing through the room. "I don't know—"

"Where would your grandfather take him?" Caitlyn leaned in closer. "You claim you're sorry for not helping Thomas. For letting the man die when you could have given him the means to kill Byron. Prove that now. Tell us where he'd take Riley." When the woman didn't speak, Cait slammed her hand on the rail, shaking the bed. "You must have some idea. A best guess! Give us something. Anything."

Tears streamed down Beverly's face as she pulled her knees up, rocking in place.

Deacon gave Cait a pat on the arm, motioning for her to let him handle it. Cait's chin quivered before she stalked away, spinning once she'd reached the wall. She leaned against the window frame, her unshed tears glistening in the waning light as she stared out through the glass.

Deke lowered the rail, sitting on the edge of the mattress. He placed a gentle hand on top of Beverly's, dipping his head to make eye contact. "I know you wanted to help my father. That you wanted to end this even then. It's hard admitting that someone you love is beyond help. That the kindest thing you can do for them is to let them go. The last thing you said to us the other day was that there was nothing left of the man. Only evil." He gave her an encouraging smile. "Help us save the man your grandfather once was. Destroy the demon that made him into a monster. Give Byron the peace he deserves."

Her chin quivered as more tears spilled over her cheeks. "He was a good man. He didn't ask for this."

"I know. And we'll kill the bastard that took him from you, if you'll help us. Talk to us."

"I don't know where he is."

"But you know *him*. His habits, his needs. You said consuming a soul during the full moon gave him more power. Why?"

She glanced at Cait, breaking eye contact as soon as Cait focused on her. "There's more energy available during the full phase, which means not only is the demon more powerful, humans also have heightened awareness. Which gives the demon more raw energy when it devours the soul."

"So, he'll wait. Even though this is his sixth victim?"

"He's injured. Hardly at full strength. And now that you know who he is, he'll have to go into hiding instead of merely blending in again. The increase in energy is worth the risk for him to wait. Especially when it's only a few more hours."

"What's stopping him from simply leaving?"

"Rinikarhus are bound to a small area around where they are created. Their immortality is linked to the place they first possess the host. If it leaves, no amount of souls will sustain it. That's why it doesn't hunt for long periods of time. It can't afford to draw too much attention to itself."

"Which means we're not too late. We just need to know where it'll take Riley."

She cringed. "I don't know. I swear. He never told me. It's someplace sacred to him."

Cait moved to the end of the bed, gripping the rail until her knuckles whitened. "He must have said something over the years. A casual remark that would hint at a place."

Beverly frowned, glancing off to one side before meeting their gazes. "The only thing I remember him ever saying is that in order to possess the future, he had to make homage to the past. That the increased energy doesn't just come from the person, it's derived from the surroundings, as well."

Cait released the rail, ducking in beside Deke. "So he needs to go to a specific location in order to harness the added power."

Beverly nodded. "But I don't know where. He never told me, and I didn't want to know."

Cait raked her hand through her hair. "We've only got a few hours. We need to narrow it down."

"Wait!" Deke held up one hand. "Shit, why didn't we think to look at this once Beverly mentioned the whole full moon thing?" He pulled out his phone, launching a page of lunar cycles. Then he typed in a date. He waited as the information appeared on the screen, the answer staring at him with painful clarity.

Cait crowded him. "What?"

He held out his phone to her so she could see the screen. "The night my dad was killed. It was a full moon."

Her eyes widened, her mouth gaping open slightly. "Which means—"

"The bastard took Riley back there." He inhaled sharply, reaching into his pocket again and removing the photo he'd shown Doris. "Fuck! I knew there was something familiar about this damn picture." He angled it toward Cait. "Look behind Byron. It's the same damn house as in my father's file." He focused his attention on Beverly. "Why this place?"

More tears gathered in Beverly's eyes. "I'm fairly certain that's where he was first possessed. After his youngest child drowned. I think that's why he didn't try to have the demon exorcized. It helped lessen the pain. Made him feel nothing at all, but I'm not certain. He never said much, and I didn't ask."

Deke turned to Cait. "There's no guarantee he's there. It could just be a coincidence my dad died during a full moon. Byron might not have been after the added energy."

"I don't believe in coincidences. Why would your dad have gone to a deserted house on the edge of town when every other killing happened in the city?" She shook her head. "He was taken there. Or lured. Something. But it wasn't by accident."

"Then I say we call in your SWAT team. Fuck, the bureau's SWAT team, too. I say we call everyone."

Cait paled. "What if we're wrong? You've got every available agent your department can spare manning roadblocks. Half of the Seattle PD is out searching for Riley's car. If we're wrong and we call them off the search… We could be taking away Riley's last hope."

"So we face this thing alone? Just the two of us?"

"Your brother is dead if you go in there with anyone else." Beverly sighed as they focused on her. "Byron isn't stupid. He hasn't survived this long by making poor decisions. As much as he needs the extra power, if he thinks he can't control the situation, he'll just kill your brother and target someone else. But if there are just two of you—if he doesn't feel threatened because he's beaten you both before—he'll stand and fight. And I know he wants Deacon's soul more than anyone else's. He won't pass up a chance to get it. Not when the odds are in his favor."

Deacon met her grim expression. "If he wants my soul, then let's offer it to him, because this time, I'll be ready."

# CHAPTER TWENTY-ONE

Caitlyn sat in silence as Deacon pulled onto the dirt road leading up to rundown house where his father's body had been found twenty years ago. She glanced at the clock, then the horizon. Only another thirty minutes before the moon began to rise, and she lost her brother forever.

She closed her eyes, praying they were right. Deke had insisted on stopping at the precinct first—going over some traffic footage in the direction of the house. It'd taken nearly an hour, but they'd spotted Riley's Jeep on a road heading east before it'd vanished from the video. While she knew Byron could have ventured damn near anywhere after that one brief flash on the screen, the fact he'd been heading in the right direction had convinced them to take a chance. And it beat sitting around waiting for Riley to die.

Bile burned a path along her throat as her stomach roiled. She'd never been this scared. Never felt so helpless and on edge at the same time. Not even that night she'd ended up in the ER. But it wasn't just Riley's life that had her stomach in knots. Knowing Deke was going to face the creature, that he could die as well, hurt just as much. And after finally allowing herself to fall in love, the thought of having it ripped away made her want to scream.

Gravel crunched beneath the tires as Deke eased the car off to one side. A darkened house sat a few hundred yards ahead, the roofline just visible against the indigo sky. He turned off the engine, hands trembling slightly, before twisting toward her.

A volley of emotions played across his features, most of the color draining from his face. "This is it."

She nodded, placing her hand over his. "Are you okay?"

His lips quirked. "I just..." He huffed. "I never thought I'd come here. Never *wanted* to come here."

Her chest tightened at the desolate quality of his voice. "Shit, Deacon... I never stopped to consider how you'd feel having to come here, knowing..."

He smiled, lifting his hand to brush the corner of her mouth. "You're worth it. And Riley's your brother so..." He visibly drew himself up. "I'm thinking we'll do a quick recon of the outside. If they are here, Riley's car should be close by. From what I read on the report, there's the main structure plus a barn near the rear of the property. He could be in either."

She nodded, afraid her voice might crack. Deke handed her a bottle and the knife they'd gotten from Beverly, before clipping his supplies onto his belt. He'd claimed the knife she'd first picked up, the blade still slightly stained from their other encounter.

The notion sobered her, and she welcomed the feel of the earth beneath her feet. She needed something to ground her. Keep her focused on the task instead the fear trying to claw its way through her defenses. Smother her with images of how she'd find her brother if they failed. If they were wrong.

Deke whistled softly, waving her over. She rounded the car, kneeling beside him.

He pointed to a set of tracks. "These are fresh. And I doubt it's a coincidence or someone else just visiting." He motioned to a small shack off to their left. "Wanna bet the car's hidden in there?"

She followed as he struck off, keeping to the shadows as he made his way to the far side of the shed. He circled around, cursing at the padlock on the metal door before making his way back to a small, dirt-smeared window. He wiped off some of the grime, flicking on his flashlight then swinging the beam around the inside.

"What are the chances that's someone else's red Jeep?"

"That's Riley's. His hospital parking sticker is on the windshield, upper corner."

Deke nodded, killing the light as he turned to face the house. He pursed his mouth as he stared at something, darting ahead slightly, then kneeling again. He placed his hand in one of two long ruts. "Someone was dragged."

Cait's stomach roiled again. God, just thinking... She pushed it out of her mind. She needed to stay focused before she got Riley or Deacon killed. "I wouldn't have thought a demon would have to drag a man. I mean—he lifted you up by the neck with only one hand. Tossed me twenty feet across that warehouse. And I don't think he uses a knife to rip up his victims. I think he does it by hand."

"Beverly said he was hurt. She must have really weakened him. That could definitely give us an advantage."

"I just hope the silver and holy water are enough. That they work."

"Me, too."

He stood, once again keeping to the shadows as they followed the tracks around to the rear of the house. Muddy footprints led to the back door, but the ruts continued toward the barn. Even in the dark, it was obvious that the structure was massive, the wooden building nearly twice the size of the house. Deacon made a series of signals, skirting to the far side of the yard as he raced toward the barn. He bypassed the closed, main doors, heading for the other side, stopping at another locked door.

"Shit." He kept his voice low, his words barely reaching her. "They're probably all locked."

"Hay loft, upper floor? Can't lock what doesn't have windows."

"That's a ways up there."

"If I stand on your shoulders, I should be able to reach that rope hanging from that old pulley. I can climb to the loft then lower it for you."

"No." He stepped in closer, knocking her back a bit. "What happens if it's not long enough? If you're stuck in there alone? I won't risk that."

"Fine, then you'll have to stand on my shoulders."

A hint of a smile teased his mouth before he frowned. "I weigh damn near a hundred pounds more than you. I'll crush you."

"Which brings us back to plan A. Unless you have

another way to access the loft." She motioned around them. "I'll be fine. And I'll make the rope reach. Promise."

"Fuck."

Deacon cursed again, slotting his hands together to give her a boost up. She grabbed one shoulder, balancing her other hand against the barn as he lifted her waist high. She did her best to climb onto his shoulders as he stayed poised beneath the dangling end.

She grasped it, hanging just long enough to swing her feet against the side of the barn and shuffle up to the open area. Deke stayed vigilant below her, looking as if he planned on catching her if she fell. The rope scratched at her hands, drawing a bit of blood before she was able to reach the loft. She pushed off, swinging out then back as she lifted her feet, slipping through the opening then skidding to a halt. Bits of old straw and dust billowed into the air, and she covered her mouth, praying she wouldn't start coughing or sneezing—giving away their presence before they'd gotten close to freeing Riley.

*If he was still alive.*

She cursed the fearful voice in her head, focusing on untangling the rope from the pulley. She gathered the long length, wrapping one end around a post before tossing the rest down to Deke, praying it he could reach it. She braced her weight, holding her end when the post creaked as the rope pulled tight, nearly yanking her off her feet. She held on, losing a bit of ground when Deke's head appeared above the opening. He placed one hand on the wood, then pushed himself in, easing the pressure on her hands.

He huffed as she moved over to him, brushing off some of the debris. "Remind me not to let you talk me into something like that again. I swear I just aged ten years."

"At least we're in."

"I just hope we can get down without alerting anyone. Let's see if there's a ladder."

She trailed behind him, placing each footfall carefully, hoping they weren't sending clouds of dust and hay down from the rafters with each step. Deacon made his way along the edge, finally stopping at a set of rungs.

He glanced down. "Darker than shit down there. I'll go first. If anything comes at me, keep your ass glued to this loft."

"If anything comes at you, I'll launch myself off of here and stab it."

He sighed with forced patience. "You're determined to do the opposite of everything I say, aren't you?"

"Only if it means you're going to get yourself killed trying to protect me. I'm not fragile." She smiled. "Though, I am touched you want to keep me safe."

"I can't spend the rest of my life with you if get yourself killed, sweetheart. Stay close."

He moved onto the ladder, seemingly oblivious to her wide-eyed stare as he slowly climbed down, fading into the shadows. His words rattled through her head, making her chest constrict. Had he really just said he wanted to spend his life with her?

She shook off the shock, making her way to the bottom, taking up point when he moved out in front of her, using one flashlight to find their way. He was obviously determined to stand between her and anything they might face, a fact that battered at her heart. His sense of honor was awe-inspiring, but it also frightened her.

What would she do if she lost him? If he died trying to save her or Riley? How would she ever find someone who made her feel a fraction of the way Deke did?

Feel loved?

She used the thoughts to strengthen her resolve. She'd have his back, no matter what. And when they made their stand, he wouldn't be alone. She could be just as determined, just a sacrificing.

Deacon paused, bouncing the beam around the space, stopping when he illuminated a pile of bones. He glanced back at her, leaning in close. "I'm starting to think we didn't find all his victims."

Cait frowned. "How has he been able to stockpile bodies all this time?"

"Probably only started since the last round of serial killings. Maybe my dad injured him enough before he died that Byron hasn't been able to go without. And there wasn't any reason for anyone to come back and check once the case went cold."

"I say we add the bastard's corpse to the pile."

"I agree."

Deke moved ahead then stopped when he reached another closed door. He looked at her, holding up his hand as he signed down from three. When he reached zero, he twisted the handle and threw the door aside, striding through as he swept the area with his gun. A large open space spread out before them, a single lantern hanging on a post at the far end. The light flickered across the wooden floor, dancing long, finger-like shadows along the slats. Riley was slumped on his ass against the post, head bowed, scratch marks oozing blood along his chest as he took a labored breath. His arms were bound above his head, his feet splayed out in front of him.

Cait inhaled, fighting her natural instinct to run to his side. Instead, she moved into a dark recess with Deke, gun still at the ready. Deke inched forward, constantly scanning the area when a silhouette stepped out from the shadows behind Riley. The pungent stench of sulfur filled the air as a wicked grin split the man's face.

He walked to one side, gaze centered on where they hid in the darkness. "You might as well come on out, Agent McGraw. I can smell you from here."

Deke motioned for her to stay, then moved into the dim circle of light cast by the lantern. "I don't believe we've been formally introduced…Byron Howard, right?"

"Don't play me for a fool…Deacon. You know far more about me than anyone else ever has—other than my granddaughter. I never should have assumed she'd die."

"She didn't know you'd be here. But I did." He took a few more steps forward. "That was your mistake. Once you discovered I was on the case, you made this personal. Stopped doing what had been working for you all these years. Now, here we are."

"Right where your father was twenty years ago." Byron laughed. "He'd figured it all out, too. Just a bit too late to save himself, I'm afraid. Let me guess…that's a silver knife on your belt."

"Everyone has a weakness. Even you."

Byron raised his hands to his shoulders, palms out. "Silver's a bitch. Thankfully, not as prevalent as it was when I really was twenty. Everyone carries guns these days. But I think you've discovered that those bullets won't even slow me down."

Deke holstered his gun, letting his hand rest on the knife's hilt. "Old habits." He nodded at Riley. "So if it's me you want, why take the doctor?"

"It's like you said. Everyone has a weakness. And I know yours, as well."

Deke's focus drifted to her brother then back. "Riley's my weakness?"

"No. But his sister is. Detective Caitlyn Decker. I assume she's around here somewhere." He tapped his nose. "I'm not quite as attuned to females, not that it matters. I'll gut her before she can get close to me."

Caitlyn stilled. Either Byron was lying and knew she was still cloaked in the shadows, or he really couldn't sense her the way he did Deacon. Which meant they had an advantage. She put away her gun then drew her knife, edging closer to where Riley was still tied to the post.

Deke didn't even register her motion, taking a few steps in what she assumed was an attempt to hide her progress. "Why would Caitlyn be my weakness? She's just a temporary partner. Jurisdiction protocol."

"That's what I thought. Until after she saw me drive away from the apothecary, and I made the point of following her home that night. I'd planned on sending you a message. A bloody one. But she didn't stay home. She went over to your place, and she didn't come back out until the next day."

He tsked. "Who would have guessed you both had so much stamina. That's when I realized she was the most satisfying way to hurt you. I'd planned on killing her, just for fun, when I discovered she had a brother. A man so damn perfect I couldn't help myself. I had a feeling you'd eventually figure it all out, which meant I'd get two souls tonight."

Byron shrugged. "Either way, it was worth the risk. And now, as you said, here we are."

Deke held his ground. "We both know it's me you really want. Let Riley go, and we can settle this. Just the two of us."

Byron laughed. "I'm a demon. I don't give a shit about settling things or honor. I just want your soul." He nodded at Riley. "His, too. My bitch granddaughter drained what I'd worked so hard to achieve, much like your father did that night. I've had to supplement my usual diet with whatever's been available. People who wouldn't be missed, while I waited for enough time to pass so I could go on another spree. Who knew McGraw's son would follow in daddy's footsteps? Consuming both of your souls will give me more than enough power. And by the time I need to feed again, you'll just be another forgotten file, collecting dust on a shelf somewhere."

Deke drew the knife. "That's assuming you can kill me."

Cait jumped as Byron grinned, appearing in front of Deacon in the space of a heartbeat. Deke took a surprised step back, somehow avoiding the bastard's first strike before he dodged to his left. He motioned for her to get Riley, advancing toward Byron and blocking the man's path.

Cait cursed as she ran for her brother, using the knife to cut through the rope binding his hands. A series of grunts sounded behind her before Deacon landed on the ground beside them, a single gash marring his chest.

She spun, catching the demon across the shoulder when it lunged at her. Blood sizzled along her blade, bubbling and spitting as it seemed to boil on contact. Byron howled, retreating a few steps. He stared at her, growling in defiance before his human features faded into his demon form. His skin bleached blue, long grooves scouring his flesh as he grew in size, his arms out of proportion to the rest of him.

The creature charged, deflecting her next strike before its fingers curled around her throat, lifting her off her feet then tossing her across the barn. Pain blossomed through her shoulder and head when she hit hard, skidding a few feet before stopping. Black dots pitted her vision as she rolled onto her knees, reaching for the bottle of holy water.

Deke shouted her name, and she looked up as he managed to land a blow, sinking his blade into the demon's back. The creature swung at him, connecting with the side of his head and sending him tumbling against another post. A dull thud filled the room as Deacon bounced off the wood then onto the floor.

The demon yanked the knife out, growling at the blade before tossing it at Deacon's feet as if taunting him. Close, but useless. It rushed the man, shoving him upright against the post before palming each side of his head. The creature's body shimmered to life, a blue glow covering its skin as it bowed its head toward Deacon's.

Cait staggered to her feet, uncapping the holy water as she stumbled across the space, tossing the liquid at the demon. Steam curled off its skin on contact, drawing a painful cry. It batted at her again, its overly long arm catching her shoulder and sending her back across the room. She rolled to a stop, the glow of the demon's skin shining off to her right.

Fear ate at her gut, the cold reality of the situation hitting her hard. She pushed to her feet one more time, fighting the pitching of the floor as her equilibrium shifted, knowing none of them would survive if they didn't kill the bastard now—while it was starting to feed off of Deacon. She scanned the floor for her knife, inhaling when Riley swayed to his feet, the silver blade grasped in one hand. He looked at the demon then raised the knife, notching it back then throwing it across the short space. It struck Byron in the shoulder blade, arching the bastard's spine as its head tipped up, an ungodly shriek rattling the windows. The blue glow dimmed but didn't vanish.

Cait lurched forward, determined to yank the knife out then shove it back in, when the demon gasped, clutching at its chest as it stumbled backwards, another hilt sticking out of its chest. Deke gained his feet, following the creature's retreat. He palmed the handle then twisted, drawing another guttural cry from the beast. The demon tripped onto its back, slowly morphing into the man. Deacon knelt beside him, looking as if he was going to stab the guy again, when Byron placed his hand over Deke's, a small grin lifting his mouth.

He shook his head. "It's already too late."

Deke stilled. "Byron?"

"Thank you." The man's head lolled off to the side, his eyes staring blankly at the ceiling.

Riley fell to his knees beside Deacon, checking Byron's vitals before shaking his head. "He's gone."

Deke merely nodded, collapsing back on his ass. He caught her when she fell into his lap, wrapping her arms around him as she lost herself in the steady thrum of his heart against her chest. He dropped a kiss on her forehead, smiling when she released her hold, turning and yanking Riley against her.

Her brother muttered something under his breath, one hand curving around her back. "Easy, sis. I'm okay."

She swatted him on the shoulder as she eased away, still braced against Deacon as she shook her finger at Riley. "Don't ever fucking do that again. Don't scare me like that. I thought…"

Her words dissolved into a series of raspy gasps as she tried not to fall apart. Riley's forehead pressed against hers, his heavy sigh rustling the strands of hair around her face.

He lifted one hand, thumbing her cheek. "I love you, too, brat."

She managed a smile, focusing on Deacon again. Those weird markings bruised the skin by his temples, the gash along his chest still oozing. She pursed her lips. "You're hurt."

He chuckled. "Beats being dead."

"You should have stabbed it sooner, instead of letting it feed off of you. I know you did that on purpose."

"It needed to establish a link. Make itself vulnerable. It was the only way." He glanced at Riley, arching a brow. "Besides, I didn't plan on Jason Bourne, here, throwing a damn knife at it. Where the hell did you learn to do that?"

Riley merely shrugged. "My dad spent the first half of his career as a doctor in the Army. He passed along a few moves he'd picked up." He nodded toward Cait. "Did you really think she got that good at ass-kicking just by being a cop? Please. Joe made sure Cait could take out a punk long before she started wearing her blues."

Deke smiled at her. "Just another reason to love her." He chuckled when her mouth gaped open, pressing a finger across her lips. "We'll talk about that, later. Right now, we need to call this in." He glanced at Byron's limp body. "There should be more than enough evidence here to wrap this all up."

Cait sighed. "Those bones he left behind should substantiate the whole family pact theory. That fathers groomed their sons from an early age."

Deke's expression fell slightly. "Nice and clean. And normal."

She palmed his jaw, wishing she could take the pain from his eyes. "I'm sorry. If there was a way to make this right…"

He shook his head, pulling her into a firm embrace. "You already made it right. And my dad wouldn't want either of us throwing our careers away just to make him look good. That's not why *he* became a fed. We'll play this out the way it has to be."

She leaned in, giving him a slow kiss. "You did it. You stopped this. Stopped him. Saved my brother's life and proved your father was smarter than all of us. Even if we're the only ones who'll ever know it. I'm thinking he'd be real proud of you."

He snorted. "Didn't do any of that alone. We make a damn good team, sweetheart."

"And that's my cue to leave." Riley stood. "Is my Jeep around here somewhere?"

She nodded, leaning against Deke when he wrapped

his arms around her. "Shed, in front of the house. It's padlocked, but that shouldn't be too hard to break."

"Good. I'll go grab my bag before your boyfriend bleeds all over the evidence. You, too. Stay put. I'll be right back."

She watched Riley unbar the main door then slip out before focusing on Deke, determined to finally confess her feelings when he blocked her with a hard kiss.

He held up his hand. "Hold that thought." He pressed his finger against her lips again. "I mean it. Wait until we're back at my place. Or your place. When your words aren't colored by the fact we actually didn't die." He tucked some hair behind her ear, grinning. "Then you can tell me how much you love me, and that you'll say yes when I ask you to move in with me."

Her heart fluttered, a warm feeling spreading through her chest. She smiled beneath his finger, giving it a light kiss when he eased it away. "Deal."

# CHAPTER TWENTY-TWO

"Decker! McGraw! My office. Now!"

Deacon cringed inwardly at the firm bite to Captain Rankin's voice as it echoed through the precinct. The steady din of conversation faded away as the other officers shifted their gazes toward them, tracking their progression through the room until they stopped at Caitlyn's desk. Shit, they'd just walked in the damn door.

Caitlyn snorted. "We should have stopped at Stacy's and gotten the man some coffee. Nothing like a bribe of caffeine to soothe the savage beast." She tossed her keys and phone on her desk. "Might as well see what he wants before he gets any angrier."

Deke sighed, following Caitlyn toward the open door, praying he didn't trip over his own feet. Fuck, he was tired. And it was more than just the side effect of having some of his life force drained. By the time they'd cleared the scene last night, filled out a few reports then ensured Riley made it home, they'd barely had enough time to pass out at Cait's for a couple of hours before heading back in. Though, he had to admit, just holding her in his arms for that short amount of time had made everything worthwhile. Knowing she was safe, that it was over...

He pushed the thoughts out of his head as he entered Rankin's office, cursing under his breath when Assistant Director Jamieson moved out from the side and closed the door. He'd somehow missed his boss' vehicle in the parking lot when they'd pulled up. Jamieson flashed him a knowing smile as he crossed his arms over his chest, motioning for them to sit.

Cait smiled back but remained standing, drawing a chuckle from the man. "Assistant Director Jamieson. Nice to see you again."

Jamieson shook his head. "How do you manage to lie to my face and still make it seem convincing? You are definitely one of a kind, Detective."

"I wasn't lying..." She snorted. "Not much, anyway." She turned to her boss. "Captain? Everything okay?"

He arched a brow, looking proud and pissed at the same time. "I guess that depends on your definition." He held up the preliminary reports they'd filled out the previous night. "The Assistant Director and I were just going through your account of the events that led to Byron Howard's capture and unavoidable demise last night. I have to say...it made for some interesting reading."

The inklings of doubt slivered along Deke's spine as he glanced at Cait. As far as he knew, their reports should have been identical. They'd gone over what they were going to put in them while waiting for the cavalry to join them last night.

Cait seemed unaffected by the man's comment. "I'd

assumed you wanted an accurate description of the events both leading up to and encompassing the confrontation last night."

Rankin narrowed his eyes. "Don't play coy with me, Caitlyn. You know what you put in here."

Caitlyn glanced at Deke, giving him a quick wink. "I'm well aware of what I wrote. It's the truth, sir."

Jamieson snorted, opening his copy and thumbing through the pages until he reached a section he obviously found troubling. "You said, and I quote, 'Mr. Howard displayed inhuman strength and speed, which was directly attributed to his possession by a...rin-ik-arhu." He paused to arch a brow at her before looking down at the page again. "This enabled the suspect to maintain a youthful appearance, allowing him to commit over seventeen murders during a sixty-year time span and thus, establishing Special Agent Thomas McGraw's theory of a single killer to be correct'." He glanced up at her. "Did I get any of that wrong, Detective?"

Deacon's mouth hinged open as he stared at Cait, dumbfounded.

She merely nodded. "That about sums it up."

The man huffed. "You can't be serious. This..." He shut the file. "It's grounds to get you suspended pending a psychiatric evaluation." He turned his attention to Deke. "Well, McGraw? Any comments? Because I couldn't help but notice your report omits all of that. Something along the lines of a family pact theory. Which confuses the hell out of me as I thoroughly expected your account to be the one filled with mystic bullshit."

Deacon firmed his stance, allowing his hand to move

to the small of Cait's back in a visible show of support. "Then my account is wrong, sir."

Jamieson took a calculating step forward. "Deacon—"

"Enough." Rankin stepped between them. "Both of you just stand down. Caitlyn...an explanation, please."

She turned to fully face the man. "The truth is, sir, some pretty weird ass shit went down. That report...it really is true." She held up her hand, stopping anyone from interrupting her. "I know. Trust me, I know how crazy it sounds. How crazy it actually was, but Riley will back my account, as will Beverly Howard. Now, I realize the fact they're directly related to the people involved doesn't put much stock in their reliability in this matter, though I doubt the media would care about that particular detail too much. However, I'm willing to recount my report and file one identical to Deacon's on one condition."

Rankin raised a brow. "Go on."

She focused on Jamieson. "I want the bureau to erase any black marks staining Thomas McGraw's record as an agent, and I want the man given a commendation for giving us the tools and information to solve a serial killer case that spanned six decades. A case he died trying to solve."

Jamieson huffed. "You want me to publicly confirm that demons exist and are running around sucking the souls out of people. Not likely, Detective."

"I didn't say you had to divulge the true nature of the case, sir. It's easy to explain that, due to the limited technology even twenty years ago, Agent McGraw made a plausible conclusion based on the evidence at hand, even if it was unpopular. And that his unyielding determination to find the truth provided us with the necessary means to finally solve the case. In exchange, I'll be happy to allow the bureau to take full credit for Howard's apprehension." She took a step toward the man. "Thomas McGraw died trying to kill that bastard. Damn near did, according to Byron Howard. Don't you think the man deserves to be recognized for the hero he was?"

Jamieson pursed his lips, looking over at Deke. The man shook his head. "Detective Decker, you should run for office. You'd make an excellent politician. Fine. I'll gladly recommend Agent Thomas McGraw receive a commendation for his previous work in this case...just as soon as I receive your *corrected* report."

Cait grinned. "Hold that thought." She darted out the door, auburn hair bouncing behind her.

Jamieson turned to Deacon. "Not sure what you did to win that girl over, but...I wouldn't let her go if I were you, Deacon."

Deke smiled. "I have no intention of letting her out of my sight anytime soon, sir."

Jamieson schooled his features when Cait returned, handing him a beige folder. He placed it on top, nodding when she gave an identical one to Rankin. "Do I need to worry I'll see the first version plastered on the evening news?"

She scowled. "I don't go back on my word."

"Fair enough." He extended his hand. "Excellent work. Can't say I really thought these cases would get the closure they deserved." He turned to Rankin. "I have a feeling our agencies will be working together far more often in the future. You were right. Once your detective sets her sights on something, she doesn't back down.

Deacon, take a few days off then see me in my office. I'll make arrangements for an appropriate ceremony for your father. Perhaps Detective Decker will do us the honor of being on hand to help present the award."

Caitlyn beamed. "It would be my pleasure, sir."

Jamieson chuckled as he left, whistling to himself.

Rankin cleared his throat, giving her an exasperated sigh as he leaned against his desk. "Christ, Caitlyn. You could have gotten suspended for that stunt you just pulled."

She glanced at Deke, understanding shining in her eyes. "It was worth the risk. Deke nearly died saving my brother's life. I couldn't offer him any less in return."

"Which makes you both my best and most reckless officer." He stood, moving around to the other side of his desk. "Finish up your other reports then go home. Sleep. Whatever. Take the rest of the week off. I'll see you back in here Monday morning."

"Yes, sir."

"Oh and Agent McGraw?"

Deacon turned at the captain's call. "Yes, sir?"

"See that she makes it safely home. And then back again on Monday."

He grinned. "Certainly, Captain."

Caitlyn rolled her eyes, muttering something about her not needing a babysitter, as they headed back to her desk. They focused on completing the last of the forms, handing the file into Rankin before heading out again. Deke smiled when Cait tossed him the keys, sliding into the passenger side and relaxing as he started the car. She closed her eyes, seemingly content to go wherever he took them.

He pulled into traffic, humming along with the music

as he made his way across town, finally turning into his driveway. While he would have gladly gone to her place, he had the sudden urge to see her tucked in his bed, her hair pooled on the pillowcase, her skin still flushed from making love.

He smiled at the thought, willing his dick to stand down until he got her inside. Though having her ride him in the front seat of her car definitely had potential.

Cait blinked when he opened her door, scrubbing her hand down her face as she gave him a sheepish smile. "Sorry. I didn't realize I'd dozed off."

"I consider it a miracle you've been able to function at all, today. Come on. Let's slip into something more comfortable."

Her lips curled into a devilish grin. "Like you?"

He tsked, helping her out of the car then lifting her into his arms. He ignored the irritated swat she gave him as she insisted she could walk, enjoying the feel of her pressed against his chest. The constant reassurance that he hadn't failed her, and that he had a lifetime's worth of chances to show her how much he cared. That he'd fallen hopelessly in love with her.

He smiled as the thought settled peacefully in his gut, warming his chest. He was done running. Letting his past predict his future. Cait had vanquished his demons. He only hoped she'd let him slay hers.

Cait chuckled when he headed straight for the bedroom, finally setting her on her feet beside his bed. Her eyes closed on a hum when he leaned in closer, brushing his lips along her nape then across her jaw. She opened for his tongue when he sealed his mouth to hers, completely giving herself over to the kiss.

Deke moaned at the addictive taste of her, knowing he'd never get enough. Never touch her enough. Love her enough. He let his forehead rest on hers once he'd eased back, drinking in her increased breath, the way her hands linked together behind his neck. "God, I love you."

Her sharp inhale had him pulling back just enough to make eye contact. Wide eyes stared up at him, her bottom lip snagged between her teeth. He laughed, knowing he'd give her all the time she needed to get to where he was. To trust him enough to say the words in return.

She huffed when he shook his head, placing his finger across her lips. She released one hand, gently moving his finger aside. "Deacon…"

"It's okay. I know you need time to trust that I'm not merely saying what I think you need to hear in order to control the situation. I'm fine giving you that time. I can love you enough for both of us, for now."

Her gaze softened as her eyes teared up a bit. She shook her head, using one hand to brush his hair back from his temple before tangling her fingers around the strands. "I thought you promised you wouldn't stop me the next time I tried to declare my undying love? Are you breaking that promise, G-man?"

His heart tripped at her words, and he took a stumbling step back before he could recover.

Cait laughed, reclaiming the lost inches. She reached up, cupping his jaw. "I don't need time. Or proof. I trust you. With more than my heart. You have my soul." She thumbed the corner of his mouth. "And my love."

She smiled when he simply stood there, staring at her, wondering if he'd really died and this was heaven.

"Deacon…"

He swallowed whatever else she was going to say, tracing every inch of her mouth until dots flashed behind his closed eyes and he gasped in a much-needed breath. He nuzzled her nose, feeling whole for the first time in twenty years. "Say it again."

"I love you."

"Love you, too. Which means, it's playtime." He reached into his back pocket, removing a set of cuffs. "I seem to recall you saying something about being put over my lap while wearing these?"

She laughed, palming his chest when he went to make a move. "I only have one question. Do you want to play before or after you help me move in?" She grinned again. "That offer still stands, right? Because I can't think of anything better than going to sleep in your arms every night, then waking up the same way."

He dipped down, kissing her again, wrapping his arms around her with the intention of never letting go. He nipped at her lip when he finally pulled back. "Technically, I said *when* I asked you to move in with me."

She swatted his chest, wrestling playfully against his hold. He let her gain a bit of ground before launching them both on the bed. She gasped as they bounced, and he used the opportunity to lever up with her spread out across his thighs. Then he grabbed her arms, cuffing her wrists together behind her back.

Cait wiggled on his lap, moaning when he landed a light slap across her ass. "Deacon."

"Oh, sweetheart. I love how you inject just enough authority into your voice to make me think you don't want to be exactly where you are." He leaned over, licking the shell of her ear. "And we can move you in *after* we play.

Because I can't wait another minute to see your ass flex beneath my hand."

She smiled, relaxing onto him. "Then get me naked because turnabout is fair play. And I have a set of cuffs, too."

"That's right. Which means I'll get to restrain more of you." He chuckled at her feigned huff. "I love you, Cait. Now get comfortable. As I recall, you've been a very bad girl."

*Damn, she's fine.*

Master Sergeant Rick "Cannon" Sloan, Army retired, eyed the blonde across the bar. V-neck crop top, tight black skirt and biker boots—the lady was dressed to kill. She had her elbows propped on one of the bar tables, showing off a healthy dose of pale cleavage as she leaned forward, dainty fingers absently skimming up and down her cooler. She'd hooked the heel of one black boot in the lower rung of the chair, her other foot tapping the floor. If it weren't for her steady hands and even expression, he'd have pegged her as being nervous. And she should be. She was seated next to the reason Cannon was at the bar. Biding his time. Hunting.

Nigel O'Mally. The bruiser in the leather jacket, who seemed determined to get his hand on her crotch. Cannon had to admit, she was good at deflecting the asshole's advances without pissing him off. Just enough to make O'Mally work harder—shift tactics. Up his game. Too bad he wasn't going to score tonight. And just as well. Most of the women he ended up leaving with didn't make it home alive. And the ones who did, wished they hadn't.

Not that anyone could connect him to the murders. Bastard seemed to have a horseshoe shoved up his ass. That, or he'd bought enough blue uniforms he didn't need luck. But, he'd been caught trying to pull off some lame-ass robbery—had managed to trip just about every security measure in the process—and was currently out on bail. Of course, he'd missed his court date, giving Cannon the excuse he needed to drag O'Mally's ass back in—profit in the process. And if there was any kind of justice, the U.S. Attorney's office would find a way to pin the murders on him while he rotted away in a cell.

"Hey, buddy. Are you going to order a drink or just sip soda water all night? This *is* a bar, ya know."

Cannon glanced at the bartender, keeping his eyes narrowed. Mouth pinched tight. He didn't answer, just stared at the guy until the other man took a step back. He swallowed—hard—then moved down the bar.

Good. The bartender recognized that Cannon was dangerous. Could sense he was someone accustomed to death. To fighting. And the guy had acted accordingly. Even now, he didn't make eye contact. Barely looked Cannon's way. Which suited him, because the last thing he needed was a scene. Something to out him before he was ready. The night was slowly coming to a close, about twenty patrons still left in the bar. He'd hoped more would leave once midnight had come and gone, but at least it wasn't still overflowing with bikers and gang members.

He looked over at the blonde, again. While her clothes definitely blended in with the other women in the room, something about her seemed...off. And it was more than just the color of her hair—her piercing green eyes begged for auburn locks, not blonde—it was her mannerisms. She didn't move like the other women—loose. Unsteady. Her actions felt calculated. And there was still that tapping foot...

Nigel wrapped an arm around her while twisting in his chair and dropping his other hand onto her thigh. Blondie's lips quirked, and her fingers tightened on her cooler bottle.

Shit. Cannon was good at reading body language. And the lady was about ten seconds away from smashing the bottle over O'Mally's head. If Cannon didn't intervene before that, it could ruin the entire takedown—cost him the fifty-thousand in bond money.

A bounty hunter.

If his teammates had told him he'd end up tracking down scum for money, he'd have flattened them. Punched them in the face then walked away without a second thought. He'd spent his entire adult life in the Army. Had worked his way up from a lowly recruit to lead in his unit. Was trained in hostage rescue, extreme weather survival, hand-to-hand-combat. There wasn't a vehicle he couldn't drive. A threat he couldn't address. And here he was, sitting in a bar that smelled like old beer and stale peanuts as he waited to make his move. One that wouldn't put the remaining patrons in danger.

Or her.

Fuck, he needed to stop focusing on the woman. She was lucky Nigel wouldn't get more than a grope out of the evening. Cannon couldn't waste his time worrying if she might get shoved aside. Maybe knocked down. Just as long as the asshole didn't have the chance to take her as a hostage, the night would end pretty much as Cannon had expected—Nigel cuffed and unconscious in Cannon's truck. The money he needed to start his own company all but in his pocket. Everything else was just a roadblock. And he had a way of dealing with those—he just hit the gas and barreled right through.

Blondie shifted in her seat, and he knew she was giving herself a better exit strategy. A way to slip out without getting caught up in Nigel's arms. Which meant, it was time to end this charade.

Cannon eased off the chair, scanning the bar, again. Not much had changed. Two redneck boys were still playing pool in the far right corner. A handful of college-aged kids bumping and grinding on the dance floor. There were two men at a table close to O'Mally. Similar clothes, though, they hadn't so much as looked at the man all night. Still, Cannon made a mental note to continue tracking their movements. He needed to be ready to react if they turned out to be the asshole's bodyguards.

That left only blondie as a wildcard.

Cannon walked forward, seamlessly shifting into warrior mode. Gone was the unobtrusive observer. The guy who'd blended in for the past two hours while waiting to strike. Now—he was primed. Muscles ready. Every sense honed on his progression across the bar. The feel of the floor beneath his boots. The slide of his jacket across his gun. He wouldn't draw unless forced. He planned on getting close to O'Mally. Too close for the bastard to get the jump on him, but perfect for taking the creep down. Bare-handed.

Oh yeah. He'd enjoy that part. Giving the man a taste

of what he dished out. If there was one thing Cannon despised it was men like O'Mally who preyed on women. Who thought, because they were bigger and usually stronger, it was their right to treat them however they saw fit. O'Mally was a threat. And Cannon had made a career out of eliminating threats.

He stalked across the floor, senses alert. The two men playing pool started shoving each other, voices raised. No doubt one of them would throw a punch. Though, based on the size difference, it would be over in all of two seconds. Not that he was in the habit of judging an enemy's skill by their size—he'd witnessed guys fifty pounds lighter than him and a good six inches shorter take out a bar full of bikers—but... He'd studied their mannerisms, too. The short guy didn't stand a chance.

Something clattered to the floor by the pool tables, and O'Mally looked over. Perfect. The asshole wasn't even watching Cannon. Sizing him up. If he had, O'Mally would have been puffing out his chest—making himself look bigger. Maybe scowling, showing a hint of teeth. Guys like him knew threats when they moved in close. Not that he'd necessarily peg Cannon as a lethal one but possibly competition for the blonde.

The one Cannon couldn't seem to get out of his head. There he was, about five seconds away from confronting his target—when all his attention *should* have been on the mission, on all the ways this could go down. Ensure he was in complete control—and a part of him was focusing on her. On the slight rustle of fabric as she slid one leg over the other—tights. Flesh colored. Nearly invisible against her skin. Or how a light flush had crept across the upper swell of her breasts. Not arousal. More frustration or anger, considering there was also a slash of red across her cheeks. She was sizing up O'Mally, the way he should be looking at Cannon—her eyes narrowed. Lips a thin line across her face. One hand slipped inside the purse hanging at her side, and Cannon saw a glint of something metallic on the inside.

Shit.

His instincts had been right. She wasn't like the other women here, after all. She was a plant. Maybe a cop or a fed. Hell, he wouldn't rule out assassin. Though, more likely another bounty hunter. Not a lot of women chose that route, but she definitely had the "calm and collected" vibe going. Now that he was closer, he picked up on more. Her muscles were primed, much like his, ready to strike. And she hadn't positioned herself for an easier exit. She'd turned so she had a clearer opening to grab O'Mally— slam his head into the table. Get behind him before he could react. She'd most likely been waiting until the crowd thinned out enough she could make a move. Cannon just wasn't sure if she was an ally or another mark he'd have to deal with. If she wanted O'Mally dead or alive.

Either worked for Cannon, but damn it—he could really use the bond money. Allow him to rent a space, hire a buddy or two to start expanding his services. Men he trusted—who he'd bled with. And if she was a threat, a hired hand... Shit, he wasn't sure he could take her out. Just the thought of hurting her...

Another step, and her head whipped around, her green eyes finding his and staying. Christ, she was beautiful. Made his damn chest tighten, his lungs fight to inflate. She was all smooth, pale skin, with full lips and high cheekbones. She wore more makeup than anyone needed, though, he suspected it was all part of her cover—to look the part. Blend in.

He had to hand it to her, she was a hell of a distraction. As long as she struck at the right time, she'd have a real chance at bagging the bastard. *If* she had backup. Surely, she hadn't come alone. Getting the jump on the guy was one thing. Dragging his ass out to her car —facing any possible company the creep might have hiding in the crowd. Like those two guys sitting behind her—it was suicide.

But, she hadn't so much as made eye contact with anyone else in the bar since Cannon had sat down. Hadn't focused on anything other than O'Mally and her phone when she'd gotten what he assumed were a few texts. Cannon knew. He'd been watching. But no one had been busy with their phone at the same time she had, which suggested...

Fuck. She *was* alone.

But, it was too late. He was already past the point of no return—inside his strike radius. Ready for battle. O'Mally had turned back, had finally caught sight of him. The bastard immediately straightened. Fisted his hands— one on the table, the other across the back of her chair. A fucking game changer just waiting to happen. It put her within reach. A possible target. Or a hostage. Either was bad.

Blondie read O'Mally's intentions—swiveled a bit more. Just enough the bastard would have to lunge out to grab her shoulder.

*She's got good instincts.*

Too bad it might not be enough. Unless she was a

professional. Then, he might end up on the wrong side of a gun. He was ready, but there were too many variables, and he didn't have enough intel. He'd just have to go in. Adapt.

He'd spent the past ten years adapting. If he'd learned one thing during his time in Delta Force, it was that no plan ever truly translated into the field. Sure, his team made a best guess. Tried to account for all possible outcomes. But there was always something that wasn't on the schematics. That hadn't been factored in. A family member when the mark should have been alone. Weapons that hadn't been accounted for. Murphy was always out there, just waiting to fuck things up.

And he was sure as shit sitting on Cannon's shoulder, right now—itching to throw a wrench into the entire mix. One with stunning green eyes and a killer smile.

Cannon stopped in front of the table instead of simply grabbing the guy, knocking him on his ass then carrying him back to his truck. The short confrontation—letting the jackass know, not to mention the woman, that Cannon was there to take him in—would give him some useful information. How she reacted, consciously or not, would be just enough to tailor the rest of his takedown.

He hoped.

It could also blow the entire op right out of the water. If she made a move right then... He'd be adapting to some deadly changes. The kind that might get one of them killed.

No doubt about it. Adapting was a bitch.

O'Mally sneered at him, gaze clearly assessing him. "Fuck off."

Cannon stood still, hands at his side—within reach of

his M9. Or the Ka-Bar on his thigh. Fuck, the asshole looked wasted enough Cannon could probably go for the twenty-two in his ankle holster and still out draw the creep. "Nigel O'Mally?"

"Whatever it is you want, I ain't interested. Now, fuck off, before I get nasty."

Cannon's lips twitched, and it took him a moment to realize he was smiling. Fuck, he couldn't remember the last time he'd smiled. Maybe Indonesia in '14. It felt odd, tugging at muscles he rarely used. But just the thought that the bastard would throw a punch—or, better yet, draw—it warmed Cannon's chest.

He took a moment to glance at the blonde, but she hadn't reacted. Not so much as a twitch of her lips or a raise of her brow. Stone. Cold.

So much for getting a read. Gaining the upper hand.

He palmed the table. Showtime. "There's nothing I'd enjoy more than having you get nasty. But... I don't have all night. And your bounty isn't getting any higher. So, you can either come quietly or—"

O'Mally moved. Reached inside his jacket as he lunged for the girl. But she was already sliding right, slipping out of the chair. Two seconds, and she was out of reach, backing toward the wall. Cannon shifted left. A quick swing of his fist, and O'Mally's arm was knocked away, his gun clattering to the table. A step, a reach, and the bastard was in his hands—squirming, trying to find purchase.

Cannon twisted, brought the fucker's head down on the corner of the table. It cracked hard, left a bloody smear, then he was falling. Crumpling on the ground at Cannon's feet.

Four seconds flat.

Until the men behind O'Mally's table jumped up. One grabbed Blondie—yanked her against his chest. His beefy arm wrapped around her shoulders, a fucking Sig Sauger pointed toward her head. The thing was massive—more firepower than the bastard looked like he could handle. But it didn't matter. No one missed a target that close.

His buddy was still drawing—the silencer on his gun catching on the pants. Another two seconds, and he'd have it free. Possibly firing off rounds in a panic, because his eyes were like white saucers. Huge. Unblinking. He most likely had tunnel vision—couldn't see past his boss getting slammed into the table. That made him dangerous. Unable to process whether he *should* fire, only that he *could*.

But Cannon was already working through steps four and five. Already had his M9 in one hand, his knife in the other—his sights on the asshole holding the woman. A quick shot, and he'd clip the man's shoulder—or better yet, peg him right between the eyes—eliminate any chance of the jerk shooting her. Cannon would have to be quick—catch the prick's buddy with his knife before the idiot fully drew. Started shooting whoever moved.

Until the woman punched up her arm, caught the creep holding her in the chin. A drop of her weight, a twist and shove, and she had him spread out across the table, face smashed into the top. She pivoted just enough to kick the other guy in the knee, buckle his leg. Another shift, and that gun Cannon had glimpsed was in her hand —pointed at the guy stumbling against the wall behind her.

Her hair fluttered around her face, tilting off a bit to

one side as she huffed, one hand holding the asshole to the table, the other leveling her Beretta at his friend. She spared Cannon a quick glance before focusing on the guy she'd kicked. "Freeze, asshole."

The guy blinked, glanced at the O'Mally, around the bar, then nodded.

She motioned to his weapon. "On the table."

He all but dropped it, wincing when it nearly clattered to the floor.

"Gently. Now, unless you want to go to jail with your two buddies, here, I suggest you get lost. Fast."

He nodded, again, looked over once at Cannon then took off. Bumping into several people on his way to the door. It bounced off the wall, a cool swirl of air breezing through the bar.

She waited until the door closed then focused on Cannon, slamming the guy she was holding against the table, again, when he shifted. "Move, again, and I'll let him deal with you."

The asshole looked at Cannon, paled, then stilled.

Blondie smiled, finally gazing up at Cannon. She studied him for several moments then arched a brow. "Pretty sure I know most of the local hunters. You're new. You got a name?"

"Most people call me Cannon."

"Cannon? That's it?"

"It's enough. And you are?"

"Nash. Deputy U.S. Marshal Jericho Nash. And it looks like we just collared the same guy."

## ABOUT THE AUTHOR

Author, single mother, slave to chaos—she's a jack-of-all-trades who's constantly looking for her ever elusive clone.

And don't forget to subscribe to her newsletter to get the latest scoop on new and upcoming releases as well as exclusive free reads.

https://www.subscribepage.com/krisnorris

Kris loves connecting with fellow book enthusiasts. You can find her on these social media platforms...

krisnorris.ca
contactme@krisnorris.ca

www.ingramcontent.com/pod-product-compliance
Lightning Source LLC
Chambersburg PA
CBHW020252200626
46816CB00001BA/261